GW00382086

Ice and a Slice

Della Galton

Published by Della Galton
www.dellagalton.co.uk

Copyright 2013 Della Galton

All rights reserved.
No part of this publication may be reproduced, in any
form, without the prior permission of the copyright
owner
Please visit dellagalton.co.uk
for contact details

For all the other SJs out there

About Della Galton

Della Galton is a freelance writer and tutor. Ice and a Slice is her third novel. She is also the author of How to Write and Sell Short Stories, The Short Story Writer's Toolshed and Short Story to Novel – Moving On, as well as How To Eat Loads and Stay Slim.

She is a popular speaker at writing conventions around the UK and is also the agony aunt for Writers' Forum.

When she is not writing she enjoys walking her dogs in the beautiful Dorset countryside where she lives. Her hobby is repairing old cottages, which is lucky as hers is falling down.

Find out more about Della, her books, and her speaking engagements at www.dellagalton.co.uk

Chapter One

The first thing she noticed was the tinny metallic taste in her mouth. And then came the thirst. The thirst was so bad it had got into her dreams and forced her awake. No, not awake, aware – a slowly growing awareness which was coming, sense by sense.

Like sound. She could hear an echoey blur of footsteps and voices, which rolled in and out of her head. Closer by, something electronic beeped. *Beep, beep, beep* – steady and rhythmic – *beep, beep beep.*

Where was she? She opened her eyes and was hit by a wall of light. She shut them swiftly. She felt as though she was made of crystal, cool and brittle. She was a thin glass person who could be shattered by the slightest touch.

After a while she tried opening her eyes again. This time the room swam in various shades of light, but she managed to squint long enough to focus. To her left was a tall metal stand with a clear bag of fluid clipped to the top. To her right was some kind of machine, which seemed to be the source of the beeping. Close to her cheek was the edge of a thin blue woven sheet, but it felt more like a tablecloth than a sheet. She shifted a little to get away from its roughness and her head spun.

"So you're awake then?" A blurred face leaned over her. She made out red lipstick, a thin line of a nose, kind eyes.

"Drink?" she gasped.

The face moved away, then loomed back in and she was aware of a straw close to her mouth. "Take it steady."

Ignoring the advice, she sucked greedily and her throat was suddenly awash with coolness – the wonderful coolness of water – and then she was retching, choking, drowning. A firm hand supported her back. "Easy does it." She tried again, more carefully, and this time with more success.

"You're in ICU," the voice went on. But she wasn't really listening, didn't really care; there was nothing more important than water; the need for it blanked out every other sense, every other feeling.

It was about thirty seconds later that the pain kicked in.

There was a deep, deep ache in her lower back, sparked off by the movement of leaning forward to drink. She moaned and the voice returned. "Gently does it, love. Slowly, slowly…"

The other voices – the further away voices – were still rumbling in the background and now she could make out odd snatches.

"She's in a very weakened condition – I really wouldn't advise visitors."

"I want to bloody well see her. Tell him, Jim. Tell him we want to bloody well see her now."

Oh God, that was her mother. What was her mother doing here? And why was she swearing? She never swore. Something bad must have happened. Something very, very bad.

Beneath the awful aching her heart began to thump harder and the beep of the machine sped up to keep time.

Then all at once they were there; the lumbering shadows of her parents sliding into the light. Her father bulky and silent – he never said much, he couldn't get a word in edgeways most of the time – and her mother in her Evans black and white knitted jacket.

"Oh, Sarah-Jane, whatever are we going to do with you? Whatever are we going to do with her, Jim?"

Her mother's usually ruddy cheeks were pale and she didn't look as though she'd combed her hair lately. She was shaking her head now, a frown creasing her forehead, and her face was reproachful.

"It's okay," Sarah-Jane began, desperate to reassure them, but she only managed the very first bit of the 'it' so her voice resembled that of a mouse – a very small mouse caught in a trap – and the hand she'd meant to lift to calm her mother seemed to be attached to a wire. She glanced at it, which turned into a painful and rather shocking moment as there was a needle in the top of her hand which led to the wire which, in turn, led to another machine that looked like an old fashioned typewriter.

"Oh," she said. "Oh…oh…"

"What's she saying, Jim? Do you think we should call the doctor?"

Something niggled at the back of her mind. It was something to do with a party. Had she been at a party? A snapshot of memory drifted in. Herself draped on a chair watching someone walk across the terracotta carpet. They were carrying a tray of mushroom vol-au-vents.

"SJ, love, can you hear me?" The kindness of her father's voice brought a sharp ache to her throat. "SJ, lovie?" He'd moved closer to the bed and was holding her hand in a fumbling, awkward kind of way. They

3

had never been a touchy feely family. And when she looked up at him she saw that his eyes were full of tears and the ache in her throat intensified. Dad never cried. He was trying very hard not to do it now. He sniffed twice and rubbed his cheek with the side of his index finger, a tiny little movement that broke SJ's heart.

She couldn't speak and she couldn't bear to see the pain on his face. Shutting her eyes again she let herself drift backwards into the soft black space of her mind.

The next thing she was conscious of was someone lifting the wrist that wasn't wired to the machine and taking her pulse.

It was the nurse who'd given her the water. She had tiredness lines around her eyes and spoke gently. "How are you feeling?"

"Quite bad," SJ said, hearing her voice come out hoarse and unused.

The nurse nodded and wrote something on a clipboard. "You've got a visitor if you're up to it."

As she spoke another woman slid into SJ's line of vision. She was small and serious-looking with bobbed hair and Yves St Laurent glasses.

"Hello, Sarah-Jane. I'm Doctor Maria Costello; I'm from Clinical Medicine. I'd like to have a little chat with you if I may?"

SJ nodded, although her consent was clearly not required. The doctor had already pulled up a chair.

"Do you know why you're here?"

"No. Have you come to tell me what's wrong with me?"

"Would you like me to tell you what's wrong with you?"

"Yes please." SJ lay back on her pillow, exhausted with the effort of speaking. Everything still hurt and she could smell antiseptic hand wash. It was beginning to make her feel sick.

She watched the doctor's face through half closed eyes. Shadow memories lurched at the back of her mind and suddenly she wanted to say, "No, stop, I've changed my mind. I don't want to know."

But it was too late. The doctor's mouth was moving again, her words crisp and precise. "You are suffering from alcoholic poisoning. On Sunday your husband found you unconscious at home and he called an ambulance. If he hadn't acted as quickly as he did, you wouldn't be here now. The quantities of alcohol we washed out of your stomach were more than enough to kill you."

SJ covered her face with her hands. The memories were taking form, becoming less shadowy, forcing their way up to the surface.

There had been some terrible argument with Tom. She'd been trying to stop him leaving the house. She was holding tightly onto his arm and he was trying to shake her off and his face had been grimmer than she'd ever seen it. As if he really hated her. As if he couldn't bear to be married to her for a moment longer.

She could feel herself starting to shake, in a place deep inside. Because there were other images coming too, only these were more detached. She was watching herself from a distance. She was watching herself cross the hallway of her house, go into her lounge and unclip the gin bottle from the optic behind Tom's bar. She could see her own hands getting out glasses and lining them up – a long line of glasses on the bar.

Four crystal tumblers, two pewter tankards, five little shot glasses Tom used for whiskey chasers if ever he was in the mood, and one commemorative wine glass with the words *Sarah-Jane and Tom, on their wedding day, May 2009* inscribed on the side.

"I did this to myself," she said, closing her eyes.

The doctor's voice was very serious. Almost cold. "Are you conscious of the danger you placed yourself in? Last Sunday afternoon you drank almost a full litre bottle of gin. I'd like you to tell me why."

Chapter Two

Two Months Earlier

The terrifying part was pressing the button on the intercom system beside the grimy frosted-glass door. Before that she could have been any other office worker on the busy Soho street with nothing more important on her mind than where to go for lunch: Daddy Donkey for a burrito or Malletti for a slice of pizza? Oh, what she would have given to have been making a choice like that.

She could still run away. Phone up later and say she'd been ill or had to work. She probably needn't even phone. These kinds of places must get loads of people who made appointments and didn't turn up. No doubt they were used to it.

Her legs were too rubbery to run anywhere. She glanced over her shoulder. No one was paying her the slightest attention. Thank God. Her outfit, overloud floral leggings and her hideously expensive Monsoon jacket, red for confidence, had been a mistake. She should have worn a wig and dark glasses and one of those great big overcoats so no one knew whether she was male or female. On second thoughts, that would have attracted a fair bit of attention in the June heat – everyone else was in summer suits or mini dresses. A few hundred yards away two bare-chested council workers had coned off a section of kerb and were digging up the road. The faint smell of tar mingled with traffic fumes on the summer air.

Taking a deep breath, she stabbed at the intercom button, which she missed first time because her fingers were shaking. Now she was committed – please let them open the door quickly before someone she knew strolled by and spotted her.

A buzzer indicated the catch had been released and she hurtled inside and found herself in a hallway with a discreet sign, S.A.A.D – that was appropriate – and an arrow pointing upwards. A guy in a baseball cap was coming down the stairs. He smiled and she smiled back and hoped he'd mistaken her for a counsellor.

Her shoulder length dark hair was pinned up in a look which aimed to be grunge, but she had a sneaking suspicion looked more 'dragged through a hedge backwards', and she wore the Miss Dior Tom had given her for her birthday. She was not a shambling wreck. She hadn't even had a cigarette before she came – well, one quick one when she'd got off the tube – but she'd had three mints since then.

Another man carrying a file met her at the top. He smiled too, and she gave him what she hoped was a friendly nod. Pretend you're here for a doctor's appointment – nothing to worry about. Just a routine visit to the doctor – no, not a good idea: she hated going to the doctor. She realised suddenly that he was speaking and she hadn't responded.

"Sarah Carter?" he repeated.

"Yep, that's me." Her face blazed with embarrassment. She'd always been hopeless at lying.

"Hi, I'm Kit. Go straight in – door at the end. I'll be right with you. Can I get you a coffee?"

"Thanks." She escaped into a cell-like room, furnished with a two-seater settee, an armchair and a small table, which was home to a box of economy tissues and a wire tray of leaflets. On the wall was a Van Gogh print, one corner peeling away from the frame. It showed a small child, supported by his mother and heading towards his father on tottering toddler legs. It was titled *First Steps*. Well, even she could see the wry aptness of that one. In any other circumstances she would have smiled.

A spider plant spilled out of a pot on the table. The earth around it was bone dry. Poor little plant must be desperate for a drink. Oh God, perhaps the spider plant was some sort of in-joke between the counsellors. That couldn't be right. They shouldn't be taking the piss. They were supposed to be sympathetic and nice. She remembered the sign downstairs – so it was an acronym, but it was pretty appropriate.

Shuddering, she chose the armchair by the table and picked up a leaflet from the stack. *How to get help if you or your family is suffering from alcoholism or drug abuse.*

Oh crap! She crammed it back in the stand, opened her bag, switched off her mobile and tucked an escaping Tampax back into its compartment – why was it that anything embarrassing in your bag always gravitated towards the top, ready to fall out and humiliate you next time you opened it? Fleetingly, she considered escape, but before she had the chance to move, the door opened and Kit reappeared with two mugs.

"Sorry to keep you waiting." He put them on the table and she thanked him numbly. He didn't need to apologise; he wasn't late – she was early. It still wasn't quite midday. She'd been so early she'd actually gone an extra two stops on the tube and walked back, not wanting to arrive too soon in case she bumped into anyone she knew and they asked her where she was going.

Kit sat opposite her on the settee, looking relaxed - no closed body language there. She put her bag on the floor so it looked less like a shield and made a conscious effort to unclasp her hands, uncross her legs and look natural. She knew all about body language. They wouldn't get her on that one.

Having rearranged herself she turned her attention back to Kit. He looked a bit like a young Bryan Adams, dark eyes and a craggy lived-in face. It had been a waste of time dressing up – he wore jeans and a white T-shirt. Still, at least he wasn't some shrink in a suit with a load of psychobabble to throw at her. She wondered if Kit was his real name. Probably not. She had a feeling people who worked in these places didn't give clients their real names in case they turned out to be nut-cases. Well, Sarah wasn't her real name either. So they were on an equal footing. Hah!

"Anything we discuss in this room is completely confidential…" His voice was Bryan Adams too – gravelley from years of smoking. "…And won't be disclosed to anyone else without your permission."

She nodded, relieved he didn't have a notebook or pen. She didn't want anything she said recorded and kept on some central government database – far too many people had access to government databases these days.

"So where would you like to start, Sarah?"

"Where do you usually start?" Her voice sounded normal – hey, she could be at the doctor's discussing her blood pressure. Good job she wasn't; it must be sky high. She could feel her heart pounding away in time with the faint sounds of the drill, which had started up again outside the window.

"You said on the phone you were concerned about your alcohol consumption. So how about you tell me how much you usually drink?"

"Sure." She picked up her bag, more comfortable with it on her lap. "Well, I don't drink at lunchtime – apart from the odd Sunday if we go out for lunch. I don't drink in the day at all, actually. In fact sometimes I don't have one until nine or half past. I'm too busy, you see." So far, so good. In a minute he'd start asking her why she was here and she could say she wasn't sure, it had all been a mistake – a phone call made after a particularly bad night when she was feeling depressed. But that was probably more age than excess. Everyone got hangovers when they got past thirty-five, didn't they?

He nodded. "So when you do drink, after nine, what would you have on an average day, say?" His voice was mild and not at all judgmental.

That was easy. "Wine. White wine, usually. With dinner, you know – like everyone."

Another little nod. "How many glasses would you have?"

"Two or three, it depends on the size of the glasses – they vary so much these days, don't they?"

"Would it be easier if you told me in terms of how much of the bottle you had? Would you drink maybe half a bottle, or more than that?"

"More than that," she said without thinking. "I mean, half a bottle is nothing, is it? Everyone has half a bottle of wine with dinner."

He smiled. "Three quarters?"

"Yes, I'd say it was usually three quarters, occasionally the whole bottle, but not always. Maybe if I'd had a particularly stressful day, or if I was up late."

"Do you drink on your own or with a husband or partner?"

She was ready for this one; it was the same thing they asked on the *Are you an alcoholic?* questionnaire she'd found on the net. If you drank alone you were a saddo alky, but if you were sharing the wine with someone else you were okay. Not that she exactly shared the wine because Tom didn't like white much – luckily – but he did quite often have a glass of red.

"My husband's usually around," she said firmly.

"But not always?"

"No, he sometimes works late, so I might have the odd glass before he gets in."

"But not the whole three quarters of a bottle?"

"Well, possibly I might – if he was working very late." How had she fallen into that one? "I mean, if I didn't I wouldn't have a drink at all, would I?"

"And would that bother you, not having a drink at all?"

"No, I don't think so." Her hands felt slippy on the leather of her bag – she didn't remember picking it up, but it was on her lap and she could feel sweat dripping down the back of her neck. Flustered, she stared at a paperclip on the grey carpet just in front of Kit's trainer.

The truth was she couldn't remember the last day she hadn't had a few glasses of wine – so she didn't actually know whether not having it would bother her. After a slight pause she told him this. After all, she wasn't in denial about how much she drank. If she was an alcoholic she would have been in denial. That was a big part of the illness – it was almost the definition. If you thought you were an alcoholic then you probably weren't. She'd been clinging to that little truth for a while now.

But instead of condemning her as an alcoholic Kit changed tack. "Do you ever drink anything else besides wine, Sarah?"

The fact he'd called her Sarah reminded her that whatever she told him would be attributed to someone else and, feeling a strange sense of liberation, she told him she drank gin and tonic, too – not much – a litre or two of gin every couple of weeks. She knew this because she put at least one empty bottle in the green recycling bin every fortnight. Never any more than two bottles. She was quite proud of that, although occasionally she put the recycling bin that contained innocuous plastic shampoo bottles and milk containers over the one that contained glass - in case the neighbours took more than a passing interest.

"So you're mixing your drinks?" he asked unexpectedly, and she stared at him.

"Is that bad?"

He paused, and suddenly she'd had enough. In the cold light of day listing all her drinks like this sounded a lot worse than it felt. It wasn't as though she ever got drunk – well, very occasionally she did, but hardly ever. Not one of her friends had ever commented on how much she drank, although, come to think of it, she'd had an awful lot of jokey drink-related birthday cards this year. Not even Tom had commented. Mind you, he didn't comment on much she did; he was too tied up with his job to notice.

She wanted to get out of here – she'd only come to reassure herself her drinking habits were normal. For heaven's sake, if you were French you drank gallons of wine, didn't you - not just the odd bottle. The French had the stuff with every meal. A ten-year-old French child probably drank more than she did. But before she left she really needed to establish she was fine and didn't have a problem. Otherwise the whole embarrassing experience would be a waste of time.

"Am I drinking too much?" she asked, glad her voice sounded perfectly calm. "I mean, I know I'm not teetotal, but I'm not too OTT, am I?"

"Do you know what the recommended amount of alcohol units for women is?" Kit smiled as he spoke, as if they were about to share some private joke.

Reassured, she smiled back. "Yes, it's something absurd like twenty-one units a week, isn't it?"

"A bit less than that – it's fourteen units for women."

She waved a hand, feeling in control again. "Everyone knows that's ridiculous. It's like the government recommendation for eating five portions of fruit and veg a day – a nice idea, but utterly impossible in reality. I mean, no one lives like that." Her stomach rumbled at the thought of food. She'd been too anxious to eat breakfast. At least she didn't feel sick any more. She glanced at the clock – soon this would be over and she could escape and get something to eat.

"Sarah. From what you've told me, you're drinking at least fourteen units a day. So in a week you'd be drinking – what – almost seven times the recommended limit?" His voice was soft, completely non-judgmental, but the words hit her like a bucket of ice.

For a few seconds she was too shocked to speak. The little room felt oppressive and her head was spinning. No longer caring about body language, she grabbed her bag again and closed her eyes for good measure so she didn't have to look at him.

"Shit, am I?" she whispered, opening her eyes and staring at a point to the left of her shoes.

"According to what you've told me, yes. I could list all the damaging effects of alcohol - what it's doing to your body - but you don't need me to do that, do you? You're obviously bright. You can work it out for yourself."

When she forced herself to meet his gaze, his eyes were gentle, but he was no longer smiling.

She nodded, wondering if she looked as shaken as she felt. "Yeah, I can work it out. But just because I drink a lot, it doesn't mean I'm an – an – *alcoholic.*" She had to force the word out. "I mean, I don't get through a bottle of spirits a day. I can still do my job fine. I'm good at it."

"I can't tell you what you are or what you aren't. You came here because you were worried. All I can tell you are the facts. It's up to you to decide what you want to do from here."

He let that sink in and she chewed the inside of her mouth, longing for a cigarette and trying to get her head back into some kind of normal thinking pattern. Everything seemed distant now. The sound of the drill, the drone of traffic, all muted. As if she was in a little bubble of unreality while the real world went on outside the window, unconcerned.

"We can help you if you want some help. It's up to you."

"What do I need to do?"

In answer, he got up and came across the small space between them. He had some papers in his hand.

15

Where had those come from? He crouched beside her chair and showed her the forms.

"This one's a confidentiality agreement. We'll need you to sign it. This one tells you what we're about and gives you information about our appointments system, our aims and objectives and our mission statement."

"Everyone has a mission statement these days, don't they?"

He rocked back on his heels and smiled at her. "Yeah, I guess they do."

She was relieved she could still joke about things like mission statements. Paperwork, she was familiar with. The Adult Ed courses she taught at City College were riddled with paperwork. They were on the same side. They could laugh at mission statements together.

"This other form's self-explanatory. But I would like to go through it before you go. Then you take it away with you. You don't have to put anything personal on it. But you will need to fill it in. Then you bring it back next week so we can discuss it. If you're coming back next week. Are you? Would you like me to make another appointment?"

"Yes," she said slowly. "I think maybe I would."

Chapter Three

Twenty minutes later she was outside again. The roadworks team had downed tools and disappeared. People in suits were hurrying along the pavements, juggling their mobiles with takeout coffees – lunch on the run. A Big Issue seller was arguing with a black cab driver about change. On the opposite side of the street, a man with mad black hair and a scruffy denim jacket was staggering out of The George. When she'd phoned the helpline, the girl who'd answered had told her the drop in centre was opposite a pub. "Bit ironic," she'd said.

Ironic wasn't the word for it. She gazed back at the drunk. He could hardly stand up by the look of him and it wasn't yet one o'clock. He lurched against the wall of the pub and almost fell.

She felt an unexpected wave of sympathy, which she hastily suppressed. He was a proper alcoholic – she didn't even think about drinking in the day. How could she possibly be the same as him?

Everything around her looked normal, but she didn't feel normal inside. She felt as though a part of her world had been jolted off its axis. It was ridiculous; she was still the same person she'd been when she went into S.A.A.D. She didn't ever have to go back. Even though she'd made another appointment – she could cancel it – they just needed twenty-four hours' notice. Then someone more deserving, more in need of their services could take her place. Like that man across the street. He probably didn't know the place was here.

Perhaps she should go back in and tell someone and they could hook him in and dry him out or whatever they did to people with real problems.

Remembering her mobile, she switched it on and a text message flashed up on the screen.

Hi hun, long time no c. When can u do lunch? Tanya Xx

She lit a Silk Cut and phoned her. It was a relief to hear her friend's voice, a thread of normality through the weirdness of the day.

"So how's it going, SJ?"

"Fine, absolutely fine," she murmured, giving the usual response. The required response. No one ever expected you to say anything else, did they? It was just politeness to ask. One of those stupid English traditions. You'd say you were fine if your leg was dropping off. "How's you?" she asked. "Keeping busy?"

"Mad busy. As ever." Tanya was an accountant, although she was as far from the stereotype as it was possible to get. "How about you? You up for lunch some time?"

"Yeah. Sure. Hey, I don't suppose you fancy lunch now, do you, Tanya? Are you in your office? I'm near Chinatown – say if you're busy."

"I'm never too busy for a girlie lunch." Her friend laughed throatily. She had the sexiest laugh on the planet and it wasn't a cultivated thing. From her wild red hair to her outrageously short skirts, nothing about Tanya was cultivated. Tanya's laugh put some perspective back into things and SJ relaxed a little. She hadn't been aware she was so tense until she felt her neck muscles unknot.

18

"I'll meet you in *All Bar One* in around ten minutes," Tanya was saying. "Mine's a white wine if you get there before me. Standard – not one of those bucket-sized glasses you drink. I'm seeing a client this afternoon."

"Okay," SJ said, feeling guilty and thinking of the form she was supposed to fill in. She was pretty sure people with drink problems, even minor ones, shouldn't go into wine bars. It was the equivalent of a dieter going into a cake shop and drooling over the cream donuts – far too much temptation. Bollocks, she could have a Diet Coke. It wasn't like she needed to drink.

Minutes later, she pushed through the plate-glass doors of the bar. To be honest she didn't much like *All Bar One*. It was a bit too well-lit, a bit too fresh faced and samey. But then to be fair she didn't much like bars of any description. She preferred old fashioned pubs like The Red Lion, which was where she taught Poetry and a Pint on a Wednesday night. The Red Lion was all beams and dark corners, with a landlord called Brian who was a bit grumpy but let her have the room out the back dirt cheap on the proviso she encouraged her students to drink as many pints as possible without falling over.

Maybe she didn't like *All Bar One* because she was too old, SJ thought with a pang. The place was staffed by pimply lads who didn't look old enough to be serving and bored-looking teenage girls who made her feel about a hundred. She went to the bar, dry-mouthed and tense, and heard herself ordering two dry white wines. "Yes, that's standard ones, please." How had that happened? She'd meant to order Diet Coke.

She fumbled for her purse – that damn Tampax had escaped again. Her rummaging caused it to spring to the top of her bag and poke out like some proud paper erection. Shoving it back down and ignoring the barman's smirk, she extracted a fiver and a couple of pound coins. Thinking about it, she'd save a fortune if she only drank what she'd agreed this week. If she gave up smoking too, she'd be a millionaire. There was always a bright side, wasn't there?

Not that she paid for much of the wine she drank at home. Tom ordered it by the case and refilled the fridge every time it was empty. He never complained she drank too much. He only complained if she opened one of the reds he was saving for a special occasion. Expensive reds weren't for midweek drinking. Not that she ever did drink red; she didn't like it so much – unless she ran out of white.

"That was good timing," Tanya said from behind her. "Thanks – shall we find a table? Are we eating? Shall I grab a menu?"

Handing them leather-bound menus, the ten-year-old barman stared at Tanya's legs. Oblivious to his gaze, Tanya sashayed across the room like a catwalk model. SJ wished she had legs like Tanya's – the women were about the same height, but while Tanya had legs to die for, hers were too thick – and hairy if she didn't shave them constantly. The downside of having nearly black hair and olive skin – SJ wished she was red haired and glamorous like Tanya.

High maintenance legs, like hers, were best kept covered up with jeans or leggings – although perhaps slightly less floral overload would have worked better. Nevertheless, no one should be subjected to her legs without a government health warning.

"So what's new?" Tanya asked, pulling out two stools at a table near a window. "You sounded a bit weird on the phone."

"Did I?" SJ stared at her drink. The pale liquid glowed enticingly in reflected sunlight. Never had it looked so much like nectar but, inexplicably, she was scared to take a sip.

"Yes, you did. Are you all right? Come on. Give. What have you been up to? Is it work?"

SJ looked into Tanya's concerned green eyes and frowned. She thought she'd hidden her feelings better than that. She had no intention of telling Tanya where she'd just been. Already, the shame of her appointment was sliding into the past. She'd just go there for a few more sessions, get some tips on how to cut down and then, with luck, she'd be sorted and there'd be no need to tell anybody – ever. She took a sip of her drink and glanced around. There was no one at any of the nearby tables. Perhaps people didn't go out for lunch on Tuesday lunchtimes. And this place was huge anyway. Even if they'd been busy, you could have a perfectly private conversation without anyone overhearing.

"I'm fine, work's fine. Only another couple of weeks and the summer is mine – well, apart from 'Poetry and a Pint' of course, but that's a walk in the park compared to Macbeth and Wuthering Heights. Everything's cool."

She stretched her hands above her head to demonstrate just how utterly cool everything was and narrowly avoided falling off her stool, which was designed for perching on and looking good, but not relaxing.

But Tanya, who was one of the most perceptive people she knew, didn't look as though she would be easily deflected.

"You're a rubbish liar, SJ. Come on, I'm your best friend. Tell me what's up. I might be able to help. And even if I can't – well…" She spread her hands apart. Her fingernails were painted white with little red crosses – in honour of the England football team who were playing someone or other on Saturday.

Another contrast, SJ thought uneasily, glancing at her own chewed nails and hiding them in her lap. Not that she'd have painted her nails with red crosses even if she'd had any to paint. Most of the black cabs sported flags sticking out at right angles. She was surprised there was no big screen in here – you couldn't usually get away from the football when England were playing.

"Something's obviously wrong," Tanya continued. "You look like you need a hug. You're not having problems with Tom, are you?"

SJ shook her head and put her glass back on the table – it was empty, she realised with a small shock.

Tanya followed her gaze. "You needed that, didn't you? You little alky…" Many a true word spoken in jest. "…Want another?"

"NO!" SJ knew the 'no' had come out as a yelp. "I can't, I'm working later. Tanya – do you think I drink too much?"

"Sometimes maybe, but no more than anyone else I know. Why? Are you worried?"

SJ took a deep breath. Tanya was bound to worm it out of her sooner or later and to her surprise she had a strong urge to confess. This morning's honesty, even though she'd lied about her name, had been quite cathartic. "I've just been to an alcohol advisory place. I

22

was a bit worried, that's why I went. To put my mind at rest."

Tanya rested her chin on her hands and looked interested and concerned simultaneously. "And did they put your mind at rest?"

"No, they seemed to think I was right. I am drinking too much."

"So what did they suggest?"

"That I cut down." SJ stared at her empty glass and wished she didn't want a refill quite so badly.

"That's going well then." Tanya gave her a wry smile. "Do you want to cut down?"

"Not at this particular moment, no. What I really want to do is get absolutely blotto. I think it's the stress. It was a shock finding out that I might have – you know – a problem."

"Why did you go there in the first place?"

"Because over the weekend when Tom was away I got a bit drunk – well actually I got very drunk. And then I couldn't remember what happened. It was awful."

"Oh, you poor darling." Tanya's voice was all concern, which made it worse. "We've all been there, you know. It's the kind of thing that happens at parties. You get carried away and don't realise how much you've drunk. It doesn't mean you're an alcoholic."

"I wasn't at a party." SJ could feel her face heating up, but now she'd started she wanted Tanya to know the whole story – well, nearly the whole story. "I was at home watching a movie. It was just a normal Sunday night."

"You mean you were on your own?"

"Mmm. Are you shocked?"

"No," Tanya said quietly. "Of course I'm not shocked. Well, maybe a bit surprised. I knew you drank, but I didn't know it had got out of hand. Were you upset about anything?"

"No, I don't think so. I just opened this bottle of wine and it was going down well, so when I finished it I opened another one. I drank most of that. I mean, I felt fine, I didn't even feel particularly drunk until I got up to let Ash out – I'd locked him in the kitchen by mistake, poor love, and he was barking."

"Then what happened?"

"I think I went to the loo and then I finished the wine – well, maybe not all of it. There was about a glass left." She hadn't told Kit that little snippet, she thought with a stab of guilt. That had certainly been more than a fourteen-unit night. Mind you, she'd felt too ill to drink much the following day – which probably cancelled it out.

"But that was a one-off – right?" Tanya probed.

"Well, I don't get that drunk very often, obviously..." SJ hesitated, wondering whether to tell Tanya what else had happened. No, she couldn't. It had been awful enough first time round; she didn't fancy reliving it. Not now. Preferably never.

"What does Tom say about it?"

"I don't think he's noticed. He's never said anything. I didn't tell him I was going to that place today."

"Will you tell him tonight when he gets in from work?"

"Yeah, I guess. If he gets back before midnight."

Tanya looked worried. "You two aren't having problems, are you, SJ?"

"I don't really see him enough for that."

24

"I see."

SJ stared at her empty glass. Tanya had been married for fifteen years. According to Tanya, Michael was her soul mate and she'd never looked at another man since they'd met. SJ had always admired her for that. She and Tom had only been married three years and they didn't have the same closeness. At least they didn't these days; he was too busy. A part of her suspected they never had.

"Me and Tom are okay. It's just me who has the problem." She had a sudden urge to cry. What on earth was the matter with her? She swallowed hard, the longing for another drink increasing. She was desperate for a cigarette too. Perhaps she should suggest they sat outside.

"But if you have got a problem, then surely you've done the right thing. You've asked for help. That's a positive step, isn't it?"

"Yeah, I guess." This was not at all what she wanted to hear. Tanya was being far too sensible. What she was supposed to say was of course SJ wasn't an alky – she just drank socially like everyone else. If Tanya had been a really good friend she might even have suggested they get a bottle and go back to hers. Then she could get as drunk as she liked. They'd done that a lot when they were younger - had the day off and gone to the pub for an extended lunchtime and then finished the day at one or other of their houses, sitting in the garden on sun loungers, gossiping and giggling. SJ brightened at the thought of doing the same now, before remembering Tanya didn't have the day off.

"I don't suppose you fancy another drink, do you?"

"I haven't touched this one yet."

25

The truth of that stood between them on the table and suddenly SJ was ashamed of herself. "I'm sorry. No, of course you haven't. I don't know what's wrong with me."

"I think you've had a wake-up call," Tanya said gently. "Look, I'm sorry, too. I'm not judging you. Do you want to talk about it?" As Tanya spoke, her mobile buzzed with a text and SJ felt a flash of relief as, momentarily distracted, her friend picked it up.

Now she'd started, she did want to talk, but the sense of unreality was back. Was she really sitting here telling her best friend she had a drink problem? She'd been drinking for years – they all did – it was the fabric of their social life. A girlie chat over a lunchtime drink, a bottle of wine with dinner, a summer barbecue when Tanya and Michael were staying over and none of them were driving. How had it suddenly become a problem?

It hadn't until she'd gone into that place, she reminded herself. In fact, if she hadn't made the appointment it still wouldn't be a problem. She wished fervently she could rewind this morning and go back to blissful ignorance. Everyone she knew drank loads – Kit would have a field day with some of her friends. They couldn't all be alcoholics, could they?

Aware that Tanya had finished reading her text and was waiting for her to answer, she decided it was time to change the subject.

"Who was texting you? Was it business or pleasure?"

"Oh, just a friend." Tanya looked flushed, two bright dots of colour reddening her cheekbones, but before SJ could follow this up Tanya put her phone back in its case and slipped it into her bag. "We're talking about you, not me. Come on, give. I want to know what happened. What else did they say? Are they going to tell your doctor?"

"No way. They couldn't, even if they wanted to. I didn't give them my real name."

"What did you say your name was then?"

"Sarah Carter."

Tanya raised her eyebrows incredulously. "Well, that's okay then. No one can *possibly* work that out. Sarah-Jane *is* your name. And Carter's your maiden name, isn't it?"

"Yes, but I'm not Sarah-Jane any more. No one calls me that – well, no one except Mum. And I'm Crosse, not Carter. It's different."

"Hmmm." Tanya shook her head. "Wouldn't it have been better to tell them your name was Debbie or Carol or something?"

"Probably," SJ said miserably, thinking that Tanya was right and it was a rubbish alias.

She kicked off her shoes, which were trendy, but crippling. They went with her Sarah Carter image. Cool city girl – someone who doesn't have to try too hard. Someone who doesn't care too much – except the image, like the shoes, didn't quite fit. A shrink in a suit would have had a field day with that. Good job Kit wasn't a shrink in a suit or she definitely wouldn't have agreed to go back.

She realised she was already searching for a reason not to return. Then she could forget all about this morning's little chat which, as well as being cathartic, had brought some very unsettling feelings to the surface, and carry on as normal. Well, she'd cut down, of course, but not quite as much as Kit had suggested – everyone knew the government guidelines were unrealistic.

27

"Why don't we head back to mine? It's more private there and we can talk properly." Tanya's voice was soft and SJ nodded, glanced wistfully at her glass and wondered whether she should suggest getting a bottle to take with them. It was much easier to talk about problems over a few glasses of wine.

"Maybe I could get …"

"Don't even think about it," Tanya interrupted with a frown. "I wouldn't be much of a friend if I encouraged you to get into even more trouble than you're already in."

"Look, I've probably made this sound worse than it really is," SJ muttered, deciding she'd actually prefer to go home after all. She had some nice cold Chardonnay in the fridge and it was calling to her. "They didn't actually say I was an alcoholic – they didn't even say I had to stop drinking."

Tanya looked sceptical.

"Anyway, what about your client?" SJ asked, frantically changing tack. "You can't let him down. He's relying on you."

"I'll phone him. It's not urgent. I'm going to help you out with this one, SJ. You won't have to deal with it on your own." She gave a sweet smile of solidarity, which was probably meant to be reassuring but had the effect of making SJ reach for her fags as they got to the door.

"I can catch up with work tomorrow," Tanya added, as they stepped out into the sun. "I think in the circumstances, this is more important, don't you?"

SJ was about to say it wasn't when Tanya touched her arm.

"When I lost Maddie you were there for me, SJ. You were there every step of the way. Every hospital appointment, every phone call, even when I called you in the middle of the night."

"That was different. You were grieving."

"It was not different. It was the worst thing that ever happened to me and I… well, I wouldn't have got through it without you."

SJ swallowed. Tanya hardly ever mentioned Maddie – the baby she and Michael had longed for and planned and then lost when she was born three months prematurely. And now, as she looked into her friend's green eyes, she could see tears glittering. She took a deep lungful of smoke, blew it out into the summer air and felt some of the tension leave her shoulders.

"Okay, thanks. If you're sure you don't mind I'll come back to yours. I could really do with a chat."

Chapter Four

Talking had been good, SJ thought, as she left the crowded tube station later that afternoon and walked the last part of her journey home through the beginning of the rush hour.

She and Tanya had been friends for what must be coming up twenty years, but she'd never been as frank with her friend as she'd been today – and knowing Tanya would never divulge her secret, not even to Michael, had strengthened the bond between them. It was an 'us against the world' feeling, similar to the one she'd had when she'd become blood sisters with the girl next door when she was ten.

Tom's car wasn't in the drive, SJ noticed as she reached their house. Climbing up the marble steps that led to the front door, she let herself in. Not that she'd really been expecting him to be home. He'd said he'd probably have to work late when he'd left this morning.

Ash was in his favourite position, on his blanket by the range cooker, and he thumped his tail lazily, but didn't bother getting up to greet her.

"Garden," she told him, unlocking the back door. "Come on, you lazy lump – out."

Yawning, he stretched and reluctantly strolled across the kitchen, blinking and pausing for a head-stroke when he reached her. He was old now for a greyhound; they didn't know exactly how old because he'd been second-hand. "Dumped on the North Circular," the dogs' home had explained when SJ and Tom had chosen him. But his soft grey muzzle was flecked with white, and he'd developed a little paunch lately – too many titbits, probably; he was a terrible scrounger and she couldn't resist his melting brown eyes. Still, everyone was entitled to a little paunch when they got older, weren't they?

Thinking about it, she was getting one herself. That was another thing that hit you when you got past thirty-five – although actually she was only thirty-six. It got harder and harder to keep off the weight, especially round the tummy, which was her weak point. She'd been as thin as a racing snake when she was younger, but now she was size fourteen (on a good day). Fortunately she was tall so it didn't look too bad. Although she had noticed lately if she told someone she was planning on going on a diet they didn't look amazed and say, "Don't be silly, SJ, you don't need to watch your weight, there's nothing of you," as people had done when she was younger. Well, apart from her mum, who was also tall and had to go to Evans for most of her clothes. But mums didn't count – they saw you with 'mother eyes', not objective ones.

Perhaps she could try slimming club again. She'd had to give up on it last time because the only way she could keep within the calorie allowance and still drink was to eat virtually nothing at all. But if she was going to cut down the wine, then it might be feasible. She could actually get to eat something this time and still lose weight. Another advantage of not drinking so much. Ha – she'd be slim and a millionaire. Wasn't there a saying about that – something like you can never be too thin or too rich? SJ had never cared much about money, but it would be lovely to rediscover her hip bones.

From the doorway she watched Ash cock his leg leisurely on the forsythia and marvelled at the size of the bladder he must have. He only ever went in the garden if she made him, and then he could wee for a good sixty seconds non-stop and not need to go again until the next day. She lit a fag and went outside to join him. She'd promised Tom she would give up smoking this summer, but she hadn't quite managed it yet.

Behind Ash, the sun cast a golden light across the rose-trellised arch that led up to the furthest reaches of their narrow, but beautifully secluded long garden. The garden was one of the things that had sold them this place. It was big for a town house garden and was an oasis of tranquillity, edged by rose bushes and surrounded by hedges and mature trees that shut out the prying eyes of neighbours.

There was a wooden summer house with its own patio in the middle section that you couldn't even see from the house, and at the far end a lily pond lay in the shadow of a willow tree. When they'd first come to view the place, they'd stepped out of the back door and been captivated. Tom had put his arm around her and said, "Think of us coming back from a hard day's work to this place, SJ, and sitting outside the summer house with a nice bottle of wine – what could be better? Our own little garden of Eden."

And she'd leaned against the solid, secure bulk of him and thought, *yes, a Garden of Eden.* It would have been better, of course, if Adam had actually been present a little more often, as opposed to Eve having to flit around Eden by herself, but you couldn't have everything. Tom was busy working – he was trying to get a promotion. It wouldn't be forever.

"Good boy," she praised Ash, before wandering back inside and reaching absently for a wine glass from the old fashioned oak dresser – there was nothing to stop her having a glass of wine on her own. On second thoughts, perhaps she'd better not start just yet – what was it she'd agreed with Kit? The form he'd given her was in her bag; she and Tanya had been discussing it earlier.

"Why have you got to put all your thoughts and feelings down on it?" Tanya had asked curiously. "Why would they want to know all that stuff? I thought they just wanted to know how much you drink."

"They're trying to establish whether your drinking follows a pattern," SJ explained. "To see if there are trigger points – certain emotions you're trying to avoid by drinking. You know – all that 'unresolved issues' stuff I studied in psychology. Which there aren't in my case, obviously. I just like the stuff. Like any busy person. It's relaxing, isn't it?"

"How about unresolved issues with Alison?" Tanya had asked with one of her irritating 'raised eyebrows' looks.

"Everyone has unresolved issues with their sister. It's par for the course."

"I don't."

Luckily, Tanya's mobile had buzzed with another text at that point – she seemed to get an awful lot of them. By the time she'd read it and switched it off, the unresolved-issues-with-your-sister moment had passed.

Now SJ retrieved the creased form from the bottom of her bag and stared at it. She'd agreed to drink no more than three quarters of a bottle of wine a night. Hmmm, well that shouldn't be too difficult; she had exactly that amount of Chardonnay in the fridge left over from yesterday.

Earlier, she'd told Kit this when he'd asked what she was going to do with the left over quarter bottle.

Neither of them had mentioned she'd have the same problem the night after, but that was probably because it was so obvious. She'd just put the unfinished quarter back in the fridge – easy!

She glanced at her watch – still only six thirty-five. It was going to be a long night at this rate. She'd have to do something to distract herself. There wasn't much point in cooking dinner yet. Tom was unlikely to be home before nine. Perhaps she could take Ash for a stroll up to the park.

That was another thing she liked about living just north of the river – the surfeit of parks to walk Ash. Hampstead Heath was a stone's throw away – in the mornings the car park was choc a block with the transit vans of commercial dog walkers, exercising their city charges – and there was another smaller park in the opposite direction that didn't tend to get quite so busy.

Maybe she could take him there now before dinner. She pictured herself power walking around the exterior while Ash dawdled on a sniffing bonanza, which was his favourite thing in the world to do. Bloody hell, she felt virtuous. An evening of exercise and abstinence, at this rate she'd have no vices left. Apart from the fags, of course. She seemed to have got through rather a lot this afternoon. Oh well, she could power walk back via a detour to the corner shop to restock. Good plan.

When she got back with a slightly surprised and panting Ash – he wasn't used to power walks - it was still only just gone eight. SJ grabbed a ready meal for two from the freezer and put it on a baking tray in the oven. As she straightened up, she just missed knocking herself out on Tom's latest acquisition, an earthenware pub jug that he'd hung on a brass hook just to the left of the oven. He was a fanatical hoarder of breweriana – his beer mat collection was huge, and he was forever picking up bits of old pub junk to add to his collection.

The beer jug would have to find another home, SJ decided, rubbing her head as she set the timer on her mobile phone and wondered what to do next. It was still a bit early to start her three quarters of a bottle. She went and had a look at it instead. Tom had installed a feature bar in their lounge, behind which was a wine fridge that also contained tonic and soft drinks. Above the bar was a row of optics he'd got from a friend who'd just sold his riverside pub to developers, along with Tom's display of corkscrews, which were much more useful than anything else he collected.

Tom occasionally had an after-dinner Scotch and the bottle was half full. It had been half full for ages, but the gin optic was nearly empty. Perhaps she should finish it now so it wasn't a temptation. That was a good plan – Kit was bound to tell her not to drink gin sooner or later. She'd managed to sidestep the issue today by telling him they had hardly any left.

She took a crystal tumbler from behind the bar, and also a wine glass - well, she'd need that in a bit. Then she fetched the frozen lemon slices from the freezer and went back into the lounge. Expectation of the first drink of the day – marvellous. The first one was always the best: no matter how many more you had you couldn't beat that first feeling of liquid relaxation seeping through your body. BLISS.

The flashing light of the answer machine caught her attention and she pounced on it, hoping it wasn't a message from Tom saying he'd be even later than planned.

The first brief message was from Tanya's husband Michael, confirming a squash court booking with Tom at the weekend. The second message was lengthier.

"Good evening, Sarah-Jane, this is your mother here. Thank you very much for the car boot sale contribution – we raised another thirty pounds for the Cats' Protection League." SJ suppressed a smile. Mum had her telephone voice on, which was posh and slightly self-conscious. She hated talking to answer machines. "So thank you. Anyway, I'm phoning because your father and I are trying to finalise the party arrangements. I know you're very busy, but could you please call me when you get a minute." A small pause. "We need to discuss things." Another pause. "It's quite urgent, Sarah-Jane." The posh accent was slipping a bit. "No, she's not in, Jim, I'm just leaving a message. Oh, bugger, you know I hate talking to these things. Phone me back, love. Bye-ee."

Another distraction. Excellent. SJ dialled her parents' number and settled on the settee.

"Hi, Mum. What's so urgent? The party isn't till September."

"It's early September, love, and it's a lot to organise. It's a big day for us – and we want to do things properly. Make sure everything goes without a hitch – you know."

SJ was pretty sure the hitch referred to herself and her sister, Alison, whom she'd managed to avoid being in the same room as for the last five years. No mean feat, when their parents had a thing about Proper

Family Gatherings. So far she'd been 'ill at the last minute' for three Christmases, four birthday celebrations and one meal out to celebrate Mum and Dad's Premium Bond win.

The rest of the occasions she'd either had cast-iron-can't-possibly-miss prior engagements or just turned up so late that Alison had already left. Up to now, things had worked out just fine, but she had a feeling her parents' ruby wedding anniversary was going to present problems. She should be there. She'd feel guilty if she wasn't there. It was her daughterly duty to be there. Unfortunately, it was also Alison's daughterly duty to be there – and no way was SJ going within a five mile radius of her sister, especially not with Tom by her side.

"I wish you'd forget this silly feud," her mother went on quietly. "You know Alison feels terrible about what happened." SJ doubted that very much. The only thing Alison ever felt terrible about was if she accidentally broke a nail, or her hairdresser put the wrong shade of highlights in her hair, or she put on an ounce or two. "She's really sorry she hurt you. She'll regret it for the rest of her days…"

SJ mouthed her mother's next words at the phone. *"And it's all such a long time ago."*

"And it's all such a long time ago. We would so like you both to be there. At the same time, I mean. It would really make our day."

"That's emotional blackmail, Mum."

"It's not emotional blackmail. It's a mother wanting to be with her family on her special day. You'll understand when you have your own children."

"Mmm," SJ said, hoping they weren't going into the *when-are-you-going-to-give-me-a-grandchild?*

37

routine. That was another sore point between her and Tom. She'd wanted to try before she was too much older and he was worried they couldn't afford it.

"Why don't we meet up for a drink, love? It's been ages since we've seen that lovely husband of yours."

"Good idea," SJ replied absently, reminded of her gin and tonic mission. "Why don't you come over for dinner and I'll get Tom to cook for us? It's a bit soon to organise it for this Saturday." She'd need a lot more than four days to think up a good enough excuse to miss the ruby wedding party. "How about the one after that? We can have a good chinwag then."

"That sounds lovely - if you're sure you don't mind. All right, we'll see you then. We'll bring a nice bottle of wine."

SJ put down the phone with a sigh of relief. Saturday week was certainly far enough away not to have to worry about it. Right – back to the business in hand. It was still too early to start on the wine, but a gin and tonic would fill the gap nicely.

Having extricated a double from the optic she could see there wasn't enough for another whole measure so she added what was left and reached for the tonic. There wasn't any room for the lemon – oh well. She was mid-pour when the front door banged and she heard the double thump of Tom's laptop and briefcase on the solid wood floor of the hall.

"Hi, darling," she called, torn between relief and, for some reason, guilt. "Had a good day?"

By the sound of his answering grunt he hadn't, and he didn't come into the lounge but went straight upstairs.

He'd probably cheer up after a beer. SJ hooked one out of a stack behind the bar. She was halfway through the gin and tonic, enjoying the glorious taste of juniper berries – people said gin didn't taste, but it did – when she remembered she was supposed to fill in her form about how she felt before she had her first drink. Damn.

She knew how she felt now – pretty relaxed. How had she felt before? Thirsty probably; what else were you going to be just prior to pouring yourself a drink? She had a sneaking suspicion Kit might not find that as amusing as she did so she decided to think about it tomorrow and put something sensible like 'needed to relax'.

Having got this sorted she stood at the bottom of the stairs and called up: "Dinner will be ready in ten minutes, Tom. Are you having a shower first?"

"Uh huh. Won't be a tick."

She slipped her empty G&T glass into the dishwasher just before he reappeared. Well, there was no point in keeping it out as she wasn't having any more.

"Hi, sweetie. That smells nice. What is it?"

"Salmon in white wine sauce," she said, glancing at the packet. Bloody hell – more wine. She hadn't noticed that. Blimey, it was going to be difficult to cut down if manufacturers were putting the stuff in food. How irresponsible. She turned to smile at him. "Mum phoned. I invited them for dinner Saturday week, is that okay?"

"Sure. Are we having wine now? Or is that a silly question?"

What on earth was he on about? They didn't have wine every night. SJ frowned. Actually, yes, they did.

"I think there's some Chardonnay left over. I might as well finish that off."

"Okay, I'll get it." He raked a hand through his rumpled dark hair, which looked damp from his shower. "If we're having fish, SJ, I might join you. I fancy a glass of white with fish."

This throwaway line caused her to drop the serving spoon in alarm. "I don't think there's much left," she called after his retreating back. There certainly wasn't enough for him – not if she was going to have her three quarters of a bottle. Not that it would matter if she had a glass less, of course, but she'd psyched herself up for the full three quarters. She was allowed it – she was entitled to it. Kit had said so – she had it in black and white on her form.

"Don't panic, I can always open another one," Tom called over his shoulder. "You're not going to miss out."

That was an even worse idea. If he opened another bottle she might be tempted to exceed her limit. SJ gave herself a little shake – for goodness' sake – get a grip. It's not like you need to drink a certain amount. You could skip it altogether if you wanted and then the problem of when to stop wouldn't arise.

Then she remembered the glass she'd had at lunchtime. Thinking about it, that probably counted towards the three quarters – so technically it'd be better if Tom did have a glass. Having finally got that sorted out, she relaxed.

Then Tom ruined everything by coming back with a bottle of Moet in his hand. "I thought we'd open this as well, as it's a special occasion."

His whole face was a smile and she smiled back cautiously, pleased he was pleased, and wondering if she'd forgotten something. Anniversary? Birthday?

40

Nothing sprang to mind; surely her memory hadn't got that bad.

"Don't look so worried." He waved the bottle in the air. She hadn't seen him so animated for ages. "I wasn't expecting to hear so soon, but I got the nod from old Wilson today. I got the promotion." He put on a silly voice. "Hey, babe – you are looking at Barton Aerospace's new regional sales manager. How cool is that?"

SJ smiled, delighted for him. Despite the fact he was a very good salesman he was touchingly modest about his own success. He'd always been like that. It was one of the things she really liked about him. "That's brilliant news, congratulations. Why didn't you tell me as soon as you got in?"

"I only got in twenty minutes ago. Do I get a hug?"

"Course you do." She felt torn in two as she went into his arms. She was thrilled for him; he'd worked hard for this – he deserved it. It would mean more money too, which would be helpful as they had a humungous mortgage. It would also mean he'd spend more nights away and she tended to get herself in trouble when he was away. The time she'd told Tanya about hadn't been the first.

More pressingly, there was the little matter of the champagne. The gold foil glinted tantalisingly. She loved champagne – why, oh why did they have to celebrate just when she'd decided to cut down? Perhaps she could have one glass and then revert to wine. It was probably about the same strength – and made from grapes, so it wouldn't be counted as 'mixing your drinks'. But she'd had the gin as well. That definitely mixing. Actually, she was beginning to feel a

41

little light-headed. She and Tanya never had got round to eating earlier.

"Let me get dinner served before it burns," she said, extricating herself from Tom's arms.

"Just turn the oven off for a minute. I want to open this first."

SJ did as he said. Of course, she could just tell him she was worried she was drinking too much – she had planned to tell him where she'd been today – but she couldn't do that now. She couldn't spoil his moment.

Oh, by the way, Tom, I think I might have a drink problem – nothing to worry about – just need to cut down a tad. I'm not a raging alcoholic – ha ha. Well – not yet.

That was something else Kit had said that had hit home. If she didn't control her drinking then things would only get worse. SJ had believed him. She knew she drank more now than she had before her marriage. She wasn't sure why – certainly not because of 'unresolved issues' – more likely because she had more opportunity these days, and more money. Or rather, Tom did.

The popping of the champagne cork jolted her back to the present and she watched Tom pour the pale golden fizz into flutes. He handed her one, smiling proudly, the brightness in his eyes rivalling the sparkle of their champagne.

"To future success," he said, and downed the drink in a few gulps.

"To future success," she echoed, hoping the bleakness she felt hadn't found its way into her voice.

And then she followed his example.

42

Chapter Five

SJ had met Tom at a fortieth birthday party thrown by one of her A-level students. Julie was an older mum who had worked with a travelling theatre company before she'd decided to put her career on hold to concentrate on her IVF twins.

"They're gorgeous, don't get me wrong, but I miss adult company and I thought English Lit might stop me from ending up completely brain dead," she'd told SJ with a smile when they'd first met.

Julie was smart and lively with a great sense of humour and SJ had always liked her, although she hadn't immediately accepted when Julie had invited her to the party.

Although Adult Education wasn't like teaching children, there was still an unwritten rule about getting too involved with individual students. It could cause conflicts in classes: SJ knew more than one tutor who had lived to regret getting over-friendly.

"Oh, please come," Julie pressed, sensing her hesitation. "It'll be fun. I've invited the whole cast from Jack and the Beanstalk. They're doing the Hackney Empire at the moment."

It had sounded like fun. And it looked like fun, SJ thought, as her cab dropped her off outside the pub annexe that Julie had hired for the party.

It was nerve racking going into a room full of people she didn't know, but a very nice lady - Julie's mum, she suspected - met her at the door.

"Actor? Friend from school? Or miscellaneous other?" She greeted SJ with a grin.

"Miscellaneous other," SJ said, just as Julie spotted her and ran over with a squeal.

"SJ – brilliant. I'm so glad you could come. Mum, this is the tutor I was telling you about. She can make the dullest of literary tomes sound fresh and new." She kissed SJ on the cheek. "Honestly, Mum, if it wasn't for SJ I'd have gone stark raving mad …" She broke off as someone tapped her on the shoulder.

SJ was slightly relieved. She'd never been good at receiving compliments and English Literature wasn't exactly a life changing course. Not like *Hypnotise your way to Happiness*, or *Slim your way to Success*, which were two other courses City College did, and ones she fancied trying herself if she ever had time.

Julie's mum turned to greet someone else so SJ made her way towards the bar. The oblong-shaped annexe, which looked like it had once been a skittle alley, was already packed and was loud with the thrum of music and chatter. She felt a little intimidated; it was ages since she'd been to a party, and then she hadn't been on her own. Everyone seemed to know everyone else and the new pink top she was wearing, which had seemed fine in the shop, now felt too tight and revealing. This was mostly thanks to the cab driver, who had both told her breasts the fare and also thanked her breasts for the tip.

Hot as it was, SJ wished she'd worn a jacket. She was still trying to attract the barman's attention when she heard Julie's voice behind her.

"Sorry about abandoning you."

"Oh, that's okay." She turned to find Julie clutching the arm of a tall man with a sheepish grin and very blue eyes.

"This is my cousin, Tom. He doesn't know a soul either. Tom, this is Sarah-Jane, my English tutor. SJ for short."

"Hello."

"Can I get you a drink?" They spoke at the same time.

"Gin and tonic, please."

Tom was managing not to stare down her top, which was a relief. He was obviously a man of subtlety.

"Are you an actor?" she asked.

"No. I sell bits of aeroplanes – not very exciting, I'm afraid."

"Don't be afraid." SJ studied his side-view discreetly as he stood at the bar. He was wearing a cobalt-blue shirt, and his dark hair was untouched with grey. He had nice ears: very flat and neat and clean. He looked older than her, maybe late thirties, but he was wearing well.

She liked the way he attracted the barman's attention without being pushy, and then gestured her ahead of him back through the throng of people.

There weren't any unoccupied tables and the chairs that were free were festooned with bags and coats. SJ berated herself for arriving so late.

"We could sit outside if you like?" Tom suggested. "There's a lovely pub garden. And we'll be able to hear ourselves speak."

She followed him past blown-up photographs of Julie at various ages, and on through a fire exit, which gave way to a patio area, set up with bench tables and chairs. Silver helium balloons emblazoned with the

45

number 40 floated from several tables that were occupied by clusters of people, deep in conversation.

Tom led her across the lawn – a square of dark velvet in the shadowy dusk – to a table on the edge. Just beyond it was an oak tree and there were rose bushes somewhere. She could smell their sweet scent drifting across the summer air. Tom was right. It was beautiful out here.

They sat on a slightly damp wooden bench and he quizzed her about her work. She found herself relaxing with the help of the wine and telling him all about her love of poetry – she never told anyone about that – and how she'd always fancied starting up a class which made poetry fun and not the dry boring subject many English teachers would have you believe it was.

"Poetry and a pint – I think it could really take off. You know how some poetry gives you this pain here," she said, touching her left breast to demonstrate and suddenly realising that Tom, who was now obliged to look at her cleavage, still wasn't gawping. He was going up and up in her estimation.

"Like the sort of pain you get when you listen to sad music or look at a beautiful picture," he offered, proving that not only was he a good listener, but that he was sensitive and possibly artistic, too.

"Exactly like that." SJ was warming to her theme. "Well, having a pint in your hand would help, wouldn't it? It would be a sort of drowning your poetry sorrows. A pint is the perfect accompaniment to a poem. What do you think?"

Tom nodded thoughtfully and SJ liked him more and more.

"So how about you?" she said, realising she'd been monopolising the conversation. "Tell me about your life. What do you like doing?"

"I like good food and wine; eating out in pubs – the old-fashioned type with flagstones and log fires and preferably Egon Ronay."

SJ nodded approvingly.

"I like going to antique fairs too – I collect vintage beer bottles."

"What – full ones?" she asked in fascination.

"Sometimes – but mostly it's the labels I'm interested in. My granddad used to take me to antique fairs when I was small. He was a great wheeler dealer – he used to collect breweriana – and he left me his entire collection when he died."

"I'm sorry," SJ said. "I mean that he died, not that he left you his collection."

Tom smiled. "It was a long time ago."

She watched him sip his pint. He had nice hands too: stubby fingers, but neat nails, and a thick gold ring on his middle finger with some kind of crest on it.

"There was a time when I thought I might go into antiques; they're a bit of a passion. But then I ended up selling aeroplane parts instead. Which is probably better paid."

"Money isn't everything."

"No, I agree. But I love my job. Salesmen are born and not made, some say. But then teaching's a vocation too, isn't it? Julie speaks very highly of you. Apparently you're by far the most inspiring tutor in the place."

"I do love it," she said softly. "I love seeing people's confidence grow as they realise that the classics aren't as dry and inaccessible as they seem –

that all literature is basically about people and their problems, their loves and their heartbreaks. It's brilliant watching people fall in love with words. I guess that's why I like poetry too."

"And how about your loves and heartbreaks?" Tom asked softly. "Have you never wanted to get married, SJ?"

Oh blimey, she'd walked right into that one. "I'm divorced," she said, wondering if it would put him off. "I got married too young. It didn't work out."

"Was it long ago?"

"We've been separated for over a year, but the divorce was finalised in March." She shifted her gaze from his as a group of teenagers spilled into the garden and lit up cigarettes. One of the lads, who had over-long curly hair and a Byronic look about him – definitely an actor – tilted his head and blew smoke rings up into the purple sky.

SJ breathed in appreciatively and Tom looked ever so slightly pained. So that was something they didn't have in common. Oh well, she planned to give up soon. He was right; it was a horrible habit.

"Do you get on with your ex-husband? Are you still on speaking terms?" He rested his chin on his hands and studied her, his eyes curious.

It seemed a strange question. If she'd got on with him that well, they wouldn't have split up.

"I'm sorry. I don't mean to pry." For a moment he looked vulnerable.

"It's okay," she said. "And no, we don't speak any more." Her hands felt sweaty in her lap. Suddenly she longed for a cigarette. Inside the party they were playing a Robbie Williams song, *Let Me Entertain You,* which had always reminded her of Derek.

48

She swallowed hard, forced her ex-husband's image out of her mind and concentrated on Tom.

"So how about you? Have you ever been married?

He shook his head. "I work long hours. I don't have time for a lot of socialising."

"Workaholic?"

"Julie thinks so. She insisted I came tonight. I'm glad I did."

"Me too," she murmured, feeling an unexpected sense of security steal over her. There was something very peaceful about Tom; something solid and steady like the bulky old oak tree behind them. He was nothing like Derek, who'd always fizzed with energy and impatience. He was nothing like her usual type of man at all.

There was no obvious chemistry between them. Yet she did like him. She liked him a lot. Maybe subconsciously she was searching for someone as different to Derek as possible. Someone she could be comfortable with. Someone who wouldn't let her down.

Chapter Six

It was several weeks before they moved beyond friendship and SJ found Tom's patience both sweet and unsettling. Her overactive imagination went into overdrive. She began to worry he might have some hidden reason why he didn't want to seduce her. Perhaps he had a complex about his body, like a guy she'd been out with at college who'd insisted they always make love in the dark. Then on one memorable morning when he'd stayed over and all the covers had fallen off, she'd woken up to find herself face to face with a life size tattoo of Margaret Thatcher's head on his back. That had been very disconcerting.

One evening, about two months after her first date with Tom, when they were having an after-work drink at The Feathers, she asked him if he had any tattoos.

"Yeah, I have actually," he confessed, smiling at her. "I had it done when I was on an eighteen-to-thirty holiday with the boys. I was drunk at the time – I've regretted it ever since. Why? Don't you like tattoos?"

"It depends," SJ replied, feeling her heart start to thud. "It's not a person, is it?"

"No." Tom looked amused. "It's no one's name either – I wasn't that drunk."

"Phew," SJ said, although she hadn't considered girls' names. That wouldn't have been too good either – finding a girl's name tattooed down your lover's manhood would be very off-putting. Not, of course, that Tom had said where the tattoo was – but she'd seen most bits of him. It had been a blazing summer and they'd sunbathed in the park quite a bit, as well as visiting the gym when she was feeling industrious – Tom loved the pool – and she'd seen no sign of any tattoos, so it had to be somewhere quite discreet.

"Where is it?" she pressed.

"On my bum."

"Can I see it?"

"I don't see why not. Although I don't think I ought to show you in here. We might get kicked out."

"Let's go back to your place." SJ gulped down her wine, her inhibitions having vanished with the second glass, and wondered if she'd have suggested such a thing if she hadn't drunk quite so much.

Tom looked at her thoughtfully.

"I've never known you so anxious to leave a pub before. Is that a proposition?"

"Yes," she said, feeling slightly embarrassed that she'd had to ask for a peek at his tattoo in order to move things on a bit. He should have been the one doing the asking. Derek had seduced her within hours of their first meeting.

On the way home, she worried that Tom might have some other reason for not wanting to take her to bed. Perhaps he had genital herpes or some other horrible disease. Perhaps he was impotent. Or shy? Or had only one testicle – or no testicles at all. Perhaps he was really a woman. Oh God, what was she doing? Perhaps she should call the whole thing off before they got to his flat.

But the real reason was so blindingly obvious it never even occurred to her. He told her what it was when they got back to his maisonette – although he was pretty oblique, even about that.

51

"SJ, are you sure about this?" he asked, one hand on his bedroom door.

"Sure about seeing your tattoo? Yes, I can't wait." She smiled at him. "Why? Have you changed your mind about showing me?"

He blinked a couple of times and frowned. "We're not just talking about seeing my tattoo, though, are we? If I'm going to strip off in front of you, then I don't think I'll have the self control to get dressed again without – well – you know – taking our relationship a stage further." He was blushing, she saw, feeling a little tug of tenderness. He was such a nice man.

"You're not a virgin, are you?" The words were out of her mouth before she'd put her brain in gear. And she wished she could retract them because they sounded so tactless, not to mention hurtful. There was nothing wrong with being a virgin, even at thirty-five. Tom was a very nice guy. He was bound to have a good reason.

"No, of course I'm not a virgin." He shut his eyes and sighed. "I just don't sleep around. As, I'm sure, you don't."

"No." She felt light-headed with wanting him, and the idea of them making love, now it was out in the air, was impossible to put back in its box.

Yet still he hesitated and suddenly she was afraid it was her. He didn't want her because she wasn't attractive, because she'd been too pushy, because he didn't see her as anything other than a friend. In an instant she was full of self doubt.

"I've never slept around," SJ said again, aching with insecurity and shame. She'd had boyfriends at college and uni, sometimes quite unsuitable ones, but once she'd met Derek that had been it – and there had

52

been no one since. Her confidence had been smashed to pieces when they had separated. It was Tom, she realised, who had helped her pick up the pieces again.

"And I wanted you to be sure you were ready," Tom continued softly.

READY? If she got any more ready she'd need another pair of knickers. She nearly told Tom that, then decided he might think that too pushy as well. But it really was amazing how a bit of drawn out expectation could heighten your arousal.

"Yes, I am absolutely sure I'd like us to make love," she said, putting a hand on Tom's arm and propelling him into the bedroom. Which she thought was incredibly restrained – because what she'd actually have liked to do was hurl him to the floor and rip off all his clothes.

"So are you going to show me your tattoo?"

He still wasn't in a hurry. He crossed the room, drew the curtains and put on the bedside light, which threw soft shadows over his red and black striped duvet cover.

She'd never seen his bedroom before. It was a typical bachelor room – neat, with a white towelling robe on the back of the door and a copy of Richard Branson's autobiography on the bedside table. The way she felt now, SJ couldn't believe he'd managed to keep her out of it for so long.

"I haven't got any tattoos," she joked as he came back across the room. "I haven't got anything interesting to show you."

"I'm sure that's not true." He kissed her and she found herself hoping he wasn't a man who spent hours on foreplay. Their slowly building relationship had been all the foreplay she'd needed – not to mention the long months of celibacy before it.

She slid her hands up his back and tugged his shirt from his jeans.

"So impatient," he said, but that was the last resistance he put up, thank God. Within a few moments they were both undressed, from the waist up anyway. He had a great body: finely muscled, with a light smattering of dark hair on his chest and a thin line leading downwards.

He let her unfasten his jeans, but he tugged them down himself. His boxers came with them, and he kicked them off onto the carpet.

"I thought you wanted to see my tattoo," he said, huskily, as she stared downwards. He had a pretty fine erection, which was much more interesting than his tattoo, but she decided to humour him and had a peek at his bottom.

"Delicious," she said, touching the curved warmth of his skin. The tattoo itself was a rose and didn't hold her attention for long. Fortunately, he didn't seem too set on giving her a full inspection of it either. He tugged her towards the bed with a slight moan, deftly removed the rest of her clothes and SJ got so carried away she forgot to hold her stomach in – ah well – he'd find out soon enough that her washboard stomach was the result of hold-you-in pants and not workouts. They collapsed on the duvet in a tangle of limbs.

After that, apart from a brief pause while he foraged for a condom in his bedside table, there were no further distractions. Considering the build-up they'd had, it wasn't the most exciting sex in the world. It was over far too soon, but SJ put that down to newness and overexcitement. Perfection came with practice. They could work on the finer details later.

"Sorry," Tom said, as he slid out of her, holding the condom so it didn't slip off. "I'd planned on lasting a bit longer than that."

"It was wonderful," SJ said. And in a way it had been. Just before he'd come Tom had told her again how beautiful she was.

Now, as she looked at the strong planes of his face, she was filled with a quiet contentment. She was not the ugly unlovable person she had felt since things had gone so horribly wrong with Derek. Maybe she would be able to love again.

Chapter Seven

The morning after she'd been to S.A.A.D SJ woke up with a hangover and a vague sense of remorse. The bed was cold. Tom must have left hours ago. His ability to head brightly off to work with a hangover had always amazed her.

They'd both drunk far too much last night. She had a vague memory of them making love too, which had been more functional than fun – at least for her. Success and sex went together for Tom. They always had, and SJ knew she should have mentioned long ago that their lovemaking wasn't always as good for her as she pretended. But telling him that had got harder as time went on. Small white lies that had seemed harmless when told had a habit of growing into whopping great big ones.

Blinking sleepily, she reached for her mobile which had just bleeped with a text and found a message from Tanya.

How's it going? Did you stick to target? Ring me.

SJ sighed. What time was it anyway? Eight thirty-five – shit, she was going to be late if she wasn't careful. Her class didn't start until ten, but she had to get things prepared and she needed at least three mugs of strong coffee to face a roomful of students.

SJ rarely had any absentees in her classes and students often came early so they could ask her questions. She encouraged it. It wasn't a chore to talk about a subject she loved.

Today, however, she could have done with just a few minutes to gather herself. She felt unravelled, probably because of oversleeping. The headache wasn't helping either. She was popping out Nurofen from their foil when Jimmy, one of her younger students, bounded into the classroom.

"Hiya, SJ. Any chance you could spare me a sec? There's a couple of things I'd really like to run by you …" He was at her desk now and she gave him her most blazing smile to make up for the fact she wasn't exactly on top form.

"Heavy night, was it?" He brushed a lock of unruly dark hair out of his eyes. "Sympathies, mate."

"Just a slight headache," SJ said, alarmed that he'd seen straight through her smile disguise.

"Tush," Jimmy said, which she wasn't sure meant he believed her or not. But at least he was grinning. He pulled a chair up to her desk, the scrape of chair legs on floor tiles overloud. SJ tried not to wince.

Jimmy smelled of aftershave and young man's hormones. SJ couldn't remember if she'd put on scent this morning. She had a routine on hangover days – one in which she metamorphosed from a bleary-eyed, blotchy-faced wreck into a shiny, bouncy professional. It was amazing what make up, a smile and a heavy dollop of enthusiasm could do. But sometimes lately, she had noticed the transformation had got harder. Getting older had a lot to answer for.

Fortunately, by the time the rest of her class had arrived – three coffees later and the Nurofen had also kicked in – she was her usual self again. Her students were a mixture. They ranged from youngsters like Jimmy, who were on a catch up from courses they hadn't completed or done at college – to people who thought A-level English Literature would be useful for their career. She also had one lady, Sylvia, who was in her seventies and just wanted to keep her mind active.

SJ loved the teaching part. She enjoyed the course preparation too. She wasn't so keen on the marking part, but the very worst bit – the bit she had complained to Kit about – was the endless aims and objectives and learning outcomes part that the government insisted every tutor do for every student on a weekly basis to secure funding – and to 'prove' that learning had taken place.

This was, as far as SJ could see, a complete and utter waste of both the students' and her time.

"I couldn't agree more," said Harry, one of the art tutors, who SJ bumped into when she took her register back to the office. "If they give us much more paperwork there won't be time for teaching. And my course isn't even an exam subject. Totally ridiculous."

"SJ, did you see that letter in your register file?" called out the receptionist in between taking phone calls.

SJ hadn't, but she pulled it out now.

Harry glanced at it over her shoulder. "Fan mail?" he joked. "Or someone having a whinge?"

SJ blushed. "One of my ex students has just got into Oxford. He's writing to thank me."

"Hey – isn't that something. You should frame that one."

SJ stuffed the letter into her bag, pleased despite herself. Letters like this one made up for the paperwork. By the time she had filled in her time sheet and walked back out into the lunchtime sunshine the last vestiges of her hangover had disappeared.

She was almost home when she remembered the text from Tanya. Yesterday, in the mood of relief, confession and sisterly solidarity, she'd promised Tanya faithfully she wouldn't lie about her drinking – well, not to Tanya anyway.

When she got back she phoned and confessed she'd gone slightly over the top the previous night, but qualified this by saying there was bound to be a certain adjustment period.

Tanya sighed. "I meant what I said yesterday, you know. I'll help in any way I can. Do you want me to come over later – so I can keep you on the straight and narrow?"

"That's very sweet of you, but I'm busy. It's my Poetry and a Pint night."

There was a small silence which, to SJ's oversensitive ears, sounded accusing, and she felt the need to fill it with an explanation.

"It's work, not pleasure. I'm teaching so I can't drink too much. I mean, the pint's practically metaphorical. Honestly, Tanya, I'm not that irresponsible. I mean, I'm glad I went yesterday – obviously – but I don't think I need any more sessions. It's not as though I've got a serious problem. Thanks for the offer anyway," she added, pleased with herself for being so open and honest.

"What did Tom say?"

"Not much. He's just been promoted."

They talked about Tom's promotion for a while and then SJ managed to change the subject before she gave herself away and let it slip that she hadn't yet said anything to Tom.

"Anyway, enough of me. We sorted all my problems out yesterday. Haven't you got any?"

She wasn't expecting Tanya to say yes, but her friend gave the slightest of hesitations and suddenly her instincts told her she was right on target.

"It's something to do with all those texts, isn't it? Oh, Tanya, I've been really selfish. What's wrong? Why didn't you say anything yesterday?"

"Because we had other things to discuss," Tanya said. "And my problems are minor compared to yours."

"Mine are minor, too," SJ said, torn between guilt that she'd been so selfish and relief that she wasn't the only one with a problem. "Do you want to talk about it now?"

"I can't on the phone."

"What if I come round? I don't have to go out until later."

"No, don't worry. It's nothing urgent. Besides, I'm working. We can talk about it next time I see you. There's no rush. It's not the sort of thing that's going to disappear overnight."

Intrigued, SJ agreed that next time they met they'd devote the entire time to Tanya's problems and her friend laughed nervously.

"We probably won't need to, but thanks, you're a good friend."

SJ hung up, feeling uneasy. It wasn't like her beautiful, self-assured friend to have serious problems. Not ones that involved text messages from someone who SJ was suddenly sure wasn't Michael. Briefly, she considered the possibility that Tanya was having an affair. But that was ludicrous. Tanya would never have an affair. She adored her husband.

She was still thinking about Tanya as she gathered her stuff together for her Poetry and a Pint class. The Red Lion was within walking distance at a stretch, but she usually caught the bus because she had too much to carry – she had a cupboard at the pub, but it wasn't very big and SJ had a fear of being under prepared. As the bus trundled through the housing estates she wondered if it was Michael who was having an affair. But that didn't explain Tanya's texts. Unless she was speaking to his mistress. No – unlikely. She'd seemed embarrassed by the texts, guilty almost, but not upset or annoyed. Still deep in thought, SJ crossed the pub car park, called out a greeting to Jim, who was polishing glasses and didn't answer, and headed up the uncarpeted back stairs to her room.

Poetry and a Pint was a delightful antidote to English Literature. There were no exams, no stress and she didn't even have a fixed syllabus – she tended to flow with the group. Her seven students were united by their love of poetry and they were a diverse bunch. At the moment she had two performance poets, Matt and Steve, whose work was quite edgy; Matt wrote rap and Steve wrote controversial free verse. An older married couple, Bruce and Sybil, published anthologies of Christian verse, but had an excellent sense of humour and luckily were not easily offended. The rest of the class were women who just liked poetry and wanted something to do on a Wednesday night. One of them, Dorothy, who was always beautifully dressed and made-up – she reminded SJ of the women who worked on the posh make up section of a department store – wrote erotic novels as her day job.

Fascinated when she'd discovered this, SJ had volunteered herself as a proof reader if ever Dorothy wanted one.

At first she'd laughingly refused. "It might change the way you see me. And besides, you're busy enough with your teaching, I'm sure."

"I'm not too busy to help you – it's always a pleasure to look at your work. And besides, it's my job."

"We both know that's not true. This is a poetry class, after all. Reading chapters of my bonk-busters does not constitute teaching me poetry."

"I don't mind helping. You know I don't. So how's the latest one going?"

"Slowly. My editor's told me I need more sex in it – a wee bit more spice – you know."

Dorothy winked, but SJ fancied she saw a trace of wistfulness behind the humour. "I must say I do find it hard going since I lost my Alfie. We used to have such fun trying out all these new positions." She shot SJ a wicked smile, and added, "I've only my memories to rely on now, hen, although I'm not complaining. I've plenty of those."

SJ giggled. She'd seen Dorothy in a whole different light since she'd read her novels. Romantic they might be; Barbara Cartland they were certainly not.

People were endlessly fascinating, SJ decided, as she set up the tables and chairs in her room and liberated the white board from its dusty cupboard. The faces they wore for the world weren't always a true reflection of what was going on underneath. All authors could be glimpsed through their writing, but poetry tended to unveil people completely.

She'd once had a student, a teenager, who had read out a poem about having a miscarriage. Towards the end of it her voice had begun to shake and by the time she'd stopped reading the entire class had been in tears.

SJ had abandoned her desk and given her a hug. There had really been nothing else to do, and the class had talked about heartbreak and life for the rest of the session.

Afterwards, Dorothy had stayed behind.

"Well done," she'd said, her soft Scottish accent colouring her words. "You were very good with that wee girl."

"I think she just needed to get it out of her system," SJ said.

"Yes, love, I think you're right."

SJ was glad that it didn't happen too often, but she was well aware of the cathartic effects of poetry – she'd written a whole heap of angry poetry when she'd been a teenager, and some more equally self-indulgent poems when she'd split up with Derek. Not that she was ever planning on showing them to anyone. They were for her eyes only, but they had helped her deal with her pain.

Her students began to arrive. She heard voices and the clatter of footsteps on the wooden stairs as they collected their pints from the bar en route to class, as was the tradition.

SJ got herself a pint of Diet Coke, despite having to put up with a flurry of teasing comments ranging from, "Are you ill, Teach?" from Matt to "Blimey, the girl's on Coke – what is the world coming to? I thought this was poetry and a pint!" from one of the women.

She ignored their good-natured jibes and was pleased to reach the end of the session stone cold sober. This was easy – she'd certainly achieve her target tonight. By the time she'd got in and they'd eaten and cleared up, it would be time for bed. And as they'd made love last night, Tom wouldn't be expecting to do it again. So they could have an early night and she'd be bright-eyed and bushy-tailed for tomorrow. Alcoholic – pah! She was beginning to feel something bordering on smugness as she said her goodbyes and headed for home.

The table was already laid when she got in. Tom had recently invested in a pasta maker, declaring that nothing beat fresh pasta – a sentiment SJ wholeheartedly agreed with. She hoped they were having pasta tonight. An open bottle of Merlot stood warming on the back of the oven. She glanced at it, suppressed the urge to pour herself a large glass and fetched a Diet Coke from the fridge instead.

While she was sipping it SJ caught herself wondering if Kit was sitting in some pub somewhere, knocking back pints. Bound to be, whispered a little voice in her head – all that stuff about her giving up when he probably drank bucket-loads. He had that kind of face, weary-worn and crinkled around the edges. He obviously hadn't spent his youth drinking orange juice.

Tanya had mentioned yesterday that Kit might be a recovering alcoholic, as people who worked in addiction places often were. SJ wasn't so sure. Surely if you were one you'd want to get as far away as possible from your past, not hang around to see what the next generation was like. You'd probably turn into a born-again Christian or something. Not that she had anything against born-again Christians – they had as much right to their opinion as anyone else. But she was a born-again heathen and it was the mention of God that had put her off the AA meeting she'd once attended.

She hadn't told Kit or Tanya about that. It hadn't seemed relevant, but she'd gone to a meeting a couple of years ago. That had been after another particularly heavy session when she'd been paranoid about her drinking. She'd looked up AA on the internet and had rung the helpline. A pleasant, very sober sounding woman had asked her if she'd had a drink today, and she'd said no she certainly hadn't, it was only four thirty in the afternoon – what did they take her for? - before lapsing into an awkward silence. It was obvious what they'd taken her for.

Anyway, the upshot was that she'd gone along to a meeting. She'd established very quickly that she was in the wrong place. The whole lot of them might be sober now, but they'd obviously been raging drunks once. Not that this had put her off particularly – drunks were quite interesting. No, the main thing had been when she found out the cliché was true. You were expected to say, "My name's SJ and I'm an alcoholic," before you could so much as ask where the loo was.

Telling all and sundry you were an alcoholic surely couldn't be a positive move. It would have been the equivalent of standing up in the slimming club and saying, "Hi, my name's SJ and I'm a big fatty." It simply wasn't the right approach. It was buying into negativity. Everyone knew that if you wanted to be something other than what you were, you simply had to repeat it. *I'm thin*, or *I'm rich*, or *I'm a teetotaller*. It was basic psychology. If you went around telling everyone you were a big fatty, or an alcoholic, or a pauper, then it would very quickly become true. And then where would you be?

"Hi, sweetie."

65

SJ jumped as Tom appeared behind her. He'd just had a shave and smelt of Paco Rabanne. Maybe he did want to make love again. The promotion must have gone to his head. Feeling guilty for such disloyal thoughts, she smiled at him.

"You've obviously been busy. What's on the menu?"

"Spag bol. I haven't been in long. Thought I'd better put in a bit of overtime to show willing, you know. How was Poetry and a Pint?"

"It was great – we did Walter de la Mare." She smiled. "On a Coke."

"Uh huh. Is he one of the druggie ones?"

"What? Oh – no, I meant me. I had a Coke instead of a pint."

"I'd better pour you a nice glass of wine then. You must be gasping!"

Now he came to mention it… Not that she was buying into that, though, obviously. If she'd been gasping, she definitely had a problem.

"Just a small one, then."

She waited until they'd finished their first course before she told him about going to S.A.A.D.

"Oh? What did they say?" He'd been about to refill her glass. That was bad timing – she should have waited another four seconds in case he took it upon himself to help her in her quest.

"Not much. Just that I ought to cut down."

He relaxed and carried on pouring, much to her relief.

SJ emptied half her glass and then, concerned he hadn't grasped the seriousness of the situation, she added firmly, and rather ironically, "I think they're probably right – but it's quite difficult to cut down when you usually drink a certain amount."

"Are you saying you've got a drink problem, sweetie?" Tom stared at her, dark eyebrows meeting in the middle of his forehead.

"No, no. Nothing like that." She laughed brightly. "I don't think I drink any more than anyone else we know, do I?"

"No – I don't think you do," Tom said, reaching for another slice of garlic bread.

SJ frowned – so that had been a damp squib then. She'd just told her husband she might be an alcoholic and he'd blithely ignored her. Everyone knew that real alcoholics lost their jobs, alienated their families, and became a useless waste of space to society. Whereas she, obviously, was far from that – even her husband hadn't noticed anything amiss. She gulped back her wine – red, as Tom hadn't got any white out tonight - refilled her glass, and settled back in her chair to enjoy it.

"You – an alcoholic? That's ridiculous," Tom muttered, reaching for the bottle and looking slightly surprised to find there was none left.

SJ smiled sagely. She knew exactly what she would say to Tanya next time they spoke.

"If you're an alcoholic, you're supposed to be in denial, aren't you? But I'm not. I confessed all to Tom and he thinks I'm fine – so if anyone is in denial, it's him. Not me."

Chapter Eight

The following Tuesday morning, SJ was looking at her Things to Do pad and trying to decide which was the most urgent: her lesson plan for Poetry and a Pint or giving some serious thought to her 'Reasons Not To Go To My Parents' Party' list, when the doorbell rang. Irritated, she glanced at the clock. Only eleven fifteen, so too early for the post, which never came before lunchtime. She got up wearily and went to answer it. Hopefully it wasn't anyone important as she hadn't got round to a shower yet and was wearing old, but very comfy grey leggings and a baggy T-shirt Tom had bought her, emblazoned with the slogan, *Is there any wine in the fridge or do I have to pretend to be happy?*

Tanya was standing there, looking as though she was going to a photo shoot in a navy pinstriped suit, her perfect skin glowing with health, and her titian hair held up in butterfly clips.

Painfully aware of the contrast between them, SJ forced a smile and said, "Hi, I didn't know you were coming over. You should have phoned."

"I did. But your mobile's switched off. And you haven't answered my last three texts."

"Haven't I? Sorry, I've been a bit busy." SJ avoided Tanya's eyes. She had been busy, but the truth was a little more petty – that wonderful feeling of solidarity she'd felt when she'd poured out her heart to Tanya had diminished somewhat when she'd realised Tanya had been in no hurry at all to confide in her.

On the other hand, perhaps Tanya had just been plucking up the courage to come round. "I'm sorry I've been out of contact," she murmured, touching Tanya's arm. "Come in, I'll put the kettle on. Are you okay?"

"Of course I'm okay. Why shouldn't I be?"

"You said you had a problem you wanted to talk about."

Tanya gave an embarrassed laugh. "Look, I'm sorry; I probably shouldn't have said anything. You must have caught me at a weak moment. I'm fine, really I am."

"I see," SJ said, feeling hurt all over again.

"Actually, I haven't come round for a chat." Tanya narrowed her eyes thoughtfully. "I've come to give you a lift to your appointment. I thought you might need some moral support."

"I don't need a lift. It's in the middle of Soho – I can get the tube."

"I know you don't *need* a lift," Tanya said patiently. "But I thought you might like one. I've got to take the car in anyway. It's no trouble."

"Well, it's very sweet of you, but I'm not going today. I thought I told you. I don't need to go to that place. It's not just my opinion," she qualified hastily, because Tanya looked as though she was going to argue. "Even Tom doesn't think I need to go. He doesn't think I drink too much."

"Have you cancelled your appointment?"

"Er no, I meant to, but I haven't got round to it. Like I said, I've been busy."

"Do you have to pay for these appointments?"

SJ shook her head.

"Then I think you should go, and at least tell them how you feel. They'll be expecting you – and if you

69

really don't think you need their help, it's only fair to let them know so they can book in some poor bugger who does. There might be a waiting list."

"I bet there isn't," SJ said, feeling uncomfortable, because Tanya was right, and she didn't usually let people down. She'd managed to put her appointment at S.A.A.D in a box marked Think About Later, and she hadn't thought about it at all.

"I can't go now, I'm not ready – look at me. Perhaps I'll just give them a ring and say I'm ill."

"Well, I agree you should probably change that T-shirt," Tanya said dryly, "but you've got time to do that. We'll still make it. I can drop you outside the door."

Oh joy, that was all she needed. One beautifully-dressed woman dropping her scruffy, alky friend off at the drop in centre – okay, so the sign was discreet, but no doubt everyone in the world knew S.A.A.D stood for Soho Advice for Alcohol and Drugs.

"I can't, Tan, seriously I can't. For a start I haven't filled in my form and that's what we're supposed to be discussing..."

"Are you scared to go back?" Tanya asked softly. "Is it like slimming, when you've put on weight instead of losing it and you know as soon as you get on the scales they're going to suss you out?"

SJ was about to make some quip about it not being anything like that – they didn't have a handy little breathalyser on the door, not that it would have mattered if they had, because she hadn't had a drink since last night anyway – when Tanya gently pushed her back inside.

"Come on, we're wasting time arguing. Go and get changed. I promise I'll never nag you again if you just go today and tell them you're okay and don't need any more appointments."

"All right, all right." SJ gave up because Tanya obviously wasn't going to let this go and besides, she'd just had a brainwave. Tanya wouldn't be able to park anywhere near the centre. Therefore she'd just get out of the car, give her a cheery wave, and as soon as she was out of sight, she could hop on the tube and go home. Okay, so it was a little convoluted and she'd still have to phone and tell them she'd planned on coming – of course she had – until she'd been unavoidably detained. But it was better than having Tanya loading all this guilt on her.

All the way there, Tanya made her feel even worse by saying how proud she was that SJ was dealing with the issue rather than avoiding it. And all the way along Western Street, where the centre was, SJ prayed that there wouldn't be any spaces Tanya could pull into. So far, so good. SJ stared intently ahead at the line of parked cars. It was going to be okay. It was going to be fine. And then, to her horror, a yellow Mini pulled out of a space just ahead of them, almost directly outside S.A.A.D's entrance.

"Parking angels," Tanya said with a happy smile, nipping the Smart Car into the space. "They never let you down."

Flaming parking angels. "What are you doing? You can't stop here. You'll get booked. I just saw a traffic warden."

"Then hurry up and get a move on." Tanya smiled sweetly and SJ wondered if she'd been sussed out. "Go on. I'll pick you up in an hour."

She hadn't anticipated that either. "No need, I'll get the tube. I've wasted enough of your time already.

Anyway, I probably won't be here very long. Once I've told them I'm fine, I expect they'll be glad to see the back of me."

"It's no trouble – I'm seeing a client round the corner. My motives weren't entirely altruistic, as it happens. Go on, you're five minutes late. You can text me when you come out."

Reluctantly, SJ stepped onto the pavement, but to her alarm Tanya showed no signs of pulling away. Even the cheery wave didn't have the desired effect. Disconcerted, she turned towards the door and then checked over her shoulder to see that Tanya still hadn't moved the car. Shit, it was even worse standing outside than pressing the buzzer. There were dozens of people out shopping today. One or two of them were glancing curiously in her direction.

Why couldn't the centre be located in some dingy little side street? Why oh why did it have to be slap bang on a main road? They might as well go the whole hog and put up a flashing neon sign. Losers Gather Here. There ought to be a law against drop in centres being in full view of everyone. Didn't addicts deserve any privacy?

Tanya still hadn't moved and, feeling a wave of panic, SJ pressed the buzzer. Thinking about it, she could always go inside and wait until Tanya had left and then make her escape. The reception was upstairs so they wouldn't even know she'd been here. Brilliant – why hadn't she thought of that before? The buzzer released and she shoved open the door and bumped straight into Kit, who must have popped down to use the Gents.

"Hi, Sarah, I was beginning to think you weren't coming. Good to see you."

He grinned at her and she pasted on a sickly smile. He was the last person on earth she wanted to see. She'd rather be going for a Brazilian, or a wisdom tooth extraction without anaesthetic, or an appointment to talk about piles – no, maybe not an appointment for piles, which would have been equally embarrassing.

"Go on up – we're in room three, same as last week."

"I er – don't think I…"

The buzzer went again and she jumped out of her skin.

"I'll be with you in a sec." He glanced at the door and then back at her. "We don't want to talk on the stairs, do we?"

Trapped, she went up, feeling her legs turn more rubbery with each step. It was worse than confessing to piles – she felt as though she was walking to the electric chair. Why on earth had she let Tanya talk her into this? She should have known Tanya didn't trust her. All that talk about being proud of her had obviously been a smoke-screen. She was going to kill Tanya once she got out of here. Some friend she'd turned out to be.

She pushed open the door of the little room and glanced at the bars on the window. The feeling of being trapped increased. Perhaps the bars were there for no other purpose than to hammer the point home. Once you'd walked in it was impossible to escape.

When had she got so paranoid? Close to tears, SJ headed for the same armchair she'd sat in last week. It seemed an eternity ago. Had it really only been seven days?

Chapter Nine

Kit didn't keep her waiting long. Perhaps he knew she'd run away if he did. His counsellor antennae were probably tuned into such things. Right now they must be twirling round at ninety miles per hour. She glanced nervously at him as he sat opposite.

At least she didn't have her bag on her lap. She'd put it behind the chair so she couldn't reach for it in a weak moment and give away the fact she didn't feel comfortable talking to him without having a nice solid shield to hide behind. She'd just have to make sure she remembered to pick it up again.

With hindsight, perhaps putting it behind the chair hadn't been such a bright idea. It was going to look awfully strange when she started shifting furniture around at the end of her session to retrieve it. He'd definitely think she was bonkers. That's if he didn't already. Oh, God. Bad move, bad, BAD move. Perhaps she should hook it out now – pretend she'd dropped it down the back by mistake. In complete turmoil, she tried to put on a casual smile.

Kit seemed oblivious to her tumbling thoughts. "So how have you been?" he asked easily. "Had a good week?"

"Yes thank you. I've done stacks of work," she said, knowing that wasn't what he meant.

"What is it that you do, Sarah?" He sounded interested – far too interested for her liking.

She waved a hand airily. She wasn't falling for that one. If he knew what she did he might be able to find out who she was. At the very least he could weasel his way into her head. "Oh, this and that – you know … office work. I'm a PA."

"Do you enjoy it?"

"Mmm, I love it. It's a great company. I've been there since I left college." There was a small silence as he waited for her to elaborate, but she couldn't without telling more lies.

The silence dragged on. He was looking at her, his gaze steady. She had the horrible feeling he could see right inside her head. She had no idea why it had been so easy to talk to him last week. It certainly wasn't now. Perhaps he knew about the bag. Perhaps they had hidden cameras in here and that's what he really did when he said he was making coffee – sat in front of the monitor with his counsellor mates for a good laugh at the loonies.

"It helps if you enjoy your work." Hah! Maybe not. So she'd won that particular battle then. She relaxed marginally, which meant that on a scale of 1 to 100 – 100 being high – she was down to about 130 instead of 180.

"How's the cutting down going? Did you manage to stick to your target?"

What to say now? If she said yes, no problem, actually she'd stopped altogether so she obviously didn't need to come here any more, then she might be able to turn things around. He surely wouldn't want to talk to her about how much she hadn't drunk. That would be wasting both their time and she could escape and go and find Tanya.

If she told him the truth and said that actually she'd drunk more since she'd tried to cut down than she usually did, he was probably going to be pretty annoyed. Last week he'd told her if she carried on as she was, sooner or later she'd end up in a treatment centre. She knew nothing whatsoever about treatment centres, apart from the fact they weren't likely to allow wine with dinner – which was one very good reason to avoid them.

"I had a word with my husband," she said, deciding a diversion tactic would be good. "He doesn't think I've got a problem at all." Hah – put that in your pipe and smoke it, Mr Counsellor.

"I know this might be a silly question, Sarah, but did you tell him what you told me?" Kit frowned, as if trying to remember something. "Didn't we work out you were drinking six or seven times the recommended number of units for women?"

"Mmm, I think we did establish that," she said, his gentle question hitting her with the same force it had the previous week– but this time a wave of guilt washed over her, too. It reminded her of a moment back in her misspent youth when she'd been called in to see the headmaster, who'd asked her if she'd attended her maths class that morning, when both of them knew perfectly well she'd been spotted in town playing truant.

"I'm not sure whether I did actually mention the details to him – no," she whispered.

"So he might not be aware of how things are. I think we talked about this before, didn't we? It's very important you get his support. You are going to need his help. I can't reiterate that strongly enough."

"Yes," she said, glancing at the door. She could probably just walk out anyway. She wasn't committed to staying. Racking her brains, she tried to remember what she'd put on that form. Nothing that meant she'd

76

signed up for a certain number of sessions, she was sure.

"You don't have to talk to me," he went on gently. Why did he have to be so damned reasonable all the time? It made it ten times harder to walk away. "But it might be a good idea if you talked to your husband."

There was another little silence and he went on thoughtfully. "Actually, I didn't expect you to come back this week."

SJ glanced at him quizzically. He'd got that right. She'd had no intention of coming back. If Tanya hadn't bullied her into it she'd still be safely at home doing her lesson plan. But perhaps that wasn't what he meant. "Why did you think I wouldn't come back? Did you think I didn't need to?"

A wild surge of hope rose in her as he smiled unexpectedly. He had a lovely smile, full of warmth and humour. She was on the verge of telling him he should do it more often when he went on. "No, as I said last week, it's not up to me. Only you know whether you want our help or not. And only you can make the changes. But it takes a lot of guts to come in here – and I could see you weren't very comfortable. You're not now, are you?"

"No, these chairs are bloody hard – they kill your back, don't they? It must be hell sitting in one all day."

He laughed and she found herself laughing with him and a lot of the tension in the room evaporated.

Then he stood up, and she thought for a moment he was going to suggest they sat on the floor instead. But he strolled across and gestured to a pie chart pinned on the wall behind her.

"Did we go through this last time?"

"No." She joined him, relieved at the diversion. The chart was split into segments, each with a heading. She read them curiously. *Pre-contemplation; preparing to change; making changes; maintaining changes; lapse/relapse.*

"Which stage do you think you're at, Sarah?"

"Preparing to change," she said thoughtfully, but her attention had been caught by the last section of the pie chart. The *relapse* section. She hadn't noticed it last time. She felt like cheering and doing a little dance round the room, but she didn't realise she was smiling until he raised his eyebrows and gave her a sideways glance.

"What's on your mind?" He was standing quite close and he used the same cologne as Tom – Paco Rabanne. Suddenly it was all she could smell and, feeling a strange mixture of trust – because he smelt familiar – and nervousness – because he was so perceptive and Tom wasn't; Tom never picked up on her thoughts – she told him exactly what was on her mind.

"I was wondering how many times I could go round. How often could I relapse? Would that be as many times as I liked? Or would you only give me so many chances before you washed your hands of me?"

He bit his lip and she realised he was trying hard not to laugh.

"You can go round as many times as you like, but relapse isn't supposed to be a good thing. Although I understand it might seem like that right now."

"Do you?" She wondered whether she should ask him how he understood that. It was on the tip of her tongue to say, "So you used to be an alcoholic too, did you?" But she couldn't bring herself to say the words.

She knew she'd be disappointed if he said he hadn't. Most of the time she did feel he understood – either that, or he was a very good actor. In fact, if they'd met in different circumstances she was sure they'd have got on well.

"Do you want to cut down – or are you happy to go on the way you are and increase the harmful effects alcohol has on your brain and central nervous system – not to mention the harm it will do to your job and relationships?" He'd got his serious face back on now, but suddenly she felt as though she did want to cut down. It was no fun having hangovers every five minutes, and seeing the chink in his counsellor armour had made her want to tell him the truth.

"To be honest, I've had a totally crap week," she confessed, meeting his eyes and reassured to see no recriminations. "I've had well over a bottle most nights. Even though I did plan to cut down – I really did – but ... well, it was a lot harder than I thought."

Bugger! That had probably been too much honesty, even for her. The same thing had happened last week; perhaps they put some sort of truth drug in your coffee. Yes, that had to be it. She resolved not to drink coffee if she ever came here again.

"Sorry," she added, as an afterthought. "I'm wasting your time, aren't I? I'm a hopeless case. Perhaps I should go now and you can concentrate on someone more deserving." She took a step towards the door.

"Hang about, Sarah." He gestured they sit down once more, and nervously she complied and waited for the lecture, which surely must be coming. It must be blatantly obvious she hadn't taken this seriously.

He wasn't quite smiling, but he didn't look disapproving either. Come to think of it, he never did. He leaned forward. "You've been honest with me, Sarah. That's a very good start. You could have strolled in here and said, 'Great news, Kit, I've stuck to my target,' – even if you hadn't. I wouldn't have known the difference."

"No, I suppose you wouldn't." She sighed.

"You could have stayed away. I think because you didn't do either of those things it proves you really do want to change. That takes guts."

God, he was an optimist. Obviously the type of person who could see good in everyone – even when they were lying through their teeth, like she was. She held up a hand. It was no good. She couldn't accept credit where it wasn't due.

"I wasn't going to come back today, that's the truth. The only reason I did was because a well-meaning friend dragged me here, kicking and screaming. If it hadn't been for her, I'd still be at home, sorting out my teaching stuff." She blushed madly; she hadn't meant to say that last bit. Now he'd know she was a complete and utter liar. She was right. He zoomed straight in.

"So you're a teacher? Not a PA?"

"Mmm – yes, I do a bit of teaching. Adult education, not children." Deciding she might as well go the whole hog, she added, "My name isn't exactly Sarah either, it's Sarah-Jane, but everyone calls me SJ – it's a nickname."

"More honesty!" To her amazement he was smiling again. "Then I reckon, SJ..." His eyes danced with amusement and she wondered if he'd known all along Sarah wasn't her real name. Or perhaps Tanya was right and it hadn't been such a clever alias as she'd thought. "...That we're making pretty good progress, aren't we? So how about we go back to the form I asked you to fill in. Did you bring it with you?"

"Mmm," she said again, not that she'd put much on it. She certainly hadn't put anything in the thoughts and feelings section. Neither had she put anything very truthful in the totals section, thinking that might be a fast-track route to one of those awful treatment centre places.

"You don't have to show me what you've written. That's personal to you. But I want you to think back to the time when you first started drinking more than socially. How long ago would you say that was?"

She considered this. Factual questions were a lot easier than thoughts and feelings ones. "About three years, I guess."

"And did anything happen around the same time – any major life-changing event you can think of?"

"I got married. I suppose that was pretty life-changing." She stared at him in alarm as she realised what she'd said and began to backtrack hastily. "Getting married had nothing to do with me drinking – definitely not. Tom's lovely. Not a bit like my first husband. He was a bastard."

Chapter Ten

There was a long pause and SJ would have given up at least a day's wine allowance – maybe even a couple of days' worth – to have been able to rewind the conversation and retract that last comment. Now Kit had an unresolved issue to beat her over the head with.

The silence stretched on and she looked at the floor and clamped her mouth shut so she wouldn't be the first to break it. She knew all about long silences – and how stressed-out people would gabble on about any old rubbish, rather than let them go past a certain point. She could feel her face burning and her throat was raw with vulnerability. It was an immense effort to drag her gaze away from her shoes and meet Kit's eyes without speaking.

"There's usually a reason why we drink," he said. "But you don't have to tell me what it is. That's not why we're here."

She breathed a huge sigh of relief. She felt like a fish that had been caught by a sportsman, carefully measured, then laid on the riverbank just long enough to think its time had come before being put gently back into the water – the wonderful, life-giving haven of its natural element. She almost felt like giving a little wriggle before she sped away downstream.

Instead, she took the lifeline he'd offered and said, "I'm sorry. I don't know what's the matter with me. I'm not usually like this." She wanted to tell him she was scared, so scared that she really did have a problem, but instead she coughed and said,

"Does it get easier to cut back after a while?"

"Yeah, it does."

"Are you sure about that?"

"Yeah." And a smile, this time, to go with it.

"Are there things I can do to make it easier – in your experience?" This was better. Her sensible head, her professional head was back in control.

"Yes, there are things you can do. We can go through some of them now, if you like?"

"Yes, I would like." She was full of conflicting emotions. It would be good to know she need never drink more than she'd planned to again – although there was another part of her that thought it would have been better if there was simply a pill you could take to prevent hangovers. If someone invented a pill like that they'd be a millionaire, billionaire, multi-billionaire even.

Perhaps some scientist somewhere was working on it at this very moment. Locked away in a white coat in some laboratory, and tomorrow's headlines would be 'Miracle Hangover Cure. Imagine the rest of your life without hangovers.' Brilliant. Obviously it would be better if someone came up with a miracle cure for cancer or Aids, though.

"Cutting down is easier if you put some strategies into your life."

"What sort of strategies?"

"Well…" He leaned back in his chair, utterly relaxed. "Things that delay you having that first drink – like, say – you could go to the gym of an evening."

She thought about the joint gym membership she had with Tom before they got married. It had been bad enough then, squeezing herself into tight shorts and T-shirts and hoping her legs didn't wobble like out-of-control blancmange on the running machine. She was two sizes heavier now. She swallowed.

"I don't think gyms are my thing."

"Have you got any other hobbies? Preferably things you can do in the evening as that seems to be your danger time. They'd be things you can't do with a drink in your hand."

"I teach one evening, as I said. I run a class called Poetry and a Pint."

He raised his eyebrows. "That doesn't sound all that promising, I have to say."

This time it was SJ who laughed. She was starting to warm to him again. And things couldn't be too bad if she could find humour in the situation, surely. That must mean she wasn't too far down the slippery slope. What a good job she'd realised she might one day have a problem while it was still soon enough to nip it in the bud.

Then he said something that brought reality crashing back into the room. "When you stop altogether, SJ, you'll find it very useful to have these strategies in place."

For a moment she thought she must have misheard. "What do you mean, stop altogether? I thought I was just cutting down."

"The idea is that you gradually wean your body off alcohol. At the levels you've been drinking – and that's if you've told me the truth…" That was a cheap shot – of course she'd told him the truth. "…Then you'll have developed a certain tolerance. What I mean is that your body will be expecting a certain amount of alcohol."

"I know what tolerance means," she said huffily.

"Yeah, sorry – course you do." He smiled and she could have sworn she saw little horns sprout on his head, whereas earlier there had been the distinct possibility of a halo.

She dragged him back to the question in hand – the important issue. The BIG issue. "Are you saying I have to stop – I mean stop altogether? No more alcohol ever again?"

After an imperceptible pause he nodded.

"You mean, not even at parties or if I'm celebrating, or if it's someone's birthday?"

Another nod.

"Not even if it's MY birthday?" This was outrageous. She could feel the hairs standing up on the back of her neck in protest.

"I'm afraid not."

"What about at Christmas?"

"Nope."

"New Year?"

"Nope."

"A girlie night out?"

"Nope."

"You're saying I can never drink anything again – EVER?"

"Yep."

"Shit!"

He didn't answer this, just continued to hold her gaze, his eyes serious.

"Are you sure?"

"Absolutely sure."

A shadow had fallen across the room, velvet soft, like some great black shroud wrapping her tightly so it was difficult to breathe. She could feel her head dizzying with shock. She had to get the conversation back on an even keel. She hadn't misheard him, so perhaps she'd misunderstood him. She was just trying to think of another way to ask the question when he pre-empted her.

"How does that make you feel?"

"Terrified," she said without thinking.

"That's what everyone says. But don't worry about that now. All you need do for now is cut down."

He glanced at the clock and she realised her hour was almost up.

"So this week, how about trying to restrict yourself to half a bottle a night. Do you think you can manage that?"

"No."

"Give it a try." He handed her another form and she reached for her bag to tuck it away before remembering with a jolt of embarrassment that it was safely out of reach behind the chair.

"Haven't you got anyone else to see?" she said brightly, hoping he'd leave the room so she could retrieve it in private.

"No rush." He gave her an odd look, as she leapt to her feet and edged backwards until she was pressed against the wall. She darted a frantic glance behind the chair – she could see her bag. Perhaps it would be possible to bend sideways unobtrusively and hook it out. If he would just turn his back on her for a few seconds, she was sure she could do it.

"Don't let me hold you up. I'm sure there must be dozens of people queuing up outside." She could hear the edge of panic in her voice.

Misinterpreting her motives to get rid of him, he said softly: "SJ, it's not as difficult as it seems. I promise. Don't worry about stopping. When the time comes, it won't be half as bad as it looks now."

86

"Right. Thanks." It was no good. She was going to have to bite the bullet and go for it. She closed her eyes, leaned sideways, bent from the waist like an athlete doing warm ups and groped around for her bag with her right hand.

"Have you lost something?"

She opened her eyes to see that Kit was looking at her in amazement.

"Nope – not permanently. I've found it now." She hauled out her bag and brushed a layer of dust off the leather. "How on earth did it get down there?" she said, smiling at him sweetly and tucking it under her arm.

He shook his head and shrugged, but not before she'd caught the fleeting look of incredulity he wasn't quick enough to hide.

So that proved it – he obviously did think she was a complete fruit loop. All that nice counsellor stuff was a front – just as she'd suspected. Not that it mattered as this was the last time she was going to see him. Because at some point during the conversation they'd just had – she wasn't sure whether it was when she'd inadvertently called Derek a bastard, or when he'd started laying down the law about never enjoying herself again – she'd made a decision. Nothing on earth would induce her to set foot in this place again.

Chapter Eleven

"How did it go? Are you okay? You're ever so quiet." Tanya's voice broke into her thoughts and SJ sighed and dragged her gaze away from a point beyond the windscreen and the London streets that she'd been staring fixedly at ever since Tanya had picked her up.

"Yeah, sorry. I'm fine. I was just thinking." Remembering was closer to the mark. Just before she'd left S.A.A.D, Kit had stressed again that she didn't have to discuss any problems that may have led to her drinking – but that she really should consider making another appointment, which she'd declined with a swift shake of her head. But it hadn't stopped the memories flooding back, unbidden, as soon as she'd got out of the place.

She hadn't thought about Derek, who'd been the love of her life – and also the hate of her life, if there was such a thing – for a very long time. And she was amazed how much it hurt. She could easily have broken down and wept, which was madness; she'd cried more than enough tears over Derek bloody Anderson.

"Well, you don't look fine," Tanya persisted relentlessly. "Where are we going for lunch?"

"Don't you have to get back to work?"

"Yes, but not for a while. Mind you, I don't think we'll bother with a wine bar this week." Tanya's mobile buzzed to announce the arrival of another text and SJ remembered why she wasn't going to confide in Tanya again. She knew she was being childish. Despite the fact she'd decided she didn't need Kit's help any more – or perhaps because of it – she felt terribly vulnerable and shaken up.

"I think I'd like to go straight home if it's okay with you, Tanya."

At least at home she could have a good cry in private and a large amount of wine now she'd decided she'd done with cutting down.

"SJ, stop shutting me out. I'm your best friend. I want to help."

"I don't need any help," SJ sniffed. "I'm not some sad little charity-case you can fit in when you get a spare moment in your hectic schedule."

"For fuck's sake, is that how you see me?" Tanya slammed on the brakes and the car behind them blasted its horn in protest.

SJ had obviously touched a nerve. Tanya never said 'Fuck'. SJ clung on to her seat belt as Tanya stalled the car, eliciting another horn blast of disapproval from behind, and rounded on her furiously. "Has it ever occurred to you that other people have problems too?"

"I thought you didn't want to talk about your problems."

"Perhaps that's because they're not mine to discuss." Two pink blotches had appeared on Tanya's angular cheekbones and her green eyes were glittery – whether with rage or hurt, it was difficult to tell.

"I'm sorry. What I said just now was totally out of order. I didn't have a very good session, but that's no excuse to take it out on you."

"Apology accepted." Tanya blinked, re-started the car, pointedly ignoring the furious driver behind her, and they set off once more.

89

"I really am sorry," SJ said again, after a few moments' tense silence, wishing she could stop apologising and, more importantly, stop saying things that meant she needed to apologise. "Whose problems are they then?"

"Michael's."

"Ah." There didn't seem much else to say and for a while they didn't speak. After about ten minutes SJ noticed they'd just gone through Shoreditch, which was a weird way to go to her house, but it wasn't until they hit Stoke Newington that she realised Tanya wasn't taking her home.

"Where are we going?"

"You'll see."

Twenty minutes later they were driving alongside Epping Forest and SJ fantasised briefly that Tanya might know some gorgeous little pub and as she wasn't working today she could have a very large glass of wine when she got there. But her hopes were dashed when about twenty minutes later Tanya drew into a Forestry Commission car park, beyond which was a picnic area set up with wooden benches and a brick-built barbecue, alongside a stack of beating equipment to put out fires.

"Er – any particular reason why we're stopping here?"

"We're going for a walk. I can think better when I walk and the exercise will do us good."

SJ could think of a great many other things she'd far rather be doing – in fact, walking along some woodland path towards the middle of nowhere came somewhere at the bottom of her list of Great Ways To Spend My Day Off. But she could see Tanya was not in the mood to argue.

At least she had trainers on – unlike her friend. "Aren't you going to find it awkward in those heels?"

"I've got some walking boots in the back." Tanya flicked her a glance and SJ decided not to mention that smart suits weren't perfect attire for walking either. For the first time since they'd met this morning she didn't feel underdressed.

And also for the first time since they'd met that morning, she realised she was being utterly selfish. Tanya had taken time off work to bully her into keeping her appointment and she hadn't even thanked her. As she followed Tanya along a path strewn with pine needles, she could see her navy pin-striped shoulders were stiff with tension.

"I'm not surprised you're pissed off with me," SJ called tentatively. "I've been a total cow."

Tanya neither answered nor turned, but a few minutes later she slowed and then paused at a point where the path opened out into a glade. The trees were mostly oaks – gigantic and ancient, their old trunks velvet with moss and the odd bright patch of yellow fungi, and even though they were still quite close to the road, it was almost totally silent.

Tanya headed towards a fallen tree, its surface soft and rotten, and, heedless of her suit, slumped down on one end of it. "I'm not pissed off with you," she replied belatedly. "Cross maybe, because you won't let me help you…"

"I'm not the only one guilty of that, am I?"

"Touché." Tanya stretched out her legs, stirring leaves with the toe of her boot. "And I know this probably seems a mad place to talk – but it's peaceful and I like it. Michael and I sometimes come here for picnics."

"I don't think it's a mad place at all. Ash would love it."

Tanya smiled and ironically it wasn't until she did that SJ noticed the fine lines of stress on her face because momentarily they'd softened.

"The other reason I brought you here," Tanya went on, almost to herself, "is because no one's likely to overhear us. I'm probably being paranoid but I didn't want to take any chances. What I want to talk about – well, it must never go any further – and I mean NEVER."

"Of course it won't go any further," SJ said gently, perching beside her on the moss-covered log and thinking she was right – this place embodied peace; it seeped out of the tree trunks. "It can't be all that bad. A problem shared is a problem halved. Remember?"

"I'm afraid you'll be shocked. And once I've told you I can't take it back. You'll always know and it will change the way you feel about Michael and that's half the reason I haven't told you about it before, to be honest. I don't want you to change the way you feel about him. He's still the same person."

Feeling a deep sense of compassion because Tanya was obviously sick with worry, SJ touched her arm. "Don't tell me if you'd rather not. But if you do, I promise I won't be shocked."

There was a small silence filled by the faint whispering of the wind through the summer leaves. Somewhere above their heads, claws scraped along a branch and a flutter of squirrel debris fell onto the forest floor.

SJ had just decided Tanya wasn't going to say anything after all when she began to speak.

"I nipped home from work early, a few months back, and I found Michael in our bedroom dressed in my clothes. Well, when I say my clothes, what I actually mean is my undies." She paused, her eyes begging SJ not to judge.

It was the last thing SJ had been expecting. She had a brief and vivid image of Michael in women's underwear. How on earth had he managed to fit into anything of Tanya's anyway? He wasn't as big as Tom – he was quite lean, with hairy legs from what she remembered of the last time they'd all had shorts on – but even so, it was hard to picture him in delicate pink lace, or cream satin or a silk G-string. All of Tanya's underwear was ultra feminine. Everything about Tanya was.

Blinking away the images, she chewed hard on her lip. It was one of those times when you absolutely must not laugh. Like when someone had just told you their beloved granny had died whilst doing a parachute jump at the age of 103. It was the most inappropriate response in the universe. Why was it that your mind led you along such dangerous tracks?

"You are shocked, aren't you?"

SJ shook her head. She must not laugh. She MUST not laugh. She snorted at the effort of keeping it in.

Think very sad stuff, think you've just been told you've put on a stone since last slimming class, think you've just lost your job, think sad. Think SAD, for God's sake. What was the matter with her?

She spluttered into her hands. It was passing. Thank heavens, it was passing. As long as Tanya didn't say anything else for a moment or two, she could get herself back in control.

"SJ, are you laughing?"

93

"No." The denial came out as a muffled squeak.

"It's not bloody funny, you know. How would you feel if you found Tom wearing your bra and knickers?"

Oh God. That was even worse – hairy macho Tom in one of her beige under-wireds and a pair of M&S hold-you-in knickers. SJ snorted again, gave up trying to control herself, put her head between her knees and howled with mirth.

When she finally stopped, the air was so stiff with silence she thought Tanya might have abandoned her in the middle of the forest and gone home. Well, it was no more than she deserved.

She raised her head warily. Tanya was still sitting in the same position, her hands curled like a child's in her lap. She was staring straight ahead and there were tears trickling down her face.

"Oh God, I'm so sorry. I didn't mean to laugh. I know it's not funny."

Looking at Tanya's stricken expression, she didn't know how she'd ever wanted to laugh at all. She was such a bitch. She certainly wouldn't have found it amusing if Tanya had laughed about her drinking.

"At least you're not shocked," Tanya said in a quiet blank voice. "I suppose that's something."

"No, I'm not. I'm intrigued." SJ delved around in her memory bank for something more helpful to say. She'd never had any first hand experience of cross-dressing – it was probably one of the last taboos. If you were homosexual or a drug addict or an overeater, or if you were into spanking or wife swapping, you could probably raise the subject with your closest friends over a drunken dinner party without too much fear of being shunned, but cross-dressing was still a pretty tricky subject to bring up in polite conversation.

94

"Do you think maybe he was trying to get in touch with his feminine side?" she asked slowly. "I mean, Michael's always been very sensitive, hasn't he? The kind of man who doesn't mind discussing his emotions. Not a bit like Tom, who'd rather chew off his own arm than tell you how he feels."

To her dismay, far from being reassured by her words Tanya put her head in her hands and burst into tears. Noisy, abandoned tears that were so out of control and so unlike Tanya that SJ was horrified. Wanting to cry with her, but doubting this would be very much help, she edged along the tree trunk and put her arm awkwardly around her friend's shaking shoulders. Why was it so difficult to touch when a hug was one of the most basic forms of comfort you could offer? She couldn't remember the last time she'd hugged anyone who wasn't Tom.

Tanya's hair smelt of coconut shampoo and Classique perfume and fresh air. SJ hoped she didn't smell too much like an old ashtray, but Tanya didn't push her away, just carried on sobbing with her hands over her face.

SJ didn't say anything else, because there was absolutely nothing she could think of that wouldn't have been patronising. Besides, crying was probably the best thing Tanya could do, and she didn't want to make it any worse. She wished she was better prepared. It would have been good if she could have whisked out a nice clean hanky from her bag to offer, but she knew for a fact it was full of bits of tatty old tissues and a few dog biscuits and three cigarette lighters and several post-its to remind her of things not yet transferred to her diary, which she'd mislaid.

Then, to her immense relief, Tanya stopped crying almost as suddenly as she'd started. She still looked beautiful – her eyes a little shiny, but no mascara smudges, none of the blotchy skin that afflicted SJ when she bawled her eyes out. SJ almost envied her – she couldn't remember the last time she'd had a good cry.

"Feeling better?"

"Much." Tanya managed a glittery smile. "Thanks, SJ. I should have told you ages ago. I should have known you'd understand, but I haven't told anyone. Well, I haven't told anyone normal," she added paradoxically, "but if I had, I'm sure they wouldn't have said what you just said." She retrieved a hanky from her own bag, unfolded its pristine white squares and blew her nose loudly. "About Michael getting in touch with his feminine side, I mean. You're absolutely right, SJ. I'm sure that's exactly what he's doing."

"Yes, I'm certain of it," SJ breathed, relieved to have said something right for a change. "What do you mean, you haven't told anyone normal?"

"I got in touch with this helpline – I found their number on the internet. And since then I've been talking to this girl called Candice in Wales – she recently found out her husband's a cross-dresser."

"Oh," SJ said. It was a shock realising that Tanya had chosen to phone an anonymous helpline rather than confide in her. She hadn't realised they'd drifted so far apart. Tanya didn't seem to notice her silence. Now she'd got started she couldn't seem to stop.

"Candice caught her husband out, too. Apparently, some of them do actually tell their wives. But most of them don't because they don't think we're going to understand. They're scared we're going to think they're perverts, or they want to be women or something."

"Hmm!" SJ didn't much like the thought of Tanya pouring out her heart to this Candice person, day after day. It hurt. In some strange way she felt as though she'd lost something precious; something that, up until that point, had been hers alone.

"What?" Tanya said.

"Nothing." She knew she was being childish. Rationally she could see exactly why Tanya hadn't wanted to tell her. Scared of saying the wrong thing now she'd actually said something right at last, she said, "So how long ago was it that you found out?"

"About six months. It was just after Christmas. A freezing cold day in January. Michael had the day off work. Remember that nasty flu virus thing he had? Well, I'd nipped back home because I'd forgotten something for a meeting. I was in a tearing hurry and I raced upstairs and…" She hesitated.

"Go on, love," SJ murmured, fascinated.

"Well, he was in bed with the duvet pulled up round his ears, but there was this really odd atmosphere in the room. I couldn't put my finger on it at first. To be honest I thought he might have been – you know – having a quick…"

"Wank," SJ supplied helpfully.

"Yes. I could have coped with that. I mean, all men do it, don't they? But then I noticed the drawer of my dressing table was slightly open. First of all, I thought I'd left it like that. But I knew I hadn't."

"No," SJ acknowledged, thinking that, had their positions been reversed, she wouldn't have noticed an open drawer – but Tanya was Miss Organised. All the clothes in her wardrobe were hung in colour co-ordinated rows.

"And when I went to close it – it was my knicker drawer – I saw all my stuff was in a mess, like someone had been rummaging through it, and I knew I hadn't left it like that. And I could smell my Classique scent quite strongly. And I'd left home a couple of hours ago so I knew it wasn't from when I'd put it on.

"I went over to Michael and he was still holding the duvet up round his neck like he was hiding something. And he smelt of Classique. He must have put some on himself. He was looking at me really strangely. I pulled the duvet off him – half-messing around like you do – and that's when I saw he had my bra on. My expensive white silk one that he'd given me for Christmas."

SJ nodded, trying to imagine what she'd feel like if she caught Tom in one of her best bras. She'd probably be more worried about him splitting it than anything else. She didn't have much decent underwear and Tom was broad-chested.

"So what did he say?"

"Nothing at first. He just gave me this stricken glance and then his face kind of crumpled. It was awful, SJ. He burst into tears. I'd never seen him cry before – except at his mum's funeral, and when we lost Maddie." Her voice fractured and she swallowed hard before she could continue. "He was sobbing and sobbing and in between he kept telling me how sorry he was, how he'd been meaning to tell me for ages, but he was scared I'd leave him if he did."

"The poor love."

"I know, but I didn't feel like that at first. The only thing that really registered was that it wasn't just a one-off. He must have been dressing up in my clothes for ages and I didn't know. How could he keep something like that from me?"

"I don't know," SJ said honestly. "It must have been a dreadful shock."

"Yes, it was. I was so angry with him. I punched him."

"Bloody hell. Why?"

"I'm not sure. But I felt so betrayed. We've been married fifteen years, SJ. I thought I knew him inside out. And he looked so pathetic, sitting up in bed, sobbing his heart out with one bra strap hanging over his shoulder. It was just gut reaction. I knew he was hurting, but I wanted him to hurt more. That's terrible, isn't it?"

"I don't think it's terrible. I think it's natural. I mean, he could have picked one of your old bras, couldn't he? Inconsiderate bugger!"

Tanya snorted and gulped and for a moment SJ thought she would cry again, but then she smiled. "You always see the funny side of everything, don't you?"

"I'm not laughing at you."

"No, I know. And actually I can see the funny side now I've had a few months to get used to it. Well, sometimes I can. Other times I just get depressed, but talking to other women in the same situation helps."

SJ had a sudden vivid image of Michael, his blue-eyed, boyish face, the way his fair hair flopped endearingly over his eyes. He was the same age as Tom – forty-two, but he could have got away with being early thirties, no problem. She'd always liked him – probably because of what she'd said to Tanya earlier. Michael was sensitive and gentle and always ready to offer a friendly ear if anyone was upset. He didn't gloss over matters of the heart with a joke and a stoical shrug, as Tom tended to do. And he was great on feminine problems too.

Tanya had once told her that Michael had searched the internet for an organic recipe guaranteed to relieve tender breasts (which she suffered from just before her period) and then he'd made it up for her.

SJ couldn't imagine Tom doing any such thing. He wouldn't even buy Tampax – well, not from the chemist. He could manage if he was going to the supermarket and he could slip a box under the frozen peas.

Tanya sighed. "I've felt a lot better since I got in touch with Candice. She's been brilliant. We email each other most days and she texts me a lot, too."

SJ swallowed another little stab of jealousy. "And there was me thinking you were having an affair," she said, and clapped her hands over her mouth – why couldn't she remember to engage her brain before speaking?

But Tanya didn't look upset, just amused. "An affair? God, no. I couldn't have an affair, SJ. I love Michael. I adore him. Even if he does get off on knicker nicking." She gave a little laugh at the weak joke, and SJ found herself joining in. It was good to laugh; it chased away the pain, as laughter always did.

"Does it affect – you know – sex and stuff?" she asked curiously.

Tanya gave her a swift sideways glance. "Actually, it's made our sex life better. Michael's much more relaxed than he used to be. Although I do draw the line at calling him Lizzie when we're in bed."

"Lizzie!"

"Mmm." Tanya went slightly pink. "That's the name he wants to be called when he's dressed up. I keep telling him I don't mind having a friend called Lizzie, but I don't fancy sleeping with her."

"No." SJ looked at her thoughtfully and wondered if she was dealing with all this quite as well as she appeared to be. Granted, she had known about it for a few months – and she'd had a chance to get used to the idea. But it must have changed the whole dynamic of their relationship. It wasn't as if Michael had just told her he'd like to tie her to the bed with pink fluffy handcuffs or try out a more adventurous position. "Are you really okay?" she asked softly.

"Yes, I'm fine." Tanya smiled a little too brightly. "I should have told you before." She folded up her hanky and put it back in her bag. Then she reapplied her lipstick – putting it on perfectly without the aid of a mirror.

SJ had always envied her ability to do that. If she'd tried to put on lipstick without looking at what she was doing, she'd have ended up with the mouth of a clown. Not that she wore lipstick much. She just bunged it on before she left the house and forgot about it. She certainly didn't carry it around with her for repeated application.

Tanya finished what she was doing. "It was worse than Maddie when I first found out," she said. "Because Maddie had happened to both of us and this was something that Michael had kept from me. I felt awfully alone. Does that make sense?"

"Perfect sense," SJ said with feeling, and Tanya gave what SJ knew to be a sigh of utter relief – the aftermath of sharing a secret carried too long.

She tried to imagine what they must look like, had anyone been around eavesdropping. Two intelligent educated professional women sitting on a rotting tree trunk in the middle of the forest discussing problems you'd usually only see bandied about on the Jerry Springer show; problems that had snuck up on them without as much as a by your leave. However had it come to this?

Chapter Twelve

Although SJ wasn't planning to visit S.A.A.D again, she thought quite a lot about what Kit had said over the next few days. And there was one question he'd asked that particularly played on her mind.

When had she first noticed she was drinking more than socially? This, she decided, was worth thinking about. She couldn't remember getting drunk very much when she was younger, or even thinking too much about alcohol. As a teenager, she'd been to the occasional college party where she'd had a few too many, but she didn't remember it ever being a problem.

As she tried to recall the half-forgotten parties it struck her that in those days it had been Alison who was more likely to get into trouble with drinking than she was.

When Alison was fifteen and SJ was eighteen, SJ had been persuaded to take her to a barbecue on Sandbanks Beach. Sandbanks Beach, according to the college friend who'd invited her, was the best place for a beach party on the whole of the south coast, if not the country.

"Ali's too young to go to a beach party," she'd told her mother. "Everyone will be drinking." And possibly smoking joints, but she'd thought it best not to mention that.

"Well, surely you can keep an eye on her for a couple of hours?"

No, actually. SJ was far more interested in keeping an eye on Jed Tyler, who had darkly attractive bad boy looks and a reputation to match. And she'd heard on the grapevine that he'd been asking about her. A beach party was the perfect place to get to know him better.

"Either you take your sister – or you don't go!"

"Mum. That is totally unfair."

"I mean it, Sarah-Jane. It won't hurt you, and your father and I are going out for dinner. I don't want Ali on her own all evening."

SJ wasn't surprised to hear that. The last time Ali had been left on her own she'd raided Mum and Dad's drinks cabinet – and she and a boy from youth club had got legless. One of them had been sick on the stairs, which wouldn't have been so bad if the stair carpet hadn't been new and beige. Now there was a conspicuous stain which no amount of scrubbing would remove.

"I don't really have a choice then, do I?" SJ grumbled.

"No, you don't."

The day of the barbecue was the hottest of the year. SJ had half hoped it would rain and be cancelled. But as they got on the Bournemouth train she cheered up a bit.

After all, keeping an eye on her sister didn't mean they had to be joined at the hip. Maybe there'd even be other kids Ali could tag along with, although SJ wasn't holding out too much hope of this.

"So what's his name – this guy you fancy?" Ali asked as they left the train station and walked to catch the bus that would take them the rest of the way to the beach.

"Who said I fancy anyone?" SJ said, startled at her sister's perception.

"You spent twice as long as usual putting on your make up. And you don't normally wear short skirts." Alison heaved the rucksack she was carrying off her shoulders and rested it against the back of the bus shelter. It clinked suspiciously and SJ wondered just how many bottles of wine were in there – and who had helped her buy them. The off licence on the corner of their road was owned by a friend of Dad's so she couldn't have got them there.

"I hope you're not planning to get paralytic, Ali, because I'm not carrying you home. Where did you get the money from anyway?"

"I used Dad's emergency taxi fund. Well – we'll be getting the bus back, won't we, so we don't need it."

SJ sighed. Luckily she had some money with her anyway. She'd got a holiday job as a chambermaid and she'd been saving for a dress she'd seen in Next. She'd nearly bought it today, but the girl had said it might well be in the sale if she waited another week.

Alison smiled disarmingly and bent to tie up the laces on her Doc Martens. Neither of them was wearing the outfits they'd planned for the evening – they'd never have got past Dad if they had. Alison was dressed in her usual T-shirt and jeans and SJ had her old baggy (but very comfy) leggings on.

"You did put my tights in, didn't you?" SJ said, suddenly remembering Alison had whisked away the rucksack before she'd finished putting her stuff in – so she could sneak in the bottles of wine without their parents seeing.

"Course," Alison winked. "Do you want to see what I spent my birthday money on?" Alison gestured to her stomach and SJ gasped as she cottoned on.

105

"You haven't got a belly button ring? Mum will absolutely kill you if she finds out."

"She won't find out." Alison smiled artlessly.

The bus arrived and SJ picked up the rucksack which was, she judged, at least three-bottles-of-wine heavy. Once they were installed in seats at the back, Alison lifted up her T-shirt and showed SJ the gold ring. "It matches the ones in my ears."

"Isn't it sore?"

"Not really. Anyway, looking good's worth a bit of discomfort, don't you think?"

SJ wriggled her toes in her favourite pumps, which were on the tight side but had been in an end of season sale, and frowned. "Sometimes, maybe."

They changed in the public loos in the car park just before they got to the beach. Alison produced a miniscule T-shirt from the rucksack and swapped it for the oversized one she was wearing. Then she tugged off her jeans, pulled on a miniskirt, even shorter than SJ's black leather one, and slipped on a pair of very pretty sandals.

"Hey, that's my ankle chain," SJ said, annoyed.

"Is it? I thought it was mine."

"Course you did." SJ tutted in irritation. "Well, just be careful you don't break it."

Alison grinned and flicked gel through her blond hair. She looked stunning – and much older than fifteen.

"Well, there's no point in having a belly button ring if you don't show it off, is there?"

"No," SJ agreed, picking up a tiny black T-shirt that was rolled up in the bottom of the rucksack and frowning. "I can't see my tights."

"They're definitely there." Alison leaned across her and SJ caught a waft of alcohol on her breath. She must have sneaked a drink earlier. Oh dear, that wasn't a good start.

"Oh," Alison said, as the T-shirt unravelled to reveal the words *Rock Star* in gold leaf on the front. "Sorry – I must have picked that up by mistake. You did say your black tights, didn't you?"

"I said the ones on the bed – the sheer ones!" SJ could have screamed with frustration. No way did she have the nerve to go bare – she hated her legs at the best of times and she didn't even have a tan.

"I didn't do it on purpose."

SJ didn't believe that any more than she believed Alison had meant to put on her own ankle chain (that's if she even had one of her own), but if they had a row about it now the evening would be spoilt before it had begun.

"Look, it doesn't matter that much, does it?" A cajoling note had crept into Alison's voice – she obviously knew she'd overstepped the mark. "You look fine. You'd be too hot with tights anyway."

This was very probably true, but SJ didn't feel any better. She'd just have to make the best of a bad situation.

"Perhaps I could keep these leggings on. What do you think?" She peered at the reflective sheet of tin that served as a mirror in the public loos, trying to decide whether the leggings were as wrinkly as they looked.

Alison snorted. "It's up to you, but I don't think you're going to pull in those!"

SJ peeled them off miserably. "I haven't even shaved my legs."

107

"No one will notice," Alison said, but SJ's confidence, which hadn't been high to start with, plummeted another few feet.

She cheered up slightly when they emerged from the loos and she saw her friend, Joanne, walking by, swinging four cans of lager by their thin plastic carrier.

Joanne was bare-legged in a turquoise minidress. She was bigger than SJ – a size fourteen at least – but she always looked brilliant whatever she was wearing.

"It's confidence, babe," she'd said when SJ had once asked her how she did it. "I just tell myself I look good, and so I do. Self-fulfilling prophecy."

This hadn't helped much when SJ had tried it and she'd come to the conclusion that there needed to be at least a grain of truth in the prophecy before it could become self-fulfilling, and that you really needed a smidgeon of fashion sense as well. Alison had more fashion sense than she did.

"Sarah-Jane," Joanne shouted, spotting them and strolling across the car park. A turquoise scrunchy held back her brown hair, and some strappy gold sandals set off the dress. Her toenails were fluorescent purple. SJ's yellow Sam and Libby flats felt suddenly out of date. She felt more self-conscious than ever as the three of them crossed the tarmac stretch of promenade to the beach.

Then, as her feet sunk into soft golden sand, SJ decided her friend had been right about this being the best beach in the country. The tide was out, and on their left a wide expanse of sand the colour of Colman's mustard stretched towards the sea, which glittered like diamonds in the evening sun.

On their right were some of the most beautiful houses she had ever seen, some with great glass frontages to give a panoramic view of the bay and many with their own private jetties.

"Oh, to be rich," Joanne said.

"I'm going to marry a millionaire," Alison giggled, "who can keep me in the style to which I'd like to become accustomed."

"You wish," said SJ and Joanne simultaneously.

It didn't take long to find the barbecue. They just followed the music (Janet Jackson) and the smell of frying burgers drifting across the fresh ozone tang of the sea. Clusters of people lounged about and a group of lads were playing with a beach ball on the hard sand. Lots of the girls were just wearing bikinis or minidresses, and the lads were bare-chested or in T-shirts and shorts.

"So how's it going?" Joanne asked, flicking a quick smile at Alison as they walked towards the main throng, where someone had set up a decorating table for drinks, its legs buried to keep it stable. "Any exciting gossip you want to tell me about?" Her eyes sparkled. She was well aware of SJ's crush on Jed.

"Not yet. Although I'm hoping I might have later." SJ glanced around, glad of the sea breeze to cool her hot face. She couldn't see Jed anywhere, and she knew without looking he wouldn't be playing beach ball. He wasn't a beach ball type of guy.

"How about you? How's Nick?"

Joanne screwed up her face, shot a glance at Alison, who was sitting on the sand and filling a plastic cup with Thunderbird, and lowered her voice. "Not so good, to be honest. We had a row last night. Nothing new there; but the making up part was good." She winked, and SJ smiled.

"Lucky you."

"He'll be down later. He went to get the burgers. Is your sister old enough to be drinking that stuff?"

"No one's old enough to be drinking that stuff. But if I say anything it'll just make her worse."

"Little sisters, eh! Hey, isn't that Jed over there?" Joanne shielded her eyes against the golden light of the evening sun and SJ followed her gaze. Way out on the hard sand, close to the creamy frill of the tide, a dark figure was sprawled on a rock. He was smoking – she could see the little breath-puffs of smoke against the pink sky – and her heart started to beat faster. Her heart knew it was him.

"Mmm, I think it is." She pretended nonchalance but Joanne wasn't fooled.

"He ought to have *dangerous* tattooed on his forehead," Joanne said with a wry smile. She ducked to avoid a beach ball that had just whizzed past her head. "Talking of dangerous," she muttered, frowning at the lad who'd raced after it. "Be careful with that, can't you?"

"Sorry." He ran past them and reached the ball at the same time as Alison, who had just bent to pick it up. She handed it up to him with a flirtatious smile and SJ saw the way he stared appreciatively at her breasts. A sigh caught in her throat. She was going to have to keep a close eye on her sister.

"Do you fancy a lager or a glass of wine?" Joanne asked. "I brought both."

"I think I'd better stick to Coke," SJ said. One of them had better stay sober. "I spotted some on the main table where we dropped off our BBQ stuff. Won't be a sec."

She was walking back towards Jo and Alison with a plastic cup of Coke when she saw that Jed was heading towards her. Smoke rose from a roll-up in his hand, which he stubbed out on the sand as he reached her.

"Hello, gorgeous." His voice was gravel and velvet and his black eyes scanned her face, her breasts, her legs while his mouth curved in approval. "I was hoping you'd be here."

"Were you?" Why couldn't she think of something more intelligent to say? He was wearing faded cut-off jeans and a black Metallica T-shirt; his arms were to die for – tanned and muscular – and he was standing close enough for her to smell the scent of him: something spicy mixed with tobacco smoke and lust.

He touched her arm. Her skin shivered in response. She knew she'd feel the imprints of his fingers for weeks.

"Who's this?" he said.

"What?" SJ turned to see her sister sashaying towards them – she must have been practising that sashay in the mirror. The sunset highlighted her hair and turned it to gold; her white top clung to her breasts (SJ realised suddenly she wasn't wearing a bra – when had she taken that off?) and her bare midriff was satin-smooth. She looked like an angel who'd been tempted away from heaven towards the dark side.

"We're sisters."

"Is that so?"

Alison looked up at him from beneath her lashes. "Are you man enough to handle two women?"

Jed laughed, a little uncertainly. SJ felt her face flame. "Pack it in, Alison." She kept her voice light and Alison giggled and then, to her relief, sauntered away towards the group who were playing beach ball.

"Sorry about that." SJ turned back to Jed.

"No worries." He spread his hands in front of him and smiled. He had a way of tipping back his head when he smiled. It made him look incredibly sexy. SJ's senses swam with his nearness. She forgot about her pale, unshaven legs.

While they queued up for burgers and hot dogs, Jed kept up a stream of banter. SJ didn't catch everything he said, partly because he had quite a strong Irish accent and partly because she was keeping an eye on what Alison was doing, but she could have listened to him all night. The texture of his voice was enough. It lilted around her, as calming as the sea. She'd always liked voices, and she liked the way he kept touching her – tiny little pinprick touches that set her skin on fire.

As the skies darkened and the moon rose to draw its shimmering light path across the black sea, SJ began to relax. The evening was turning out better than she'd dared hope. All around her was the low buzz of mellowed-out conversation and someone was smoking a joint not far away. Someone else was strumming an acoustic guitar, its melody blending with the ancient rhythm of the sea.

Alison was playing beach ball with the group of lads – they'd got progressively more rowdy, but what the heck, you were only young once. SJ could have forgiven anyone anything at that moment. Jed was being very attentive.

112

His glances were getting more lingering, his touches more daring. Considering his reputation, he was taking things very slowly. SJ was enjoying it without overtly encouraging him. She didn't want him to think she was easy, but she didn't want him to think she wasn't interested either. The last time they'd met she'd been on a girls' night out and he'd bought her a drink, but the club had been too noisy for much chat and although they'd flirted he hadn't asked for her number.

"Word is that he was seeing someone at the time but it wasn't serious," Joanne had told her afterwards. "He's finished with her now."

SJ didn't know if the 'finishing' had anything to do with her, but she did know that Jed was going to kiss her soon. Every atom of her body tingled with anticipation.

"Another cup of wine, Sarah-Jane?" The way he said her name was glorious. They were half sitting, half lying on the sand. Their shadows had already merged and become one. A prelude to the moment SJ knew was on the horizon, the moment they would touch each other, skin against skin, for the first splintering, diamond-bright time.

Jed leant across her to refill her plastic cup. In the same instant her face was sprinkled with cold water. SJ jumped and sat up. "What on earth...?"

Alison's drunken giggle smashed into the moment. "Are you coming skinny-dipping, sis? It's fan-taaaa-stic." She shook out her hair, showering SJ and Jed with another volley of freezing droplets, and her towel, which wasn't really big enough to cover her, slipped to expose one breast.

113

With a mixture of embarrassment and alarm SJ realised that a) Alison wasn't wearing anything beneath her towel and b) she was completely pissed.

Furious, she stood up. She wasn't sure exactly what she intended to do, but Alison darted away from her, stumbled on the soft sand and went sprawling.

"Oops," she called, and burst into another fit of giggling.

"I think your sister needs a bigger towel," Jed observed, leaning back on his elbows and doing nothing about finding one. He wasn't alone. Several other people were now looking in Alison's direction, the girls with disapproval, the lads with blatant interest. Alison rolled over, let go of the towel altogether and rubbed her face with her hands.

"I've got sand in my eyes."

SJ scouted around frantically for Alison's rucksack, but Joanne beat her to it. She was coming across with a beach towel, arms outstretched. SJ shot her a grateful glance as they both crouched beside Alison, shielding her with their bodies, while Joanne slipped the beach towel around her narrow shoulders. Alison was still rubbing her eyes. She'd gone very white.

"For God's sake," SJ remonstrated. "How much have you drunk?"

"Hardly any," Alison said, and promptly threw up on the sand.

SJ wasn't sure exactly when Jed slipped away into the moon-drenched night. It could have been at that point, or it could have been later on, when she was helping Alison to rinse her face under the cold tap on the prom. Either way, she was pretty sure she wouldn't see him again. Part of her ached with disappointment. She'd had such high hopes: he was so darkly beautiful, and she'd had the sense they were on the brink of something special. But a larger part of her was worried about Alison, who had been spectacularly ill several times.

SJ had forced her to drink lots of cups of water and someone had given her a couple of Paracetamol. One guy had commented that it was disgusting drinking yourself into such a state – and Alison was obviously an alcoholic in the making – and another of her more helpful friends had laughed and suggested Alison should sleep it off. But SJ daren't take her home until she'd sobered up. Dad would go spare and Mum would probably cry, and she would almost certainly get the blame.

Now, a couple of hours later, everyone but SJ, Alison and Joanne had drifted off home. The three of them were sitting in a line on the concrete steps that separated the prom from the beach.

"Thank you," SJ said to Joanne, who was pouring black coffee from a Thermos flask into a cup and handing it to Alison.

"I don't like coffee," Alison grumbled, but at least – finally – there was some colour back in her cheeks.

"Where's Nick?" SJ asked. "Is he giving you a lift home?"

Joanne shook back her mop of brown hair. "We had another row earlier," she said ruefully. "And he stormed off, silly bugger." Her voice was light, but SJ could see she was more upset than she was letting on.

"I'm really sorry." She edged along the step and slipped an arm around Joanne's plump shoulders.

"I'm not. I won't be wasting any tears on Naff Nick." The slight wobble in her voice betrayed her and for a while they sat quietly listening to the eternal swish of waves against the shore as the black sea inched its way back up the beach.

"How are you going to get home then?" SJ said at last, deciding it might be better to concentrate on practicalities.

"I'll have to ring my stepdad." Joanne didn't sound very keen at the prospect. SJ knew she didn't get on with her stepdad. "I think I've missed the last bus."

"Oh, don't bother him, Jo. We can share a taxi – we've got to get back to the station anyway."

"That's in the opposite direction," Joanne pointed out. "Don't worry. If I can't get hold of him, I can hitch. I haven't got any money anyway."

"I have," SJ said, trying not to think of the dress in Next. "We can drop you off on the way."

As they slowly headed back along the sand dusted promenade Alison spoke for the first time in ages. "What happened with that bloke you fancied? Couldn't we scrounge a lift home with him?"

"He left hours ago," SJ said, amazed that in all the kerfuffle she had managed to push Jed out of her mind. But now he was back he wasn't so easy to shift. The night breeze goose-bumped her skin and she swallowed an ache of regret that was suddenly fathoms deep.

"Do you think it was your legs that put him off?" Alison contemplated SJ's legs with a frown. "I suppose they do look a bit hairy, but they're not that bad in the dark."

SJ stared at her, open-mouthed, but before she could think of a stinging enough retort, Alison went on breezily, "He was pretty full of himself anyway, wasn't he? If you ask me, you're better off without him."

Chapter Thirteen

Would it have altered the course of history if she'd told Alison how hurt she had really felt that night? Or if she had told their mother about Alison's drunken skinny-dipping instead of keeping quiet? Would Alison have thought more about the consequences of her actions if she'd been punished?

When they'd argued about it afterwards Alison had finally confessed that she'd drunk too much because she felt left out.

"You were off laughing and chatting with your mates – and getting chatted up by that gorgeous bloke – and I was just sitting on my own, bored."

SJ didn't remember it quite like that but she'd given her sister the benefit of the doubt. Even so, the memory of Jed and what might have been was a raw spot on her psyche for several weeks. For a while she hoped he might contact her – they hadn't exchanged numbers, but they had mutual friends. Then she saw him in town with a really pretty girl on his arm. She'd pretended not to notice them and had walked swiftly in the opposite direction. And slowly the bittersweet regret had faded away.

Eighteen months later, in the canteen at university, she had met Derek Anderson. She'd been sitting at a table in the corner, immersed in a copy of *Hello,* and had barely glanced up when he approached and said softly, "Is it okay if I sit with you?"

"Sure."

"I'm not a student," he added, and now she did look up, a little irritated at this further interruption. Couldn't he see she was busy?

Her first impression was that he was quite ordinary-looking. Brown hair, brown eyes, and not terribly good skin.

"I'm working undercover for the Drugs Squad. You won't give me away, will you?"

His face was deadly serious and she frowned – she supposed it could have been true. There was always a drugs problem in universities – well, there was according to the papers. She hadn't noticed anyone doing anything untoward, apart from smoking the odd joint, which hardly counted. All students smoked dope. She did it herself at parties and had the odd line of speed if she wanted to stay up all night.

"See that guy over there – the one with the John Lennon glasses and the moustache? Don't make it obvious you're looking," he warned. "I don't want him to know we're on to him. That piece of low life is the main supplier of crack cocaine to this campus. You wouldn't believe how many innocent lives he's destroyed."

As far as SJ could tell – without making it obvious she was looking, of course – the bloke he'd indicated was Jack Watson, editor of the uni magazine and reputed to be in line for a high flying career in his father's Fleet Street paper.

"Pull the other one, it's got bells on," she muttered. "Everyone knows he wouldn't touch drugs with a barge pole." Hmm, rather a surplus of clichés for someone studying English literature, but she'd been too taken aback to think of anything clever.

"Very good cover, I'll grant you." Derek looked deep into her eyes in a way that was both off-putting and unnervingly sexy. "Do me a favour and walk out of here with me. Just act natural, like we're talking about an assignment or something. I'd really, really appreciate it."

"Do me a favour and bugger off," SJ said, sure now she was being wound up and that a group of her friends were skulking nearby to see what she would do next. "I'm busy." She indicated the magazine. "Or hadn't you noticed?"

"Please. I can't tell you how important this is. We're at such a delicate stage in operations. I've just taken several pictures of the suspect and I have to get them back to my boss." He revealed a tiny camera in the palm of his hand and SJ looked at it thoughtfully. She'd never seen one that small. In fact, she'd never seen anything like it. It was beautifully made, a little masterpiece of engineering.

As she hesitated, Derek went on softly. "If he realises what I'm doing – if he gets the merest hint, I'm dead. So are a lot of other people. All those innocent lives – wasted. You wouldn't want it on your conscience, believe me."

That was true. Despite herself, she was starting to get sucked in. And so what if she was being wound up? She wasn't actually busy at all. She put the magazine down on the table and gave him her full attention.

He smiled. Then he reached across and drew the side of his index finger across her jaw line – very soft, very sure of himself – all the while holding her gaze with his intense brown eyes. And to SJ's amazement she found the whole of her body was awakening to his touch. Never in her life had anyone had such a devastating effect on her.

It was for that reason, and not because she really believed his story, that she got up and the two of them walked side by side out of the canteen. Just outside the door, Derek flattened himself against the wall, arms and legs spread-eagled. "Oh, shit, there's another one. Don't move. Over by that bush – did you see him?"

SJ had seen something by the bush, although she wasn't sure what: a shadow – maybe a dog or cat, or something bigger, skulking on all fours. A quiver of adrenaline ran down her spine and suddenly she was caught up in the game.

"We'll have to go another way. Come on." He grabbed her hand and she ran with him down the cinder track that bordered the tennis courts and led towards the nearest accommodation. This was more interesting than reading *Hello* anyway, even if it was only because he was still holding her hand. She half expected to hear the sound of running footsteps behind them. But all was still. And when Derek finally agreed that it should be safe to walk now, they'd obviously shaken them off – she slowed to a breathless halt with him.

He let go of her hand. "Thanks for that. You've saved my life. You're Sarah-Jane, aren't you?"

She nodded, her heart returning to something like normal. "You're not really from the Drugs Squad, are you?"

"No – good crack though, wasn't it?" His eyes were full of laughter and then he snorted with mirth and doubled over. SJ was torn between stomping off and joining in. In the end she joined in. It was impossible not to. He had one of the most infectious laughs in the universe.

Soon they were rolling around on the grass verge not far from the main entrance completely out of control. Every time one of them stopped laughing the other one started them off again. Not because it had even been that funny – in the end they were laughing because it just felt so damn good to laugh. Finally SJ begged him to stop.

"I think I've ruptured something," she gasped, rolling onto her side before propping her head on her elbow and glancing at him through her lashes. "My stomach hurts."

He mirrored her movements so they were facing each other, lying side by side on the grass. SJ was vaguely aware of the distant rumble of traffic, and the closer sound of birdsong, and the smell of fish and chip wrappers wafting from a nearby bin. But most of all she was aware of the frantic beating of her heart, which for some reason was out of control again. He looked different from this angle. His eyes had little golden flecks in their depths and she could smell the indefinable scent of male skin. He looked very, very attractive.

SJ had never believed in love at first sight, particularly not when the man in question had just spent a good twenty minutes lying to you through his teeth. But it had been funny. Actually, it had been bloody funny. She couldn't remember the last time she'd laughed so uncontrollably and for so long, but she didn't feel like laughing any more. She was feeling something quite different now. Every nerve ending she had tingled in response to the look in his eyes.

For a moment she thought he was going to kiss her, but then he shifted position, moving onto his knees

121

until he was kneeling beside her, the worn fabric of his jeans making indents in the summer grass.

"A hurt stomach – huh? We can't have that. I'm going to have to examine you, SJ. You can trust me, I'm a doctor."

He grinned. His doctor voice was just as convincing as his undercover Drug Squad voice – perfectly modulated with just the right amount of concern and seriousness. "Now, perhaps if you could just lift your T-shirt up a tad for me, Miss...?"

"Carter," she supplied.

"Thank you. Now, Miss Carter. Up with the T-shirt – no need to take it right off – then perhaps you can tell me exactly where it hurts?"

Mesmerised, she rolled onto her back, lifted her T-shirt and sucked in her stomach in case he thought she was fat.

His fingers skimmed the tiny strip of belly she'd exposed and she could hardly breathe. This is madness, you barely know him, squealed the voice of reason in her head.

Who cares? contradicted another voice, a much louder, more authoritative voice.

Everywhere he touched he sparked off quivers of lust. If he could do this while touching her stomach, she didn't dare imagine what he might do given full reign of a proper erogenous zone. SJ closed her eyes in ecstasy. She could feel the sun on her face and the merest touch of breeze in her hair. What a pity they weren't in a meadow instead of a public place. On second thoughts, what a good job they weren't in a meadow.

Reality crashed in, and she opened her eyes and saw he was looking down at her through half-closed lids.

"Would kissing it better help, do you reckon?"

"Possibly," SJ breathed.

She wasn't at all surprised when he didn't kiss her abdomen, but her mouth. Neither was she surprised when the kiss took her briefly off the planet and into orbit. Later she discovered he could give her orgasms just by kissing her. No man before or since had managed to do that. No man had ever come close.

Chapter Fourteen

Reasons Not To Go To My Parents' Party
1. Massive backlog of work
2. Highly contagious fatal disease, requiring isolation
3. House move to Scotland
4. Unmoveable engagement, possibly funeral

SJ chewed the end of her pen and glanced thoughtfully at the list. Did you get funerals on Saturday nights? Probably not. She sighed. She'd had more than a week to come up with something good and she'd failed spectacularly.

Perhaps she could say she was taking Tom on a surprise weekend to Amsterdam to celebrate his promotion. It was almost worth doing – he'd always fancied going to Amsterdam. But, ironically, because of his promotion, she wasn't sure he'd be able to get away.

Or she could say she would go to the party, and be ill at the last minute again. Weak – as well as being very mean. She didn't want to hurt her parents. But the thought of seeing Alison again filled her with terror.

SJ closed her eyes. It needed to be something really good this time and she was running out of options. Her parents were coming to dinner in less than six hours – she needed a game plan. She was no nearer to a solution when Tom came in, bearing bulging carrier bags of food.

"Hello, Tom. I thought you had an appointment. I wasn't expecting you for another couple of hours."

"I know, but I've got to cook for tonight, haven't I? I wanted to do something nice for your mum and dad. Besides, I've been neglecting you lately." He plonked the bags on the kitchen table. "Come and give us a hug."

Oh no, he must want sex again – and she was too brittle to relax. Especially for afternoon sex when she didn't have the rose-tinted glasses of a few gin and tonics. She didn't mind him neglecting her on that front at all. Was it normal to find your husband attractive but not want to sleep with him? Thinking about that gave her a headache. Reluctantly, she went into his arms and was relieved to find all he seemed to want was a hug.

When they drew apart he looked at her, eyes narrowed thoughtfully. He was getting grey hairs, she noticed. Little flecks of silver amongst the brown. He looked tired, too. Eye-tired, as though he'd been staring at a computer screen too long, and there were lines on his forehead. She smoothed one out with a fingertip. "You haven't been neglecting me. You've had a lot on. I don't mind. I'm pretty busy with my poetry." Slight exaggeration, but never mind, she didn't want him feeling guilty.

"The house looks lovely," he said, sniffing the air appreciatively.

SJ smiled. Furniture polish – one quick spray by the front door and a token sweep of the wooden floor always fooled him.

"Thanks for being so supportive, love. I'd never have got this far if you'd been the type of clingy wife who was nagging me to be at home every five minutes. It will be worth it in the end, I promise. I was thinking maybe we could go away for a romantic break when I've got settled – what do you think?"

"Sounds great. They say Amsterdam's fantastic in September."

"I was thinking more Paris or maybe even Venice. We could make it a long weekend."

"Lovely." It would be even lovelier if she could manoeuvre it to be on the same weekend as the party. Especially if she could get Tom to book it up now. "Shall we go and have a look on the Internet – see if they've got any cheap deals?"

"I'm not interested in cheap – I want to spoil you. Besides, we don't want to clash with your parents' party. When is that, anyway?"

"The first weekend in September, I think." So much for that then. She hesitated. "Tom, I don't want to miss their special day either, but Alison's going to be there."

"Well, I thought she probably would." He glanced at her, his face softening. "We're going to have to meet sooner or later. Don't you think it would be better at a party? Then you can just introduce us and after that we can ignore her."

"I don't want to introduce you." SJ wondered if he could hear the tremble in her voice. She coughed to disguise it. "There wouldn't be any point." Maybe she could just trivialise the situation. "We're never going to be close again – me and Alison, we just don't have anything in common."

"You're sisters – that's quite a bit in common."

SJ grimaced. Alison had that effect on her. Little Ali, with her angelic sweet smile and blond hair and a pair of demon's horns growing out of her forehead, always got exactly what she wanted – no matter that it already belonged to someone else.

"I'm sorry," she added. "I know it sounds selfish, but I just don't want to get involved with her again."

"Not even for your mum and dad's sake? It's their special day."

SJ looked into his eyes and wished he wasn't so kind. Dear, sweet, comfortable Tom. He wouldn't stand a chance against Alison. Not once she started batting her eyelash extensions and sticking her cleavage under his nose. He'd be a pushover, she knew he would. Men always fell for that routine.

"So how about we tell them we'd be delighted to go to their party? Then I can prove to you, once and for all, that I'm completely immune to Amorous Alison. How about that?"

"All right," SJ agreed miserably, knowing it was pointless arguing with him any more. And besides, she knew he was right. She was acting like a ten year old.

She screwed up her list, aimed it at the bin and missed. It bounced off Ash's head, who was sleeping alongside it, and woke him up.

"I'm sorry." She knelt beside him and kissed his soft head. He gave a little grunt of adoration. SJ wished it was as easy to love people as it was to love her dog.

Her parents were due at seven, but as usual they were early. The doorbell rang at just gone half six and SJ went to let them in, wondering if they'd ever take any notice of her much repeated request that they just let themselves in, they didn't need to stand on ceremony.

"Hi, Mum, hi, Dad." She kissed them both and took the bottle her father was holding out. "Chardonnay – thank you, our favourite."

"Shame about the football," her father muttered. "Did you see it? Referee must've been paid off. Bloody criminal." He pronounced it "bloodeh". "Where's the man of the house?"

"In the kitchen," SJ told him, smirking. Her father, a staunch Yorkshireman even though he hadn't lived there since he'd been married to her mother, had never got used to the term 'New Man' and was even less acclimatised to the idea that SJ had married one.

"Bloodeh criminal," he repeated, and she wasn't sure whether this was a further reference to football or to the fact that Tom had just appeared. He was wearing a plastic chef's apron and had a wooden spoon in his hand – he'd obviously been mid-stir.

"So what have you done to the house since we came round last?" her mother asked, unbuttoning her coat and giving it to SJ for transfer to a hanger.

"Tidied it," SJ said hopefully, knowing this wasn't what she meant.

"I see you haven't got rid of these old floorboards yet."

"They're stripped pine, Mum, not floorboards. They're trendy."

"Carpet would be warmer, though, wouldn't it, pet? Something smells nice – hello, Tom, love. Has she got you in that kitchen again?"

"I love cooking," Tom said loyally, flicking an amused glance at SJ. "Come in, I'll get you both a drink – glass of wine, Helen? And how about you, Jim? I've got some nice real ale in."

"Sounds grand."

"Just a bitter lemon for me, if you've got one, Tom. I'm driving. Sarah-Jane, there are cobwebs on this doorframe. I've just got one in my hair."

128

"I've been busy, Mum. Try ducking, that's what I do. I'll have a glass of that Chardonnay – a large one," she called to Tom's retreating back. She'd been planning to have orange juice, but no way could she survive on soft drinks if her mother was in critical mode.

Fortunately her criticism didn't extend to dinner. Sensibly, Tom had decided not to do anything fancy, knowing her parents were both plain eaters. Mum waxed lyrical over the tenderness of the steak and the homemade pepper sauce, and even Dad waxed lyrical – well, as lyrical as he got. "Grand bit of meat, this, Tom. Is it local?"

"Local to Tesco's," SJ said, fortified by several more glasses of wine, three of which she'd drunk in the kitchen out of sight of her mother's watchful eye. They'd switched to one of Tom's special bottles of Chateauneuf du Pape for the meal. She was just topping up everyone's glasses when the subject she'd been dreading all evening came up.

"About our little bash," Mum began, with a one-glass-of-wine flirtatious glance at Tom. "We thought we'd have a buffet, rather than a sit-down meal. Nothing elaborate – it's mostly family. But some of them are coming from Barnsley, so we thought we'd better do something."

"Not elaborate, she says. Not elaborate – we're having a bloodeh great marquee in the garden." Dad laughed uproariously as if this was some huge joke. Although that was probably the wine on top of the real ale.

"It's a gazebo, Jim, not a marquee. Now then, Sarah-Jane, your sister's kindly offered to help out with the food preparation."

129

"That's nice of her. Is there anything you'd like me to do?"

"I was hoping we could rely on you to collect the wine from the off licence. We've ordered a couple of cases of plonk and one of bubbly – that's for the toast."

"Of course we'll collect it, we'd be glad to." Tom put his elbows on the table and his chin on the back of his linked hands and leaned forward. "And I insist you let us pay for it, too, as our present."

"Oh, we couldn't possibly."

"No, son, that's not on. Not on at all."

"We'll be offended if you turn us down, won't we, SJ?"

She nodded. It was typical of Tom to make such a generous gesture. Perhaps they could drop off the wine and scarper. She wouldn't feel so bad if they'd at least contributed to the event.

"That's a very nice offer, son, but you've a big mortgage to pay." Her father's neck had turned red. "You can't be going chucking money away on crates of wine. You'll need your spare cash for the bank manager."

"Cases, Jim – it's beer that comes in crates. Although I quite agree. We couldn't possibly let you." It was funny how her mother's accent got all posh when she was trying for a gracious refusal.

"We're not broke." Tom looked amused. "Didn't SJ tell you I've just been promoted? I'm regional sales manager now."

"Regional sales manager – are you? Well, I never… Sarah-Jane, why ever didn't you tell us? We'd have bought a card…" Her mother fiddled with the stem of her wine glass, looking pleased and embarrassed at the same time. "Well, I never. How

130

about that, Jim? Regional sales manager. What does it mean, Tom?"

"It means he has to work even harder," SJ said, leaning across to take Tom's hand and just missing sending her glass – which was empty again – flying. How had that happened? "Maybe we should open a bottle of champagne, Tom, to celebrate properly with Mum and Dad?"

"Well, I suppose we could." He didn't sound as keen on the idea as she was. But when she stared at him pointedly he got up and went into the kitchen.

SJ followed him, partly to ask if he minded about the champagne, out of earshot of her parents, but mostly so she could slip out for a sneaky fag.

"No, of course I don't mind. It's just I'm not sure who's going to drink it. Your parents probably won't want much more and I've had more than enough, to be honest, and…"

"Don't say it, Tom," she warned, leaning against the worktop to steady herself. "I've been cutting down all week. I've been a bloodeh saint." She hoped her father wasn't listening; he'd think she was taking the mickey. "Surely it's okay for me to let my hair down at the weekend? And I have just agreed to go to the party. That was a very hard decissssion for me to make." God, was she slurring her words?

Tom didn't seem to notice. He disappeared to get the champagne and SJ persuaded Ash he fancied a stroll around the garden. It was quite light, considering it was gone ten. A full moon sailed above the trees and Ash looked like a ghost, silver and unearthly in the moonlight.

Suddenly SJ felt giddy with joy. It was fantastic that they'd moved here to this beautiful house with its glorious garden. It was fantastic that Tom had been promoted. The meal he'd cooked had been sublime. She was so proud of him, sitting there telling her parents in his modest understated way that he'd been made Regional Sales Manager – and all because he was generous enough to want to buy the drink for their special do. She was sure he'd never have mentioned it otherwise.

She was so pleased she'd got rid of Dirty Derek and married Tom. At the thought of Derek a sliver of unease rose in her. Hadn't she thought Derek was the love of her life, once? No, she couldn't have done, because she loved Tom. Adored Tom. Beautiful Tom. She adored everyone at the moment. Even Alison – because if her sister hadn't set her sights on Derek then she'd never have realised what a two-timing rat he was.

SJ spread her arms out wide and did a little dance around the shadowed lawn, whirling and twirling in step with an imaginary partner. It felt wonderful to be so sensible and mature and forgiving. Oh, yes, she could forgive anyone the way she felt now. She could forgive the whole bloodeh world.

Twirling and dancing, pirouetting and jumping, gliding and swirling with infinite grace below the stars – beautiful stars – so many of them. She wondered if anyone had managed to count them properly without a telescope and how long it would take. And then she wondered with a vague sense of awestruck astonishment why they seemed to be swapping places with the ground. One moment they were as clear as little lights above her head and the next – curiously – they were below her feet. She experienced a brief moment of confusion before something hit her hard in the face.

132

SJ stayed where she was, shocked and hurt and not sure what had happened because although she now seemed to be stationary, the world was still moving. It must have been the ground that hit her. The dank scent of earth filled her nostrils and she realised she was lying face down. Warily, she rolled onto her back and immediately felt a concerned wet nose nudge her face.

"Sorry, Ash." She moved her head and a glorious galaxy of stars spun with renewed brightness above her. What on earth was going on? Perhaps she was having some sort of religious experience.

This theory lasted as long as it took for her to realise she felt terribly unwell. If she moved again she knew she would be sick. Clamping her hands over her mouth she tried to stay still, but it was no good, everything was moving. The lawn wouldn't stay flat. SJ hated being sick, but it was coming anyway, rising inexorably in her throat. She scrambled to her knees, some deep-rooted survival instinct murmuring insistently that it was not a good idea to vomit while lying flat on your back, however much the world was moving.

Flat on your back - supine – that was a good word, she thought distractedly, even as she threw up over and over again. There was some part of her mind that was clear. An impartial observer to her body, which was no longer under her control as it retched and heaved and retched some more beneath the velvet sky.

Being sick might not be good, it might not be dignified, but it was a marvellous relief, she realised, as at last her body was empty. Her head throbbed in a continuous thump of pain, but at least the world had stopped moving. And she was suddenly alone and shivering, on her knees in what turned out to be a flower bed, not the grass.

Somewhere nearby a voice was calling. An anxious voice, her mother's voice, over by the light that spilled from the back door. "Sarah-Jane, are you out there, pet? Only we're going to make a move now. You're not smoking out there, are you?"

Chapter Fifteen

When she woke she was lying beneath a pale striped ceiling. The stripes were pale plastic criss-crosses, a little fuzzy around the edges. SJ blinked and they came back into focus, but only briefly. For a while she played the blinking game. In focus, out of focus, in focus, out of focus – but it wasn't long before this made her feel sick. Keeping her eyes closed also made her feel sick so she was forced to open them and stare fixedly at what she gradually realised were the plastic mouldings on the ceiling of their lounge, faintly illuminated by the shards of light that poked through gaps in the drawn curtains – knife-like, evil, grinning shards of light.

She was lying on the sofa with her trousers on but no top and no bra, and the caramel-coloured throw from the spare bedroom draped half on and half off her. A heavy weight at her feet shifted and she realised Ash was on the end of the sofa. Tom must be in bed upstairs. How odd. A very slow tilt of her head revealed a glass of water and a packet of Nurofen on the coffee table, which had been pulled up close to the sofa.

Every part of her body felt bruised and sore. What on earth had happened last night? She'd obviously been run over by something very heavy. A train, possibly? Or a steam roller? Or at the very least a double-decker bus?

'You drank too much.' The voice, which was little more than a fuzzy and accusatory thought, came from somewhere inside her head. *'You really did surpass yourself last night. Feel a little sick, do we?'*

135

SJ frowned, which hurt like hell so she stopped. Perhaps it was the voice of her conscience – no, her conscience was fair and quite pleasant generally. It definitely wasn't triumphant and snide. It didn't generally tell her how useless she was, how weak-willed and pathetic not to be able to give up drinking, even for one night.

I'm never going to drink again.

'No?'

Never.

'You can't cut down – you're a lush, an old soak. Call yourself a tutor? What would your students think of you now?'

I'm cutting down.

'Yeah – right.' The voice seemed to find this intensely funny. The voice rolled and roared and hooted with laughter, hollering and howling around every corner of her head until it throbbed with the pain of it.

"Stop it. Stop it. STOP IT!" She didn't realise she'd spoken out loud until Ash, who thought she was talking to him, thumped his skinny silver tail on her feet.

"Good boy." She leaned forward to stroke him, feeling a tear slide down her cheek as she did so. She hadn't felt so awful for a long time and to top things off she was talking to herself. Wasn't that a sign of insanity? "Very good boy," she said again, to prove she was not mad and was not talking to herself. Ash rubbed his soft head against her hand in pleasure.

'Bet you do drink again.'

She shook her head.

'Bet you'll have a glass of wine in your hand by nine o'clock this evening.' The voice had softened, become cajoling, almost menacingly sweet.

136

"No." SJ shuddered and clamped her hands over her eyes to blot out the voice, although why it should be her eyes and not her ears she was covering she had no idea. When she uncovered them again, the room was still and silent. And the clock on the wall told her it was still only five thirty a.m. Far, far too early to get up on a Sunday – which was just as well, because she was fairly sure she couldn't move further than the glass of water and Nurofen.

The next time she opened her eyes, Tom was standing by the window. He'd just pulled back the curtains – the noise must have woken her – and he was silhouetted in the sunshine so she couldn't see his face.

"How are you feeling?"

"Awful."

"I'm not surprised." He moved across the room and knelt by the sofa. She would have felt better if he'd shouted at her – told her what a stupid little idiot she was. But he just picked up her hand in his big gentle one and squeezed it. His eyes were infinitely tender. "Can I get you anything?"

"A shotgun would be good."

"Don't talk daft. We've all been there."

"Some of us more often than others," SJ mumbled, trying to recall if she'd ever seen Tom raging drunk, and failing. He was moderate in all things, except perhaps for work, which he put his all into. Once or twice since they'd been married she'd thought him too moderate – too middle of the road. She'd wished he'd take the odd risk. Go a bit mad, be a bit more exciting. Now she loved his moderation. It felt safe and calming and peaceful.

"I'm sorry, Tom. Did I show you up?"

"Well – not unless you count dancing round the lounge and singing, whilst using a champagne bottle as a mike."

"Oh my God – please tell me you're joking."

He didn't smile.

"Did Mum and Dad see me?"

"Afraid so, but don't worry. You still had your top on at that point."

SJ groaned and clutched her head. "Tom, please tell me I didn't take my top off in front of Mum and Dad?"

"Of course you didn't. That was much later." He looked puzzled, but his consternation was nothing compared to SJ's dismay. She closed her eyes, trying desperately to remember something – anything – about the previous evening. But she had absolutely no recollection of dancing around the lounge. Her last memory was of being sick in the garden.

"Don't worry," Tom went on hastily. "You didn't seem that drunk to me – more happy, and your dad thought it was a laugh, he was singing along with you."

"What was Mum doing?" SJ was positive her mother would never condone drunken singing under any circumstances.

"Waiting in the car. Now I come to think of it, she did seem in a hurry to go. I must admit things are a bit hazy. I had a few too many myself. It was that champagne. Mixing your drinks is always a bad thing." He frowned, and SJ felt her heart sink to a new all-time low. She wished she shared his conviction that mixing drinks was responsible for the way she felt now – but in her heart she knew it wasn't. It was sheer quantity. Desperate to know just what she'd actually done, she steered the subject back to last night.

138

"But what about when I took my top off? Didn't you think I was drunk then?" Mortified, she covered her hands with her face.

"Well, no – I was in the loo, and when I came out you were twirling your bra around your head and singing The Stripper. I thought you were messing about, to be honest."

She would have giggled if she hadn't felt so ashamed. She hitched the throw up around her chin, which was pathetic, she knew – a bit like getting dressed behind your towel when you've been sunbathing topless on the beach all afternoon.

"Don't worry about it." Tom seemed genuinely puzzled at her reaction. "If I hadn't been so sozzled myself I'd have taken more advantage of the situation."

He winked. He was missing the point entirely. But that was hardly his fault. How was he to know she had no recollection of deciding to put on a lap-dancing routine in their lounge? She wanted to ask if the curtains had been drawn. If they hadn't, she'd probably have been strutting her stuff at about the same time as the gastro pub around the corner kicked out its noisy revellers. Deep joy – the next time she went out, the entire street would be sniggering behind their hands.

Perhaps they should move.

"Don't worry," Tom said again. "I quite enjoyed it, actually."

This was not at all reassuring. He might think she'd found a new way to spice up their sex life and expect her to do it again. And she could no more have done a striptease for him when she was sober than she could have suggested they go to a wife swapping party.

"Right," she said bleakly. "Tom, would you mind awfully if I stayed here a bit longer? I don't think I can face getting up for a while."

"Course I don't mind. Want me to close the curtains again?"

"Please." Please, God – who she didn't believe in – let him have had the sense to do that last night, too. "And, Tom, could you take Ash for a walk?"

"Sure. I'll make you a cup of tea first."

Why was he so nice? Why was he so bloody nice? She'd have felt better if he'd had a go at her. She'd have felt less ashamed. Not that she was ever going to feel better again. Not today anyway. Thank God it was Sunday.

It wasn't until six o'clock that evening that the mother of all hangovers released its grip enough for her to haul herself off the sofa, go upstairs and get showered and dressed and then go cautiously back into the kitchen.

Tom was reading the papers. "It lives," he remarked, giving her a wry grin.

"I'm so sorry."

"Don't apologise to me. I've had a productive day. Paperwork," he added, gesturing to his briefcase on the table. "I've caught up on last week's."

"And tomorrow it begins all over again. Aren't you tired?"

"Not really, no. I find paperwork quite soothing."

SJ didn't – she found it irritating and largely unnecessary, particularly the endless, inane forms that the college insisted she complete every week. Thank God that was over for the summer. Mind you, Tom wasn't talking about that sort of paperwork – tying up

140

the loose ends of sales he'd closed was probably more interesting.

"Do you think I should apologise to Mum and Dad?"

"I shouldn't think so. You didn't say anything to upset them. On the contrary."

"I said we'd go to their party, didn't I?"

"Yes, and you also said you'd help your mum with her next car boot sale because Doreen's off to Malta." He grinned. "And you told your dad you'd be a reserve for when his team plays The Cock and Bottle next Thursday."

"But I don't even play darts."

"I was a bit surprised, I must admit."

"Maybe he'll forget. Hey, maybe they'll forget we said we'd go to the party too."

"I don't think that's very likely. They were thrilled. And we're going." His voice was peaceable, but firm and she sensed he wasn't going to budge on this one. And as she had quite a lot of making-up to do, she didn't even attempt to argue.

"Are you hungry? Shall I make us some tea?"

"Just a sandwich or something will do me. SJ, if you're going to the fridge can you grab us a can? I could do with a beer."

"Sure," she said, escaping. The beer was stacked beside a bottle of Chardonnay. SJ glanced at it and shuddered. No way was she ever drinking again. She'd just wasted an entire Sunday, not to mention made a complete exhibition of herself last night – LITERALLY. Dancing around the lounge half-naked was the behaviour of a teenager, not a thirty-six year old woman.

Would she have done it if she hadn't been so drunk? She knew the answer to that one. Self-loathing tightened her stomach.

Once they'd eaten and watched Sunday night TV, and Tom was snoring softly on the sofa, she held her hands out in front of her, palms down. Her fingers were shaking. Moving and trembling with a life of their own. It was an awful feeling. A part of her body was outside of her control – perhaps she should be relieved the rest of it wasn't outside her control, as it evidently had been last night. She tried to still her fingers, but the only way to do it was to clench them in her lap. And although her hangover was all but gone she had that awful black cloud feeling that usually followed.

It was like standing in a pit of despair, with no light coming in anywhere and the sure and certain feeling you would never get out. She wanted to wake Tom so she'd no longer be alone with the blackness. But she'd been selfish enough this past twenty-four hours. Tom was still snoring, his one empty can – his symbol of moderation – on the floor beside his armchair.

Suddenly, SJ couldn't bear it any more. Couldn't bear the suffocating depression and the tidal wave of her own dark thoughts. She leapt up and went into the kitchen: opened the fridge door; stared at the bottle of Chardonnay; closed the fridge door again; re-opened it; closed it; sighed; fetched the corkscrew; drew out the bottle; uncorked it; hated herself briefly, savagely, totally; fetched a glass; poured the wine and put it on the worktop beneath the kitchen clock.

She ached to drink it, but a memory was stirring at the back of her mind. A memory of the conversation

142

she'd had with some inner voice some time around dawn that morning.

'Bet you'll have a glass of wine in your hand by nine o'clock this evening.'

SJ glanced at the clock. It was just before nine. All she had to do was wait a few minutes and she'd have won the wager. She drew up a chair and, with her gaze still fixed firmly on the glass, she sat and waited. The room filled with the quiet ticking of the clock.

How slowly time moved when you were urging the seconds to pass. It almost didn't move at all. SJ imagined herself in an anti-chamber of hell – sitting in a room waiting for a clock that ticked tantalisingly, but didn't measure time.

Waiting for a moment that would never come.

Tension stiffened her shoulders. All she needed was a sip of that wine and she'd feel okay again. She began to count alongside the ticking of the clock. Affirmation that the seconds were passing. And as the big hand inched away from the hour, SJ got up from her chair. She'd wanted to leave it till ten past, but five past would do. One minute after nine would have done – she'd still have won the wager. She snatched up the glass and downed its contents in a gulp. Perhaps one more small glass – only a small one. Then she'd put the cork back in.

"I've won, I've won." Her voice fizzed with the reintroduction of alcohol. Excitement surged around her body.

Where was the voice now, huh? Not so smug now. SJ danced back into the lounge to check on Tom. He was still snoring gently. Her gaze flicked to the clock above the fireplace and she saw with a small shock that this one said nine. The sick sense of realisation hit her

143

at the same moment as the other voice started up again in her head.

The kitchen clock was ten minutes fast. She hadn't won at all, she'd lost. And now she could hear the voice again, excitedly mumbling the same words over and over in a stream of vindictive triumph: *'Told you so, told you so, told you so...'*

Chapter Sixteen

SJ and Alison had been born and brought up on the outskirts of Bournemouth. It was SJ's fault that the entire family had ended up living in or around London. Or at least that's how it felt when she looked back over her life.

She had studied English Literature at Kingston University, moving into a flat share nearby, and Alison had quickly decided that London was THE place to be and had escaped to visit her sister at every possible opportunity. This had been both flattering – not that SJ had been under any great illusion that she was the main attraction – and worrying, because it was the party scene that Alison loved.

"London is so fab," she'd tell SJ whenever she turned up – usually without any warning. "You are SO lucky to live here. You've got EVERYTHING on your doorstep. You don't even need a car!"

By everything, she meant clubs, bars and restaurants. SJ did her best to keep an eye on her, but Alison was way too adept at giving her the slip and sneaking off to 'enjoy herself'. SJ, immersed in studying, found the responsibility of looking after her sister weighed heavy on her shoulders.

"Just let her get on with it," Tanya said. "The more you try to rein her in, the more she'll kick back against you. She'll soon get bored with clubbing – she hasn't got the money for a start."

SJ didn't have the money either. She worked in Pizza Express in her spare time, but she was still mostly broke.

"Waitressing's a mug's game," Alison told her when she suggested she might do the same. "You'd be much better off getting a rich man."

"I'm in love with Derek," SJ pointed out, slightly irritated. "And as soon as we can afford it we're getting married."

"Well, you won't catch me scrimping and saving to get married," Alison said. "I'm going to have a big white wedding, all the trimmings." She spread her hands wide. "Marquee, brass band, honeymoon in Barbados – the lot."

"Well, I hope you fall for someone who can afford all that," SJ said, knowing their parents certainly couldn't.

Alison sighed theatrically. "Durr. It's just as easy to fall for a rich man as it is to fall for a poor man. Easier in fact – as they're likely to give you a better time."

"What they're like as a person is more important than how much they earn," SJ said, wishing she didn't sound so pompous.

"Well, yes, I know. I'm not saying it isn't. But I want a decent life, SJ. I don't want to end up like Mum and Dad, living on some poxy little housing estate. I want my own beauty salon for a start. I'm not going to get that by hooking up with some loser. Not that Derek's a loser," she added hastily.

SJ gave up. It was pointless arguing with her sister. She always did what she wanted in the end anyway. She was quite surprised when Alison brought Clive back to the house one night. He wasn't what she'd

146

expected. Although he was seven years older than Alison, and clearly not short of money – he owned a house in Romford – he wasn't flash. On the contrary, he seemed quite shy and serious. And although the age gap bothered SJ a bit – Alison might give the impression of being twenty-five, but was only actually seventeen – Clive did seem to really care about her.

"I think he might actually be good for her," she told Tanya. "He might settle her down a bit."

"Or she'll get bored of him," Tanya said with a wry smile. "But I think you're right. He's not heartbreaker material, is he?"

SJ was as shocked as Alison was when Alison got pregnant two months after meeting Clive.

"For heaven's sake, I thought you were on the pill."

"I must have forgotten one," Alison murmured. "I didn't think it would make that much difference."

And so it had been Alison who got married first. SJ and Derek had in fact put their wedding on hold for a couple of years because SJ knew her parents wanted to help out and – despite the fact that Clive was able to pay for his own wedding, which had been as big and expensive as Alison had planned – they'd insisted on contributing too. And not just financially.

They'd sold their house in Bournemouth and bought a place in Romford near Alison and Clive so they could help out with the baby while Alison went to do her City & Guilds diploma in beauty therapy.

"I'm not having my grandchild looked after by strangers," their mother had declared. "Don't you worry, pet. And I'm not having you throwing your life away on a little 'un – and being cheated out of a decent career, just because you got caught out."

SJ had flinched at this – being as she'd been the 'little 'un' their mother had presumably 'thrown her life away on'. And what was the decent career she'd been cheated out of anyway? Until that moment SJ hadn't known their mother had felt cheated. She'd always seemed perfectly happy being at home with them.

When SJ and Derek finally got married, it had been low key. Even her hen night, which Tanya had organised, had been pretty low key. It had involved SJ and a group of her friends going for a meal in Chinatown. For entertainment, Tanya had organised a list of tasks which she'd had to perform (or pay a forfeit) during the evening. SJ had loved it. At the end of it she'd rolled home gloriously drunk and she'd married Derek, feeling only slightly hungover, the next day.

She'd never regretted the low-keyness of her wedding until a few years later, when she'd been invited to a hen night in Dublin by a tutor she worked with. As the minibus dropped her back home SJ reflected that if she could have relived her hen night she'd definitely go to Dublin.

It was an amazing place. But now she was back she couldn't wait to see Derek. It was the first weekend they'd spent apart. It was healthy to spend time apart, she mused, as she waved a last goodbye to the girls and tottered down her path – she never had mastered the art of heels – towards her front door. Absence made the heart grow fonder, they said. But actually it did. She wondered if he'd missed her as much as she'd missed him. It hadn't sounded like it – he'd been out with the boys last night.

They'd had more than a few drinks, judging by his slurred 'I love you' when they'd spoken on the phone around midnight. But then what was wrong with that? So had she with Jackie and the crowd. It was good to let your hair down from time to time. And lecturers were experts at partying.

"Morning, Sarah-Jane," their neighbour Norah called cheerily as SJ rummaged in her bag for her key. "Did you have a good time?"

"Yes, thank you, we did." Norah was the last person she felt like talking to, but luckily she looked like she was off to church, pristine in a navy and white suit, her horn rimmed glasses perched on her beaky nose. SJ felt dishevelled in comparison. She hadn't had time for a shower that morning. They hadn't actually rolled into bed until four, and the plane had left at some unearthly hour.

"Lovely to see Alison again," Norah went on breezily. "She hasn't been over in a while, has she?"

SJ blinked. She hadn't realised Norah kept such a close eye on her guests' comings and goings. But actually she was right – Alison hadn't been over lately. She usually only came over when there was a family birthday, or if she wanted SJ to baby-sit.

"She's ever such a pretty girl, isn't she?" Norah was practically hanging over the fence in anticipation of a good gossip.

SJ muttered something unintelligible – she was way too hungover for chit-chat – and let herself into the house.

Everything looked very tidy. Derek had obviously had a splurge, bless him – he hated housework. She paused in the kitchen, breathing in the sweet smell of home. He'd even sprayed air freshener around the place. Maybe she should go away more often.

She found him in the lounge, sprawled on the settee with the papers. When he saw her he blinked sleepily. "Hi, hun, I didn't hear you come in. You're back early."

"It's gone half eleven," SJ pointed out, gazing bleary eyed at her watch. "Have you missed me?" The sight of his crumpled brown hair and unshaven chin caught at her heart. She'd never got over the fact that she still loved him so much – after nearly six years together the honeymoon period should have been well and truly over.

She dropped her overnight bag as he stood up and then they were buried in each other's arms and she was breathing in his familiar scent and grazing her cheek against his chin. "Thank you for tidying up. You haven't been here all night, have you?"

"I'll have you know I've been up since the crack of dawn." He drew himself up to his full height, which was only an inch or so taller than her in bare feet. "I'm a regular Mr Mop, me. I'm thinking of getting a job as a domestic engineer, what do you reckon?"

"What's a domestic engineer?"

"A cleaner, my sweet lamb. Now let me take you on a full guided tour and you can let me know if my work is up to your exacting standards."

SJ giggled. They both knew her standards were far from exacting. Her *A tidy house is a sign of a sick mind* fridge magnet had pride of place between the *organised people are just too lazy to look for things* and *life's too short to drink bad wine.*

"And then…" Derek went on, biting her neck experimentally and sending shivers of lust down her spine, "if my work is to your approval, I shall demand payment in kind in the bedroom."

150

"I've got something for you," SJ muttered, wondering in amazement how it was still possible for him to elicit such a startling response from her body – particularly her hungover, party-all-night, very tired body.

A brief rummage in her bag produced a bent bar of chocolate with *A Present from Temple Bar* emblazoned across the wrapper.

"Ha ha – lunch." Derek pounced on it and then put it to one side and took hold of her shoulders. "But first, my tour. Follow me."

They didn't get any further than the bedroom. He'd even changed the sheets, she noticed, touched as he flung back the purple duvet cover that clashed horribly with the lime green walls of their bedroom.

"I really ought to have a shower first."

He brushed away her protests with a kiss and she was glad she'd at least cleaned her teeth and had been sucking mints on the plane.

"I shall lick you clean," he announced, with a wicked gleam in his eyes. Then he coughed, squared his shoulders and straightened his face as his voice took on a more formal tone.

"But first, I shall require you to remove your clothes. You can go behind the screen. Call me when you're undressed. I shall need to check your notes."

He was slipping from 'domestic engineer' into 'doctor' mode, SJ realised with a flicker of amusement as she moved around the other side of the bed and unbuttoned her jeans.

"Now Mrs Anderson, there's really nothing to worry about. My name is Doctor Clit. If you could lie back on the couch and relax – I'm going to need to examine you." He pulled on an imaginary pair of latex

151

gloves and slanted a wicked grin at her to see how she was taking it.

SJ smiled back at him and lay down obediently. They'd played this game a thousand times before. She knew the drill.

"I will need to have a very close inspection," he continued, sitting on the bed beside her and trailing a hand along the outside of her bare thigh. "Are you ready, Mrs Anderson? Are there any little problems you need to tell me about before we start?"

SJ shook her head, looked at his serious profile and went along with the game.

It was only later, when she was still reeling from her orgasm and Derek was reaching for a post coital fag, that she remembered what their next door neighbour had said about Alison.

She propped herself up on her elbows, still fuzzy and soft in the afterglow, and turned her attention to her husband.

"What did Alison want?"

"Alison?" He looked momentarily puzzled, as if he couldn't quite remember who Alison was.

"My sister, Alison," SJ murmured sleepily. "Norah caught me on the way in and she mentioned her."

"Ah – that Alison." He passed her a lit Silk Cut and nodded. "Yes, she did pop by yesterday. I meant to tell you. She wanted to know if you fancied going halves on your dad's birthday present. She's a bit strapped for cash."

Alison was always strapped for cash when it came to buying presents for other people. SJ smiled. "Did she have any suggestions?"

"She didn't really say. I told her you'd ring her some time."

"Okay," SJ said happily. The cigarette had woken her up again and she could never sleep in the daytime like Derek could, however tired she was. She clambered out of bed and showered and sorted out her dirty laundry to take downstairs.

She might as well put a load of washing on, she thought, hauling Derek's jeans out of the washing basket and emptying the pockets on auto pilot. A toffee, a fiver and a receipt. She smiled. However many times she asked him he never remembered to take things out of his pockets. Distractedly, she glanced at the receipt

Two pizzas – one pepperoni, one Hawaiian – ordered at ten thirty-five the previous night and delivered by Peter. What an amazing thing technology was. Hang on a minute. Hadn't Derek told her he'd gone out for a pizza? So why would the receipt say it had been delivered? She felt the hairs on the back of her neck prickle and a spark of unease flickered in her stomach. Alison's favourite pizza was Hawaiian.

It didn't mean anything. No doubt there was a perfectly reasonable explanation. She went back upstairs and found Derek was fast asleep. Perched on the edge of the bed, she stroked a strand of hair back from his face. "Hey, sleepy head, are you staying there all day?"

"Uh huh," he mumbled, opening one eye. "Have you brought me a cup of coffee?"

"I'll make us one in a minute. So what time did Alison come round last night? Was it before you went out with the boys or after?"

"After."

SJ frowned. "But I thought you said you went to the Jolly Sailor and had a few more in town and then went for a late night pizza."

"Yeah, we did. What's with all the questions, SJ?"

"So what time did Alison come over then?"

There was a little silence, and she could feel a nugget of anxiousness building deep within her. Something didn't add up, but then her brain wasn't exactly in gear. What she really needed was to catch up on sleep. But Derek still hadn't answered her question.

"I was quite pissed, SJ. I'm not sure of the times." He closed his eyes, indicating the discussion was over. SJ wished she could leave it there, but she couldn't.

She wished Norah had been more specific, but she could hardly nip round and cross-question her… 'Er, what time exactly was my sister here?' Although doubtless she'd be able to tell her the exact times of arrival and departure. Norah didn't have a terribly exciting life. And why was Derek being so evasive? It wasn't like him.

He couldn't have anything to hide. Nothing to do with Alison anyway – he didn't like her much. He'd always agreed with SJ that her sister was deep-down-shallow. In fact, she had a feeling he'd coined the phrase.

Downstairs she paced while she waited for the kettle to boil. Maybe she should give Alison a ring. That would clarify things.

"Hiya, SJ, how's it going?" Her sister sounded bright and chirpy. "Did you have a good time in Dublin?"

"Yeah – great, thanks. Derek said you'd popped over about Dad's present."

"That's right. I thought we could get him a season ticket for the Saints. What do you think? Mum said he'd like one, but they're quite expensive."

154

"Good idea." SJ was burning to ask what time Alison had come over, but she didn't want to admit she didn't know. She cleared her throat and heard herself saying, in a voice so casual she couldn't believe it was hers, "Did you enjoy the pizza?"

"Er – yes, it was scrummy, thanks. Look, I've got to go, SJ – the kids are fighting. Speak soon. Byee."

SJ disconnected, feeling cold. Why would Derek say he'd had pizza in town with the boys if he'd had it here with Alison?

Her heart was thudding. Her heart knew there was a problem before her hungover brain had latched on to what it was. Irritated, she stomped into the kitchen and made some coffee.

The phone rang.

"Hi, SJ, it's – um – Chalky here, is Derek about?"

"He's asleep," she murmured, wondering if Chalky had been one of the lads Derek had been out with. Probably – Chalky never missed an excuse for a good piss-up.

"Okay, no worries, I just – um – wanted to let him know I've got that Bond film he was after. I can drop it over if he's in a rush. Otherwise I'll see him Tuesday."

"Couldn't you have given it to him last night?" SJ blurted out, wishing she could think of a more subtle way of asking him if he'd been out with Derek, but unable to come up with anything at such short notice.

"Well, um - yeah – if I'd seen him last night. But – durr – I didn't, did I? He said he'd had enough at lunchtime and sodded off early. Flamin' lightweight!"

"Oh," SJ said, feeling faint. "Right, Chalky. Thanks, I'll tell him you called."

She marched upstairs, but in the doorway of their bedroom, she hesitated. Derek was still asleep on his back, half covered by the duvet, one hand flung back on the pillow like a child's. The midday sunlight slanted across his muscled upper body and highlighted his sculpted cheekbones and the lighter bits in his brown hair where he'd been out in the sun. As she stood there gazing at him, she felt a rush of love so intense she could have wept.

He loved her. He wouldn't hurt her, he wouldn't betray her – he surely wouldn't have anything to do with Alison. Derek was well aware of how she felt about her sister. Yet something was wrong.

Her heart was still on triple time. A giant hand twisted her intestines and squeezed at her bowels. At best he wasn't telling her the full story about Alison's visit. And at worst he was lying. Why?

Chapter Seventeen

Yet she knew the real reason she didn't confront him about Alison was that she was scared. More than scared: she was terrified. A fear that stretched right back to her childhood coiled and uncoiled inside her like some giant malevolent snake.

She thought back across the years. There had been a few times when Alison had inadvertently messed things up for her. She thought about the beach party at Sandbanks and the way Alison had mucked things up between her and Jed.

There had been other occasions too. Once they'd both gone to a 21st birthday party and the cream top SJ had been planning to wear ended up with a mysterious stain across the front. And another time she'd brought a group of friends back from college for an impromptu party and Alison had been ill with such a bad headache that Mum had told them they'd all have to leave.

And then of course there was her wedding, which she'd had to postpone because Alison needed to get married first. No, that was crazy. Alison hadn't meant to get pregnant – obviously. SJ had always given her sister the benefit of the doubt, but suddenly everything seemed to make a horrible kind of sense. Alison was jealous of her. She didn't like SJ having something she couldn't share or didn't already have.

SJ blinked away these uneasy thoughts. Alison wouldn't make a move on Derek – surely she wouldn't. That was too big a quantum leap. She was being irrational and paranoid.

For a start, Alison was happily married. Or was she? SJ had never questioned it before because Alison had always seemed settled with Clive. But settled wasn't the same as happy, was it? Perhaps she just put up with him because he was the father of her kids.

She'd only been seventeen when she'd had Sophie, but SJ still didn't really know whether Alison and Clive had got married because they wanted to or because Dad had threatened to knock Clive's block off if he didn't face up to his responsibilities.

"A wedding made in heaven," their mother had crooned, as Alison floated down the aisle in fraudulent white. But then their mother would say that – she'd had to get married young herself – and she'd always loved her youngest daughter best.

SJ gave herself a little shake. She knew that was unfair; Mum had always tried to treat her daughters the same. And actually when Alison got pregnant so young it had changed things between them. SJ had felt a rush of almost maternal love as Alison's belly expanded week by week. And it had been SJ who'd held her hand when her waters had broken and she'd been scared witless. And SJ who'd sat in the delivery room while Alison screamed for more pain relief and called the midwife every name under the sun.

Okay, so they'd drifted apart again since then; they still bickered and fought, mostly because they didn't have an awful lot in common, but surely Alison wouldn't hit on her husband? Unless, of course, she really was unhappy with Clive…

In the end, SJ could bear her churning fears and restless paranoia no longer. It was half term, which didn't help – she decided to ignore the piles of marking

158

she was supposed to be doing and pop round to her sister's for a little chat.

She might not be able to confront Derek, but she was pretty sure Alison would let something slip – that's if there was anything to let slip. And if there wasn't then she could stop torturing herself and life could get back to normal.

Alison answered the door with a tea towel in her hands and a guarded expression in her blue eyes. Or so it seemed to SJ, whose internal radar was on full alert.

"Well, well, and to what do I owe this pleasure?"

"I thought I'd come round and give you the money for Dad's season ticket," SJ announced as she strolled into Alison's sunny kitchen.

"Where are the kids?" she queried. Was her sister deliberately not meeting her eyes, or was she imagining it?

"Clive's taken them to his mum's for half term. He thought I needed a break and Joyce can't get enough of her grandchildren. She soon would if she had them all the time, I can tell you." She raked a hand through her immaculate highlighted hair. "It's hard work being a full time mother."

"I bet," SJ said, glancing at a pile of fashion and beauty magazines on the kitchen table.

"I'm thinking of having hair extensions," Alison said, following her gaze. "What do you reckon? I've always fancied long hair, but I'm just too busy to grow it."

SJ couldn't imagine how being busy could stop your hair growing. It was hardly something you had to have an active role in. Didn't hair just get on with the business of growing all by itself? But she nodded anyway. If she was going to have a heart-to-heart with Alison, they needed to start off on a good footing.

"When did he go?" she asked idly.

"Saturday morning. I thought I'd miss them, but I can't say I have. It's been bliss having a bit of time to myself." Alison stretched her hands above her head and smiled, her blue eyes as innocent as a baby's. "So what have you been up to, SJ? How's that hunky husband of yours?"

"You know how he is, you saw him on Saturday. I think he enjoyed having a weekend to himself, too. Plenty of time to get drunk without me nagging."

"Mmm." Alison tilted her face up to the sun that streamed in her back door and closed her eyes.

"Was he drunk when you saw him?" SJ asked casually.

"Pretty much." Alison giggled. "Men are funny when they're pissed, aren't they? Clive gets all morose, but your Derek's a right laugh."

A spike of jealousy seared SJ's stomach like a branding iron. She didn't want to think of Alison and Derek having a laugh when she wasn't there.

"He never takes anything seriously," she said.

"So I noticed." Alison's silvery laugh tinkled out. "He was clowning around pretending to be a drunk. He's great at impressions, isn't he?"

"By the sound of it he didn't need to pretend much." SJ wondered how drunk Derek had actually been. He had quite a high tolerance level – they both did; going to pubs was their main social life.

"So how come you ended up staying for pizza?"

"Oh well, the poor love hadn't eaten all day. I was just doing my sisterly duty, what with you being away and that. I know you'd do the same for me."

160

SJ couldn't imagine sharing pizza with the morose Clive, who she'd always thought was old before his time.

"I take it you weren't drunk as well," she queried, feeling the twinges of jealousy increase and concentrating hard on a picture of a leggy blonde on the cover of one of Alison's magazines, which didn't help at all.

"Me? No – I was stone cold sober. I had to drive home. I never miss the kids' bedtimes."

They must have pretty late bedtimes, SJ thought, remembering what time the pizzas had been ordered. She blinked.

"Hang on a minute. I thought you said Clive went to his mum's on Saturday morning?"

"Did I say Saturday morning? I meant Sunday morning." Alison's eyes widened in feigned innocence, but she couldn't resist a smirk, and suddenly SJ was sure she was lying. There was something going on. She was certain of it. Every instinct she had told her she was being taken for a fool.

"You stayed the night, didn't you?" She hadn't planned to come out with it like that, but her sister's flippancy was getting to her. "I know you did. Our next door neighbour saw you on Sunday morning. She told me."

Alison chewed her bottom lip, and SJ was reminded of a thousand other times she'd seen that look. Usually when her sister was trying to think up a good enough excuse to get herself off the hook for something she'd done, or not done, for which she didn't want to get the blame.

"Okay, so I stayed the night. So what? It was getting late and I did have a couple of glasses of wine.

161

Derek thought I might be over the limit. So he insisted. What's the big deal?"

"Well, that depends on where you stayed," SJ said, her mouth so dry she could hardly form the words.

"I've had enough of this." Alison stood up and sashayed across to the open door. "What do you take me for, Sarah-Jane? I'd hardly dump on my own back doorstep."

"Just tell me where you slept." SJ hated herself for begging. "And why you lied about it in the first place."

"I lied because I knew you'd go off on one – exactly like you ARE doing. And I slept on the settee – where do you think I slept? Contrary to what you might think, your husband isn't that much of a catch. The whole world isn't trying to get into Derek Anderson's Armanis ... I saw them on the line," she added, fractionally too late for this to have been true.

SJ felt sick. Even though a part of her had suspected it, knowing for sure was something else. It was like being hit by an articulated truck. She was glad she was sitting down, or she'd have keeled over right there on her sister's sunshine-yellow laminate floor.

"You're lying," she whispered. "You slept with him. You slept in our bed. How could you do that?"

There was a long pause. Alison stared out of the window. Finally, she turned her gaze back to SJ. "Oh for goodness' sake, okay, but it didn't mean anything. We were legless. I don't suppose he can remember much." A small smile played around her lips. "That's probably why he didn't tell you."

"You bitch." SJ leapt out of her chair and lunged across the kitchen, but she hadn't got full control of her legs and instead of grabbing Alison around the throat,

162

which had been her intention, she found herself stumbling and ending up on her knees on the floor.

As she scrambled to her feet again, still intent on doing damage – a lot of damage – Alison sidestepped nimbly away from her, the smugness on her face replaced by a look of alarm. The voice of reason was pounding through the anger in SJ's head. Beating Alison to a pulp would be very satisfying, but it wouldn't change anything. It wouldn't change the fact that Derek had betrayed her. It wouldn't alter what had happened on Saturday night.

She sagged into a chair and covered her face with her hands as her world caved in around her. For the first time in her life, she'd felt as though she had something her sister couldn't take, something beautiful and precious that belonged just to her. Derek was her soul mate, her true love, her raison d'etre. She thought he'd felt the same about her. But she'd been wrong.

When she finally looked up, it was to see Alison back on the other side of the kitchen with the table safely between them, her eyebrows arched in a look somewhere between amazement and concern.

"If it's any consolation, I can see why you're so enamoured," she murmured sympathetically. "He may not be much to look at – but he's quite something, isn't he? In the bedroom department, I mean. Quite the little dynamo. You'd never guess by looking at him."

SJ didn't remember leaving the house, only that she was suddenly outside and in her car. She put the key in the ignition, but she was shaking too much to drive. For an indeterminate amount of time she sat rigid, watching people drive by in their cars, or stroll past with their kids and their shopping.

163

Life swarmed on around her, even though her world had just shattered. How could she stay married to Derek knowing that Alison had lain with him, skin to skin, had held him, touched him, and enjoyed him while still managing to disparage him? It made their love seem somehow surprising, as well as sordid and worthless.

SJ had always felt she wasn't quite good enough for Derek. A part of her was sure she hadn't deserved to find someone so right for her; a part of her had been afraid it was too good to be true. Life didn't get that perfect.

Now she knew she'd been right. It didn't. She remembered with a knife-like thrust of pain how he'd changed the sheets – how he'd laid her tenderly beneath that hideous purple duvet because he and Alison had dirtied the only matching duvet set they had. Their beautiful pale green honeymoon set. And somehow that was worse than everything else he'd done. It was the ultimate betrayal.

Chapter Eighteen

After the drunken dinner party with her parents SJ had rebooked her Tuesday appointment with Kit. He hadn't seemed surprised to see her. Neither had he given any indication that he thought she was mad, or unreliable, or any of the other things that SJ was beginning to suspect she was becoming.

He'd been wearing his usual faded jeans with a black T-shirt, which had a small brown mark on the front just below his right breastbone. A burn mark maybe, or spilt food. Somehow it had made him seem more human. And his questions had been gentle.

He'd asked her if she could remember any other specific occasions when she hadn't been able to control her drinking – and she'd told him that she sometimes drank when she was afraid, or when she was alone, or when she felt worthless – which, to her surprise, seemed to happen a great deal more often than she'd ever previously acknowledged.

She hadn't told Kit or Tanya or anyone else the full story behind why she'd made her first appointment with S.A.A.D. The memories were still too raw and too painful. But as she got the bus back on Tuesday lunchtime after her latest appointment, the memories had crawled back, unbidden.

Tom had been working away that weekend. He'd phoned earlier to tell her he'd be a day or so later than planned and, disappointed to be spending yet another evening alone, SJ had decided to unwind with a glass or two of wine. It was easy to drink too much when you were watching television and she hadn't bothered with dinner – there didn't seem much point in even cooking a ready meal for one.

As she'd told Tanya she'd opened a second bottle and then things had got rather fuzzy and hazy, although bizarrely there were parts of the evening that were as sharp and as clear as the stills on a DVD:

Herself – staggering through the hall to let Ash into the garden, fiddling with the catch on the back door, cursing because it wouldn't open quickly enough and she was dying to go to the loo; Ash, standing beside her, wagging his tail patiently.

Then there was a chunk of blankness, empty as the blue screen on a television when the channels aren't tuned in.

Another picture: herself again, prostrate on the hall floor, aware of the hardness of the wooden floor against her cheek and the sour taste in her mouth; opening her eyes to see a glint of gold on blackness – one of her gold hoop earrings, not far from her face, coming in and out of focus as she blinked; a hand, her own hand, scrabbling around to reach it.

Another blue blank.

The sound of frantic knocking on the front door – and the awareness that their musical doorbell was chiming softly.

Another blue blank.

Their next door neighbour's anxious pale face looming in and out of focus.

"Oh, SJ, love. I'm sorry to disturb you, but your dog's been out on the road. He's been hit by a car. He's okay. Don't panic. I think the car just clipped him."

"Where is he?" SJ gulped, the coldness of shock knifing through the alcohol fuzz in her head.

"I put him in the back of my car. I couldn't get you to answer the door, you see." She tailed off, worried brown eyes quizzical, and SJ wondered if she could smell the drink. There were several feet between them and she had her hand over her mouth, but she must reek of it.

Her neighbour was already turning away. SJ followed her, barefoot – goodness knows what had happened to her shoes – to where her car was parked outside the house.

"He's scraped his front leg, but he seems fine apart from that. You never can tell with dogs though; he might have internal injuries. If he were mine I'd nip him down the emergency vets and get him checked over. Just to be on the safe side."

The neighbour smiled uncertainly and as the coldness of the pavement chilled SJ's feet, she wondered if it was obvious that she was in no fit state to drive anywhere.

Ash sat in the hatchback, panting. When he saw her, he wagged his tail and held out his injured paw, which looked grazed and bloodied. He'd cut his muzzle too, and flecks of blood spattered his chest.

SJ buried her head in his soft fur, imagining him being hit by some callous driver who hadn't even bothered to stop. He was trembling and she felt guilt tighten around her heart. Tears gritted her eyes as she coaxed him gently onto the pavement.

How had he got out anyway? Their gate should have been shut. Calling out a husky thanks to her neighbour, who didn't respond, she led Ash slowly back to their house. As they approached the front door, SJ saw that the side gate, which was normally shut, was wide open, and the bins were this side of it. She had no memory of putting them out, but she must have done. So it was her fault he'd gone wandering.

She was as bad as the people who'd dumped him on the motorway. No, she wasn't as bad as them. She was worse. Ten times worse, twenty times worse because she loved Ash and she hadn't kept him safe.

She remembered being sick again when they got inside. Then she'd switched on her laptop and tried to find an emergency vet but she couldn't type properly and Google kept throwing up irrelevant websites. And the next thing she recalled after that was waking up on the floor of the lounge and seeing Ash on the rug. The memories of what had happened flicked into her head like the mixed up pieces of a jigsaw, and she'd crawled across to check he wasn't dead. The utter relief that he seemed to be breathing normally had tipped her back into oblivion.

It was only when the dawn light stabbed through the undrawn curtains that she'd woken up again. Stiff and sore, with a pneumatic drill going off in her head and a foul taste in her mouth, she'd shuffled into the kitchen and downed two pints of water and some Nurofen. Ash was okay, he was fine, hardly even limping when she'd persuaded him to come into the kitchen and had sponged the dried blood off his chest. But it was no thanks to her. The remorse and self pity had kicked in big time.

She would never drink again. She would go one step further than that. She would make an appointment with someone to talk about her drinking – just in case it was becoming a problem. Frantically she'd scrolled through the list of alcohol advice websites on the internet; she'd ignored the number for AA, which she already knew didn't work, and that's when she had phoned S.A.A.D.

Chapter Nineteen

"Tom, I've decided to give up drinking," SJ announced, a few days after her fourth appointment with Kit. She moved the plates from where they'd been warming on the oven and hunted for a tea towel to get out the ready meals. She'd done a lot of thinking before she'd come to this conclusion. Not just about Alison and Derek, but about the time that had passed since, and she'd discovered quite a few uneasy little skeletons that she'd like to examine through the clear lenses of sobriety.

One of them was her marriage to Tom, which she was beginning to suspect might not be the perfect union she'd always told herself it was. Especially since he'd refused to backtrack on the arrangements they'd made to go to her parents' anniversary party, which they'd discussed heatedly the previous night.

She glanced at him and saw he was smiling benignly – probably still trying to wheedle his way back into her good books. Neither of them had mentioned the first real row of their marriage and he certainly didn't seem concerned about it now.

Last night he'd suggested that perhaps Alison could give the anniversary party a miss, which proved to SJ that either he a) hadn't grasped the facts – she'd explained several times that their parents insisted they both be there, or b) he just didn't bother listening to her at all.

Judging by that silly smile on his face, he probably wasn't listening properly to her now either.

"Did you hear what I just said, Tom? I'm going to give up drinking."

"Yes, sweetie. Is that forever or just for today?"

SJ frowned. She'd expected him to treat this momentous piece of news with slightly more gravity than that, but then she hadn't told him about Ash either. Despite Kit's insistence that she talk to her husband, she still hadn't told Tom how it really was for her. Putting it into words would have made it far too real. She could cope better if it was locked in her head.

Something had changed in her since that terrible hungover Sunday when she'd had that conversation in her head with some imaginary opponent. She'd thought about that voice a lot since. She'd even given it a name: *Alco* – the Demon King. She imagined him as an all-powerful ruler of the alcohol kingdom, sitting on a black throne on the edge of an endless black abyss, his drunken subjects crawling submissively around his feet, holding up their empty hip flasks to be refilled while he beckoned them closer, tempting them towards the edge with one more glass. '*Just a teensy weensy little glass, SJ, what harm can it do?*'

Picturing some crazy demon lord felt slightly less absurd than the idea that she was talking to herself.

"I felt really awful the night after Mum and Dad came round."

"It's called a hangover. Caused by too much *al-co-hol.*" He exaggerated each syllable as if he was talking to a child.

"Tom, I don't just mean in the morning. I mean all day. In the evening too. I – well – I thought I might be going mad." She couldn't tell him about *Alco* in case he agreed with her. "I was really depressed and I was tired

171

and ashamed, but I still had another drink on Sunday night – I couldn't stop myself."

"Uh huh." He wasn't looking at her. He was busy opening the bottle of red he'd just brought in from the bar. She wasn't quite sure why, as they patently weren't going to need it now. She sighed. "I don't suppose I'll give up forever – but I'm definitely having a few days off."

"You won't mind if I don't join you?" he queried, raising one eyebrow and pausing from unpeeling the foil around the top of the bottle.

"Of course not – you carry on." How virtuous was that? Obviously your run- of-the-mill alcoholic wouldn't be able to casually sit back and watch someone else drinking themselves silly, while they sat beside them dry as a drum – it went without saying.

"So you won't want any of this then?"

"No thanks."

"Not even a teensy weensy little glass?" He was beginning to sound like *Alco*.

"I just said no, didn't I?"

"Okay – keep your hair on. I was only asking. So what would you like to drink with your dinner? I think we've got some Coke in the fridge."

"Is it diet?"

"No, it's normal."

"Then I'll have water," SJ snapped, because she could see no point at all in drinking a calorie-laden drink, unless it was also laden with alcohol. If she had to suffer, then at the very least she expected to lose half a stone in the process.

They ate dinner in strained silence and then she escaped to the garden for a fag, which helped to ease some of the aching tension in her shoulders. Ash joined

172

her, wagging his tail joyfully as she bent to fondle his soft grey ears.

"We'll show them, boy, won't we?" she crooned. "We'll show that silly counsellor that he doesn't know the first thing about unresolved issues." She would show Tanya, too, who had taken to texting her each morning to see if she had a hangover, which actually was quite touching because she knew Tanya cared.

She hadn't told anyone how it really was for her – although Tanya knew quite a bit. It struck her suddenly that she didn't have any other close friends to tell. How had that happened? Until her marriage to Tom, she'd kept in touch with a few people from college and uni. A couple of them now had families and were too busy to socialise; Joanne had moved to London and they'd lost touch; and the rest had just drifted away.

Tom hadn't been keen on socialising with her friends – he wasn't very comfortable around groups of women, he was good on a one-to-one basis, and he was good at certain subjects, particularly sport or breweriana or his work, but he didn't really do small talk.

She could still have kept in touch with her friends via Facebook, which was what a lot of her work colleagues did. Tanya spent a fair bit of her spare time on Twitter and Facebook too. But social networking sites didn't really appeal to SJ. She'd *let* her friends drift away, she realised with a small shock. As her drinking had increased she'd become more isolated, and as she'd become more isolated her drinking had increased even more. It was a vicious little circle that she hadn't even spotted, and yet now, as she stared out across the yellowing August lawn to the sunlit trees beyond, the truth was impossible to avoid. Her friends

173

– all but Tanya, who was more tenacious than most –
had slowly been replaced by a glass of gin and tonic,
complete with ice and a slice.

The next two days were hell. Up until that point, SJ
hadn't seriously considered she might have a drink
problem. She certainly hadn't expected going without
alcohol for a couple of days would present any
difficulties. But suddenly her mind, which was
normally in a fairly scatty but comfortable and familiar
place, no longer felt as if it belonged to her. For a start
she couldn't sleep – it wouldn't let her – it raced with
unpleasant thoughts and emotions, all sorts of crawling
little demons that wouldn't be quietened.

For some reason Tom featured in many of these
thoughts. Tossing and turning, she lay beside his
quietly snoring body, hoping against hope he wouldn't
wake up and want to make love. She didn't know why
this was, because Tom was a skilled and considerate
lover. He did all the right things. His idea of foreplay
wasn't just a quick poke in the back with his erection
which, according to the problem pages she'd read in
magazines, happened to a lot of 'happily marrieds' and
would definitely have been cause for complaint. He
always took his time and made sure she was ready
before he clambered on.

'Ready' – for SJ – meant she was in that happy
fuzzy half-world of inebriation when he finally entered
her. And this took a fair bit of co-ordination. Too much
alcohol and she wasn't interested. Too little and she
was like a dry and terrified virgin. She knew from
previous experience that no alcohol at all turned her
into a nun – her sex drive simply disappeared. She'd
rather have done anything else instead – even iron

shirts or wash the floor on her hands and knees, both of which she did as little as possible in the normal scheme of things.

At four a.m. on the second sleepless night, SJ came to the conclusion that there must be something seriously wrong with her. Tom was her husband, her soul mate. She loved him. Okay, she knew their marriage wasn't quite the amazing rollercoaster of joy and pain she'd had with Derek. It was far more your dodgem car ride – mostly on the level with the odd bump, which suited her much better. Everyone knew rollercoasters made you feel sick if you spent too much time on them.

SJ sat up in bed wondering why on earth she was thinking about fairground rides. Scared she would wake Tom with her restlessness, she went on a sleeping pill foray to the bathroom cabinet. She'd bought some at the pharmacy for her last bout of insomnia which, oddly enough, had happened when she'd been prescribed antibiotics for toothache. The bottle had said 'Strictly No Alcohol'. SJ had blithely ignored the warning – as she always ignored 'no alcohol' warnings – but had then found herself throwing up repeatedly when she'd had her usual pre-dinner gin and tonic. She'd later discovered the antibiotics the dentist had given her were also known as Antabuse and prescribed to alcoholics who wanted to quit.

After two awful drink-free nights she'd abandoned the antibiotics and had the offending tooth removed instead, which had been a huge relief – in more ways than one.

This time there was no such respite. Although the sleeping pills knocked her out there was no escape from the demons, who crawled into her dreams instead. So

175

when she woke up she was more tired than when she'd fallen asleep.

By late Sunday afternoon, two more endless days until her next appointment with Kit, her hands were so shaky she could hardly type out her notes for her poetry and pint class.

By early evening she was ready to crack. She abandoned her notes and looked up alcohol withdrawal symptoms on the Internet.

- Mild shakiness
- Inability to concentrate
- Insomnia
- A feeling of dread
- Restlessness
- Mood changes

As she scanned through the list, SJ felt an increasing sense of panic. She had every symptom. The shakiness wasn't particularly mild either. It wasn't just in her hands; it was in her stomach and her legs too. However she sat at her PC she couldn't get comfortable. She was also besieged with mood swings like the kind she had before her period, when she usually stepped up her alcohol levels to compensate – for medicinal purposes, obviously.

Her period. Of course – that was it. It was due in three days. So this was what Tanya was talking about when she said she had bad PMT. It was such a relief to discover she only had PMT that she leapt out of her chair and charged down to the kitchen for a packet of Nurofen.

It would have been nice to wash them down with a glass of white wine but, quite apart from the fact she'd given up, it was only just gone five. She had water instead, went back upstairs, but still felt too restless to work. Perhaps she'd picked up the 200mg strength tablet instead of the 400mg. They must have changed the packet colour.

Twenty agonizingly long minutes later she still felt exactly the same. She got some more pills and, on autopilot, she opened a bottle of Chardonnay and poured a large glass to wash them down with. The relief was instantaneous. She could feel the pills being washed to the furthest corners of her body. Her hands stopped shaking. Her legs took a little longer to feel normal. But amazingly, wondrously, her mind came back on line.

It was such a good feeling she had another glass of wine. Then another. Now her fingers were flying across the keys. Thank goodness she'd discovered she had PMT and not withdrawal symptoms. She was reaching for a fourth glass of wine when she noticed the bottle was empty. They must be making wine bottles smaller too – she knew perfectly well you got more than three glasses out of a bottle. And she certainly hadn't drunk much. She didn't feel remotely light headed.

Humming to herself, she went downstairs to find another bottle. There wasn't one. Oh well, she'd stop there. Three glasses was well within her limit anyway. She prowled around the bar – on second thoughts, there must be something else she could drink. She really did fancy another one. Only one more – four glasses wasn't too bad. Tom would probably appreciate a nice unwinding glass of red when he got in. She could put a bottle on the side to breathe. Pleased with herself for being such a considerate wife, she opened one of his special bottles. Fourteen per cent – oo-er, better be careful with this one.

It tasted like blackberries and she was also getting notes of chocolate and wood – just as the label promised. It didn't taste that alcoholic either – certainly not fourteen per cent. It was more like upmarket Ribena. Very easy drinking. Too easy. She really should take the bottle into the kitchen to breathe. Or there wouldn't be any left for Tom. He'd be in soon. It was just after six.

The phone rang and she danced across the room to answer it.

"Hi, SJ, it's Michael. I was wondering if Tom still fancied squash tomorrow night. I've just booked a court. Can you get him to give me a ring, please?"

"Sure," SJ murmured, as a sudden picture of Michael playing squash in a summer dress, his hairy legs pounding the floor, sprang into her mind. Perhaps he shaved them. She giggled, tried to stop herself, and snorted loudly instead, which struck her as incredibly funny.

"SJ – are you still there?"

"Mmm." It was incredibly difficult to keep it together for some reason. Far away in her mind the voice of sanity urged her not to laugh.

"Do you want to speak to Tanya while I'm on? She's right here."

"Er no – bit busy," SJ mumbled. "Paperwork to do for my poetry class. You know…" She waved a careless hand and then remembered he couldn't see her. "Bye Tom. I mean Michael. Cheers."

She'd nearly called him Liz. Who on earth was Liz? Remembering his alter ego and feeling sweaty

178

with panic because she wasn't supposed to know about it, let alone start discussing it with him, she crashed the phone back on the receiver and sunk onto the sofa, which wasn't where she anticipated it would be.

She found herself on the floor instead – well, half on the floor, half on the coffee table, which was exceptionally hard. Bloody coffee table. Bloody floor. Cursing softly, she rolled completely onto the floor and sat up.

She'd been going to do something. Ah yes, she had to open a bottle of wine for Tom. Stumbling to her feet and swaying across to the bar she looked at the rack. Now what day was it? He didn't like her to open expensive wine unless it was the weekend. Was it the weekend? It had been Sunday yesterday, or was it Sunday today? Best be on the safe side and open a cheap bottle.

The corkscrew wasn't in its usual place. Not that they didn't have plenty of others – but most of Tom's collection were in locked glass display cases and she didn't know where the key was. When she finally found the functional corkscrew she discovered two empty bottles beside it. Ah, it must be Sunday then. They'd have had these with their tea. The phone was ringing again, but she ignored it and opened another bottle.

"SJ… SJ, wake up. Wake up, will you? SJ, for God's sake, please wake up …"

Fragments of voices swam through the confused blackness. They sounded urgent. They sounded cross. With an immense effort SJ opened her eyes and wished she hadn't. Tom's face loomed into focus and then out again. He wasn't happy. She felt like someone had given her a good kicking. Why would anyone do that?

179

She groaned. Something bad had obviously happened. Her body felt bruised and sore and her head was so fuzzy she didn't know what day it was – or what time. Squinting at her watch she saw it was seven thirty, which didn't help much, was it A.M or P.M?

"Get her some coffee or something, can you, Tom."

That sounded like Tanya's voice. What was Tanya doing here? Suddenly remembering Michael's phone call, SJ hauled herself into a sitting position. She seemed to be on the floor in the dining room. Glancing around her frantically for the phone and then remembering it was in the lounge, she tried to collect her fragmented thoughts. What had she said to Michael?

"It's okay, I'm fine. What's happening?"

Tanya, who was now crouching beside her, was wearing a pale blue T-shirt and jeans and leather flip flops with sparkly stones set in them. As always she looked both cool and stunning. How lucky was she to have ended up with such a gorgeous best friend?

SJ tried a gorgeous smile of her own.

Tanya didn't smile back. Her green eyes were narrowed and angry, but her voice, when she spoke, was surprisingly soft. "How are you feeling? Pretty crap, I guess?"

"Very crap. Very very very VERY crap. In fact I don't think I've ever felt worse in my whole life." At least she didn't feel sick. "What are you doing here? Did Tom ask you to come?"

"It was me who phoned Tom. I was worried about you. Michael said you'd called and you sounded odd. I guessed you might have been drinking."

180

Hang on – hadn't he called her? Something about a squash game. Oh well, it was an easy mistake to make.

"I haven't drunk much – I've been cutting down. Honest." SJ swung out an arm and hit what turned out to be a half empty bottle of red, which would have fallen over if Tanya hadn't caught it deftly and transferred it to the dining room table. "See…" She announced triumphantly. "…I'm on half bottles now."

"You didn't get in this state by drinking half a bottle of wine. We found two other empty bottles. Do you remember anything at all?"

SJ certainly didn't recall drinking two bottles of wine. There was a blank in her head where her memory should have been. But she didn't think she ought to confess to this. Tanya now looked more sad than angry.

"Are you okay, Tan?" she asked, suddenly aware of how selfish she was being – lying on the floor in a heap when Tanya had obviously come round to unburden herself.

"I'm fine, SJ – but you're obviously not…" She broke off mid-sentence and glanced up, and SJ realised Tom had come back into the room.

"Is she alright?"

"I wouldn't go as far as that. But at least she's conscious." Tanya stood up and faced Tom.

"Hey, I am here, you know. I can speak for myself."

Both of them ignored her. Tom turned back to Tanya. "I didn't know things were this bad. I had no idea."

"Didn't she tell you she'd been going to a clinic about her drinking?"

"Well, yes, but I thought she was overreacting. She is a bit of a drama queen sometimes. Hell…" He sat on

181

a dining room chair, put his head in his hands, his long fingers ruffling his dark hair, and SJ felt fleetingly sorry for him – until she realised he was talking about her. The cheek of it. She never overreacted. It was Alison who was the drama queen.

"I don't know why you're making so much fuss," she began, clambering unsteadily to her feet. "I just got a bit drunk, that's all."

"SJ, that was past drunk." Tanya came across to her. "You were unconscious on the floor. We've been trying to bring you round for the last half an hour. And I know it's happened before because you've told me about it."

SJ flicked a startled glance at Tom.

"You've been having blackouts, too, haven't you?" Tanya carried on relentlessly.

"No idea. I don't remember. What are blackouts, anyway?"

"Periods of memory loss." Tanya's lips twisted in a wry smile. She was obviously trying to make a joke of it.

SJ decided to join in. "Everyone has memory lapses at my age. It's called early onset Alzheimer's – or senior moments, if you prefer!"

"SJ, please just shut up and take this seriously for five minutes." Tanya's usually husky voice was slightly shrill.

Alarmed, SJ shut up and decided she'd feel better if she sat down again. She slid down the wall until she was on the floor once more, her legs bent in front of her. Her leggings were grubby and covered in dog hairs. She tried to remember when she'd last vacuumed and couldn't – a further example of her fading memory, obviously.

182

"Do you remember phoning Michael earlier?"

"Of course. But I didn't phone him – he phoned me. Something about squash."

"You phoned him back." Tanya bent and her fingers closed tightly around SJ's wrist. "You were rambling – you were talking about someone called Liz. But when I came on the phone you hung up. Do you remember any of that?"

SJ felt herself break into a cold sweat, as she looked up into Tanya's green eyes – eyes that, at this moment, were filled with a mixture of pain and worry.

"No... No, I don't. What did I say?"

"You were pretty incoherent from what I can gather," Tanya continued quietly, before flicking a warning glance at Tom, who looked bemused at the turn the conversation was taking.

"Liz is a student," SJ said quickly, hoping to salvage something from this awful mess. Michael might have guessed she knew something she shouldn't have known, but it was obvious Tom had no idea what they were talking about.

"I've been seeing her after class to talk about this poetry book she's interested in publishing. Tell Michael I'm sorry. He didn't need to listen to all that."

There was a long moment when, even in her befuddled state, SJ knew she was apologising for a lot more than nonsensical ramblings to Michael. She had no idea if he was aware Tanya had told her about his fondness for women's clothes. Tanya didn't seem to think so but it was no thanks to her – she couldn't even remember the conversation. Horrified with herself for being so out of control, she closed her eyes.

"I'm really sorry," she repeated. "He must think I'm a complete idiot."

183

"He's not the only one." Tanya let go of her wrist and rocked back on her heels. "You need to get this sorted out, SJ, before you really hurt someone. Or yourself – but I think you're already doing that, aren't you?"

SJ nodded, darts of shame shooting through her. It was much worse to hurt other people than yourself. And Tanya was the last person she wanted to hurt. She followed Tom's example and rested her pounding head in her hands.

Then Tom roused himself from the dining table and she heard him coming across the room. "This is all my fault. I've been too tied up with work to notice what's been going on. I haven't been here for you."

"It's not your fault," SJ glanced at him stricken, as guilt piled upon guilt. Tom looked really upset. His face was pale and there were circles of tiredness around his eyes. Had one afternoon of over-indulgence really made him look like that? She wished she didn't feel so tired and fuzzy.

"Actually – if you two don't mind, I think I'd like to go to bed. I don't feel all that well." It was the coward's way out. She knew it was. But it was true. She couldn't remember feeling so bad since… Well, probably since the last time she'd drunk too much, too quickly. The awful thing was that she knew exactly what would make her feel better – another glass of wine from the half bottle that was still sitting on the dining room table.

"Don't even think about it," Tanya warned. "Go and sleep it off. We'll talk later."

"Yes, we will," echoed Tom.

SJ slunk away before either of them changed their minds.

184

Chapter Twenty

"My counsellor thinks it might help if I go to an AA meeting." SJ told Tom this with a little shake in her voice. Sometimes she felt as though this part of her life was happening to someone else. It was someone else, not her, who joked her way through the Tuesday lunchtime appointments at S.A.A.D; someone else who had agreed to venture into the shadowy underworld of an Alcoholics Anonymous meeting.

"Do you want me to come with you?" Tom asked. He'd taken to coming home earlier, bringing his paperwork with him and doing it on the kitchen table.

SJ shook her head. "Thanks, but no, it's okay. I phoned the helpline and they've arranged for me to meet someone outside so I know where to go."

"Don't they tell you that then?"

"They tell you the name of the building, but not which part of it. I guess they can't tape a big sign on the door, can they? *Alcoholics Anonymous meets here.*" She gave a hollow laugh. "It wouldn't be very anonymous if they did."

Tom put his arm around her and she tried not to flinch away from him. Why did she find it so difficult to accept comfort from her own husband? When Kit had given her the list of meetings his arm had rested casually against hers and she'd wanted to lean against the warm broad warmth of him, hear him tell her, as he so often had, that she was doing really well, that she didn't have to cope on her own.

Shrugging away such uncomfortable thoughts, she got up. "I'm going to a meeting in Hammersmith." That should be far enough away for her not to meet anyone she knew.

"I could always drop you off and …"

"Go for a drink while I'm in there? No thanks."

"I was going to say I'd wait in the car park."

She glanced at him, saw the flash of pain in his eyes and knew he was doing his best to support her – now he'd finally acknowledged she had a problem. She felt a wave of guilt. Why did she never say the right thing?

"Honestly, Tom, I appreciate it, really, but there's no need. This is something I need to do for myself."

Anxious not to be late, SJ arrived at the community centre in Hammersmith ten minutes before the agreed time. She and the woman she'd arranged to meet outside hadn't exchanged descriptions – not even of their cars, let alone themselves – and she wondered how she'd recognise her. To her surprise, there were already quite a few people hanging around the entrance of the centre, both men and women, puffing furiously on cigarettes.

She could hardly wander up to one of them and say, "Hi, are you here for AA? – Oh sorry, you're here for the line-dancing, are you? Yeah, me too."

So she stayed in her car and spent the first five minutes trying to guess what her companion would look like. She'd sounded quite posh on the phone – she'd reminded SJ of a school teacher she once had. Oh God, what if it was her old school teacher? Her heart started beating rapidly and she had to take several deep breaths to calm down. If it was her school teacher then

186

she was obviously going to recognise her as soon as she saw her and she'd simply say she'd made a mistake and leave. Easy.

Working on the assumption it wasn't her school teacher, SJ went back to conjuring up a mental image to fit the voice on the phone. She'd probably be wearing a tweed suit: brown, with sensible brown brogues, brown perm and bifocals. Or possibly she'd have her hair tied back in a bun and her face scrubbed clean of make up in honour of her new sober lifestyle and she'd be wearing an A-line dress to cover her ample curves. Yes, she'd had a plump kind of voice so it followed she'd have matching curves.

SJ fidgeted and bit her nails while she waited and wondered if her own black trousers, pale blouse and dark jacket – even though it was far too hot for jackets – looked demure enough. She had on a trace of make up, but not much: foundation, mascara, a stroke of blusher and a conservative peach lipstick that had come free with a Woman and Home magazine. She wanted to give the right impression – middle class, but not as if she'd never had a good night out in her life.

Not that she was expecting she could compete with proper alcoholics – the ones who downed two litres of whiskey a day without as much as a whisper of a hangover. But she didn't want them to think she was here under false pretences either, in case they thought she'd just come along for a laugh at their expense. The last thing she wanted was a bunch of snubbed, demented, raging alcoholics chasing her out to her car with machetes. God, she was paranoid. Why on earth would they have machetes?

It was too hot in the car to be wearing a jacket – which seemed to be tighter now she was sitting down than the last time she'd worn it. It must have shrunk at the dry cleaners. She shrugged it off and noticed her blouse was tighter than usual too. The buttons across her breasts were under a lot of strain and the top one kept popping open.

Wanton hussy was definitely not the right look. She'd have to wear the jacket, and then she could hold the edges together and avoid any embarrassing button-popping moments. It would be even better if she could stand up all evening – preferably at the back of the room behind a cupboard. In a cupboard would be better still.

Perhaps her companion was already here. She wished they'd agreed to carry something so they'd recognise each other. Something appropriate – like an empty wine bottle, although a full one would have been better.

One thing was certain; she couldn't stay in her car. It was too hot. Maybe if she wandered across to the entrance she'd be spotted and rescued. It was like walking the plank. SJ was afraid her knees would give out halfway. At the entrance, aware of one or two curious glances, she got out her mobile and pretended to check her texts, which took all of five seconds as she'd cleared them earlier.

Then she became aware someone had detached themselves from the group and was approaching. Not a woman, but a man with a cigarette in his hand and a friendly smile. Definitely not a line dancer – he was wearing jeans and Doc Martens. She tugged her jacket around her, in case her blouse had done its button-popping trick, and smiled back uncertainly.

"Are you here to meet someone, love?"

She nodded.

"What's her name, she's probably inside. I'll nip in and see if you like?"

SJ told him and he hurried away and returned a few moments later with a woman who was tall, slim, and looked as though she might be on her way to a wedding – only she didn't have a hat. SJ felt woefully underdressed.

"Come along in," her companion ordered kindly. "You don't want to hang around out here with these smokers, do you?"

"No," SJ said bleakly, although there was nothing she'd have liked more than a fag or six to calm her nerves.

"Come in and have a drink and I'll introduce you to some of our ladies."

SJ's heart leapt at the prospect of a drink until it became evident her companion meant coffee in a plastic cup – yuck. But she sipped it obediently and smiled politely at everyone she was introduced to without trying to remember their names. There didn't seem much point as they weren't likely to meet again. There was no one in the room she knew. Thank God for small mercies.

Her plan to skulk at the back was thwarted when she was told to, "Sit here, love, next to me. It's best to sit at the front."

SJ spent the first half of the meeting wondering how quickly she could excuse herself and the second half in tears.

The tears were completely unexpected. One minute she was tapping her foot and surreptitiously glancing at her watch, and the next she had started to shake. She rested her head in her hands and then her shoulders joined in on the act and she realised she was no longer just shaking, but sobbing. Her whole body was shuddering with silent grief.

No one took any notice – perhaps they were used to people going to pieces. Then she felt a hand touch her shoulder. "Shall we slip outside for a wee while, hen?"

The voice, with its faint Scottish accent, was horribly familiar. SJ felt an increasing sense of dread as she turned to find herself looking at Dorothy from her poetry and pint class. Dorothy must have been sitting behind her all the time. What on earth was she doing here?

But Dorothy's blue eyes were kind. And through her distress, SJ noticed her exchanging an it's-alright-I-know-her kind of glance with the woman who'd brought her in.

Supremely embarrassed, because now she was bound to be the centre of attention, SJ gulped and nodded, stood up and allowed herself to be led through the swing doors and into the balmy summer evening.

They sat on the low wall outside. "I'm really, really sorry," SJ gulped, rubbing her face and blowing her nose on a tatty old piece of tissue she'd found in her bag. "I don't know why I'm so upset."

"Is this your first meeting?"

SJ nodded. It felt surreal seeing Dorothy out of context. As usual her face was beautifully made up, her black hair was pinned up in a chignon, and she was wearing the Dior suit she'd once told SJ she'd bought for a wedding and needed to get plenty of use out of to justify the cost.

Images of her favourite student flooded SJ's mind: Dorothy's steamy novels with sex scenes that were as

190

tender as they were explicit; Dorothy's tales of her grandchildren; Dorothy's passion for Byron and Pam Ayres; Dorothy's own rather clever poetry, which always bubbled with mcrriment. SJ had to admit they were conflicting images, but none of them seemed as wrong as the fact that she was here now.

"First meetings aren't easy." Dorothy's voice was gentle and SJ blinked.

"But you're not...you can't be.... You're obviously here in a professional capacity." SJ searched wildly for an explanation. "You're doing research for your books, aren't you?"

"I'm a recovering alcoholic, pet."

"You don't drink. You always have a Britvic orange." SJ had a sudden vivid memory of Dorothy laughing with the boys as they sipped pints of Guinness and she nursed her small glass with its slice of orange floating in the top.

Dorothy gave her a sweet smile. "I stopped drinking twenty-five years ago."

This news was even more shocking. SJ was about to ask her why she still came to meetings if she was cured when Dorothy spoke again.

"SJ, pet, why do you think you broke down in there just now?"

"I've no idea. Probably because I'm in the wrong place, and when that woman was speaking I just realised it." The words sounded hollow, even to her.

"Or could it be that the opposite is true?" Dorothy held her gaze. It was impossible to look away. "Be honest with yourself. Could it be that on some level you've already recognised you're the same as that woman and it was the shock of that realisation that caused you to break down?"

191

"Absolutely not." SJ stared back through the window where the circle of people – all kinds of people: men and women, some casually dressed, some scruffy, some smart, some fat, some thin, some tall, some short, some blond, some dark – sat with serious faces.

But on some level she was no longer sure. On some level Dorothy's words resonated. Then Dorothy added something that swept away the last of her reservations.

"SJ, pet. In all the years I've been coming here, I've never met anyone who walked in through these doors by accident."

Chapter Twenty-One

"So what are AA meetings like? What happens at them?" Tanya asked, her green eyes curious as she and SJ sat in Tanya's garden, sipping strawberry smoothies. Tanya and Michael lived in a lovely house in Bermondsey and the previous owners had built a huge decking, which was a sun trap for most of the day, and was where they were sitting now. Ash lay at SJ's feet, snoring peacefully.

"I'm not supposed to tell you," SJ said, leaning to stroke her dog's head. "Everything that happens at meetings is confidential." She'd been to three more since that first one – she hadn't felt the need to go daily, but she'd gone on Wednesday lunchtime, Friday evening and even to one on Sunday evening, rather to her surprise. Dorothy had laughed at her surprise and said there were meetings on Christmas Day – which was quite often one of the worst days of the year for recovering alcoholics.

Tanya didn't try to persuade her to say anything else and for a few moments SJ felt guilty. "It's not that I don't want to tell you. It's just that I can't. It wouldn't be right."

"It's okay, I understand." Tanya smiled. "What would you do if you bumped into anyone you know? I take it you haven't met that hunky counsellor at any of them?"

"No, I haven't." SJ didn't remember telling Tanya that Kit was hunky. Although she supposed he was. She'd felt attracted to him at their last session – she'd had an urge to suggest they leave the stuffy counselling room with the truth-drug infused brown drink that passed for coffee and go for a proper cup in Starbucks instead. She suspected Kit would be great company when he wasn't having to listen to all the crappy details of her life.

But then wasn't being attracted to your counsellor the oldest cliché in the book? It would be easy to fall for a man you poured out your heart to, week after week – a man who never judged or shunned you. A man who seemed to understand you better than you understood yourself. Kit certainly understood her better than her own husband. She pushed the thoughts away. She wasn't going down that route.

"I don't know what I'd do if I bumped into Kit," she said, ignoring Tanya's first question. "Smile, I guess, and give him the thumbs up. At least he'd know I wasn't lying about going to meetings.

"It's obviously working, though. How long is it since you've had a drink?"

"Five days." SJ looked at her watch and added lightly, "And about seven hours."

"Not that you're counting!"

SJ drained her smoothie. "These are nice. Have you got enough strawberries for another one?"

"I should think so." Tanya undraped herself from her chair. "You coming to help me make it?"

Helping involved heaping the remainder of the strawberries into a pristine metal sieve and rinsing them while Tanya retrieved the food processor from the cupboard, where it had been washed up and put away earlier, and took a fresh pint of milk from the fridge.

194

SJ watched her idly. "Our fridge is always full of dog hairs – they get everywhere. How do you keep everything so clean?"

"We don't have a dog?" Tanya said, shooting an amused glance out of the window to where Ash, who hadn't noticed they'd gone, was still asleep in the sun.

"No, I know, but I didn't just mean that." SJ swept out her arms to encompass the immaculate kitchen, with its polished surfaces and cream walls. You could see your face in the stainless steel oven door. Or you could if you bent down. SJ was tempted to try it – it must be handy if you wanted to check your make up and couldn't be bothered to go upstairs. There were hardly any mirrors in Tanya's house; there wasn't even one in the bathroom. She'd never noticed the mirror shortage before. How odd. Still, it probably explained why Tanya had learned to put on her lipstick without the need to see her reflection.

"Does your cleaner come in every day?" SJ asked.

"No – she comes in once a week." Tanya looked amused. "But Michael helps quite a bit. He likes housework."

"Ah." SJ felt faint heat in her face. Since the Sunday she'd made that stupid drunken phone call they hadn't discussed Michael. He was out seeing a mate tonight – or she'd never have come round. A part of her had been pathetically grateful when Tanya had phoned and suggested it.

"I'll never let you down again," she said, hearing the slight huskiness in her voice and wishing she didn't feel so emotional. That had been another thing she'd noticed in the last five days. Her emotions swung between despair and elation several times a day.

"I know you won't," Tanya said with so much sincerity in her voice that it shamed SJ still further. "It was the drink talking. I know you'd never deliberately do anything to hurt me."

"No, but it's very early days. I can't promise I'll never drink again. I can only do it one day at a time. To be honest, the thought of never drinking again terrifies me."

"Then don't think about it." That was the sort of rational sensible thing Kit would say.

Tanya turned on the food mixer, which wiped out the possibility of further conversation for a few seconds, and then handed her a strawberry smoothie.

"I don't suppose you've got any straws?" SJ asked, feeling like a child.

"In the top cupboard – with the glasses."

Tanya's mobile bleeped with a text and she read it while SJ found the straws. "That was Candice," she explained, going slightly pink. "Do you mind if I just phone her back?"

"Course not," SJ said, heading back out to the decking in order to give her some privacy. When Tanya had first told her about Candice she'd felt jealous that her closest friend had confided in a stranger before she'd confided in her, but now she understood. It was far easier to talk to someone who was going through the same life-changing experiences that you were; someone who knew how you were feeling, someone who knew exactly what the pain was like.

Dorothy had given SJ a potted history of her own twenty-two year drinking career and it had made SJ feel a hundred times better. If Dorothy could beat her alcoholism, build up a massively successful career and look like she'd stepped out of the pages of an upmarket

196

designer catalogue to boot, then surely SJ could do it too. Especially as Dorothy had taken her battle with alcohol right into the gutter.

"I wouldn't listen to anyone who tried to tell me I was on the path to self-destruction," she'd said. "My parents disowned me. So did my elder brother. I was ten years dry before I made it up with my family. Mind you, it wasn't surprising. I stole from them, I lied to them. I hurt them dreadfully. I'd have disowned me, if I'd been in their place."

Looking into Dorothy's serene blue eyes, SJ had found it hard to believe she'd ever been a hellraiser.

"My drinking cost me my first marriage," Dorothy continued softly. "Ted tried his best, but I was out of control. It's impossible to stop an alcoholic who doesn't want to be stopped. It's about as effective as standing in the path of an express train and holding up your hand."

"What happened in the end?"

"My daughter was taken away from me and put into care."

"And that was the wake-up call you needed?" SJ had asked, wanting to cry.

"I wish I could say it was," Dorothy said, "but sadly that wasn't the case. By that stage I was too far gone to care. If anything, I drank even more to quell the pain of losing her. She never lived with me again, but I didn't think it was my fault. I blamed everyone except myself and I got worse and worse."

She hesitated, her eyes reflective. "One night I was heading home with my bottle of whiskey when I collapsed. I'd started to haemorrhage, you see – my liver was shot to pieces. I'd have died there in the gutter if it hadn't been for a Good Samaritan, who happened

197

to be passing. To be honest I probably deserved to die. I certainly would have been happy to die – I'd reached that stage where I couldn't live without alcohol and I couldn't live with it, either. I couldn't see any way out. Not a nice place to be."

"No," SJ had managed, slightly overawed as she'd tried to equate the woman she'd only ever known as dignified and rather elegant with some hopeless drunk in the gutter.

"What happened next?"

"I was taken to hospital and patched up. The hospital saved my life. But I would have been straight out there drinking myself to death again if I hadn't had a visit."

"From your family?"

"No, not from my family. They didn't know I was there. I doubt they'd have come if they had. From my Good Samaritan. The man who'd found me and called an ambulance. Someone must have been looking after me that day because it turned out he was a recovering alcoholic. He came to see me and he told me about AA. To be fair, I already knew about them, but I didn't think I had a problem." She gave SJ a knowing smile. "Anyway, hen, to cut a long story short, he took me to a meeting. Not just the one; he made me go every day – sometimes twice a day. He'd come and pick me up so I didn't have a choice. At first I hated it – I didn't see how a bunch of ex-drunks could possibly help me. But I was desperate enough to go along with it. And eventually some of the stuff they said started to sink in. And here I am. Twenty-five years on – sober and loving it."

"Did you keep in touch with him – your Good Samaritan?" SJ had asked, hoping for a happy ending.

198

"Aye, I did, pet." Dorothy reached across and touched her hand. "I did more than keep in touch – I married him. His name was Alfie."

A cough and the sound of footsteps on the decking alerted SJ to the fact Tanya had reappeared, minus mobile.

"Are you okay, SJ? You looked miles away then."

"Yeah, I'm fine, thanks. Is Candice alright?"

"Yes. Thanks for asking. I was just telling her that Michael wants us to go to a party."

"Sounds nice. Where is it?"

"Soho. But SJ, it's not that sort of party..." Tanya broke off, her eyes troubled.

"Not what sort of party?" Had she missed something? Had she been so busy thinking about herself that she'd not heard what Tanya had said? Her 'friend radar' was suddenly on full alert, although Tanya didn't seem anxious to elaborate. SJ waited expectantly.

"It's...well...it's a trannie party. It's where men dress up as women. And apparently some of the wives go and...well...SJ, do you mind me talking about this sort of stuff?"

"Of course I don't mind. I'm glad you trust me – I mean after... you know..."

"I've always trusted you. It was the drink I didn't trust – well, the effect it had on you." Tanya reached across and patted SJ's hand, her face earnest. "If I hadn't trusted you totally, I'd never have told you. It would hurt Michael terribly if it ever came out. He'd feel I'd betrayed him."

"I won't tell a soul. I promise." SJ felt both humbled and afraid. A few months ago she'd have been

199

horrified if anyone had told her she couldn't be trusted. But then she hadn't been aware she'd ever had a blackout until recently. She hadn't even known what they were.

"So what did Candice say?"

Tanya shook her head. "She doesn't mind her husband going to parties; she goes with him, she says it's a laugh. But I can't, SJ. I can't bear the thought of it. It would seem like – God, I don't know – going to some elaborate fancy dress party, which is fine if you're a kid or even a teenager, but to see a lot of grown up men prancing around in stockings and dresses – well, actually it makes me feel a bit sick. Is that wrong?"

SJ shook her head vehemently and put her arm around Tanya's narrow shoulders.

"I've never been into fancy dress parties," Tanya said, a tear rolling down her nose.

"Me neither," SJ said with feeling. "Never seen the point of them. Complete waste of time."

Tanya smiled and SJ wondered if she was remembering the time SJ had organised a 60s party at college and had persuaded a reluctant Tanya to get her hair done up in a beehive.

"I don't mind him doing the dressing up bit in private. I understand that it's something he needs to do. But I can't go to this party. And he really wants me to. I don't know what to do."

SJ stared at the hanging baskets around decking for inspiration. The fuchsias over-spilled in a riot of purple and pink bells and somewhere close by lavender scented the summer air.

"Do you mind if he goes by himself? I mean, I know it's not ideal, but if you could bear that, then maybe it would be a good compromise."

Tanya frowned. "Yes, it would. That's if he would go by himself. I suppose I could ask him."

"I mean, he can't expect you to embrace every aspect of his…his cross-dressing," SJ decided directness was best, "in one go, can he? It's a complete lifestyle change, and you have to take it one step at a time." She had a feeling that line had come from an AA meeting, but it seemed to fit.

"Yes," Tanya agreed. "You're right. Maybe if I put it like that. You are quite a wise old soul, aren't you?"

"If that were true I wouldn't have ended up in this mess," SJ said with a sigh.

"But alcoholism's an illness," Tanya said. "It can happen to anyone, can't it?"

"Mmm." SJ wasn't sure she was just talking about her life being a drinking- related mess any more. She wanted to mention how things were with Tom, but it didn't seem fair. They were always talking about *her* problems. It was Tanya's turn.

"So tell me about the dressing up at home – I mean, if you want to. How are you coping with that?"

Tanya hesitated, but only for a moment this time. "He doesn't do it all the time. I mean, it's not an everyday thing. A lot of the time our life is perfectly normal." Her eyes clouded a little, and SJ wondered at her choice of words – deep down, she suspected that Tanya would have given a very great deal to go back to the normality their life had once been.

"He tends to do it when he's stressed. Sometimes if there's a problem at work – or if he's worried about something. I think it gives him comfort. We've talked

201

about it quite a lot and I've wondered if there's any connection to the relationship he had with his mum. She brought him up single-handed, you see, because his dad had left them. He never even met his dad."

"Poor little mite," SJ sympathised.

"Yes – but she also had to work for a living, so Michael used to get passed around a bit between relatives. He hated it. He was quite a mummy's boy, so she used to give him something of hers to cuddle until she got back. Usually a scarf or something. I don't know ... SJ, your psychology's better than mine, but it struck me that there could be a connection. What do you think?"

"Makes sense," SJ said. They were still sitting very close and she could smell Tanya's perfume mingling with the sweetness of jasmine beside the deck. "Childhood has a lot to answer for, that's for sure. So does Michael actually wear your clothes?"

"Oh no." Tanya wrinkled her nose. "There are shops you can go to that specialise in cross-dressing, or you can get stuff online…which is what we've been doing up until now. Lingerie's tricky. We knew roughly what size he was – from mine – you know… So we just choose stuff he likes the look of. And the feel of – textures are very important. He likes silk best."

"I'm with him on that one," SJ said, fascinated. "Silk's my favourite too – and, hey, you won't have any trouble with Christmas and birthdays any more, will you? Silk knickers beat boring old socks any day of the week, don't they?"

Tanya's face froze and for a moment SJ thought she may have taken her 'lightening the mood' comments too far but then, to her relief, Tanya nodded.

"To be honest, I'm not very keen on the actual dressing up bit. I'd be quite happy if he did that in private. But I quite enjoy helping him choose the clothes. This is going to sound strange, but it's a bit like helping out a teenage niece who's just blossoming into womanhood. Or a friend who hasn't got much fashion sense."

"Like me," SJ supplied helpfully, and Tanya smiled properly now.

"No, not like you, you walnut. You're beautiful – naturally beautiful – and it's all the more appealing because you're so unaware of it."

SJ was so startled she choked on the last of her smoothie. "I'm not beautiful. I'm a mess. I'm overweight and I've got witch's hair." She twirled a strand of it around her fingers to demonstrate.

"Good grief, you talk some rubbish sometimes. You've got the most amazing hair and beautiful eyes. You'd be stunning if you made a bit more effort. When was the last time you went to a salon?"

"I'm allergic to beauty salons," SJ muttered, having visions of fake nails and tanning beds and being uncomfortably reminded of Alison.

"I'm talking about hairdressing salons. They wouldn't need to do much. You've got naturally lovely hair. You remind me of Cindy Crawford. It's a gorgeous colour anyway, but it'd look fantastic with the right cut."

SJ felt heat in her face. She wasn't used to compliments.

"I do need a haircut, I know. I'll get it sorted. Maybe you could recommend the place you go to?" Not that she had any illusions of ending up looking like Tanya, who was always stunning.

Tanya took a card out of her bag and slipped it across the table. "I see Oliver – he's the owner. The salon's in the precinct. Tell him I sent you."

"Right. Thanks, I'll go." They seemed to have got off the subject of Michael, but at least Tanya looked happier now. Her face was open and relaxed.

"I'd tell you some more, SJ. But Michael's due back in about ten minutes."

"I should be going, anyway. Tom will be home." She felt suddenly close to tears. Tanya and Michael's marriage may still be recovering from the meteor blast of his revelations but at least they were picking their way over the rocky ground together. At least they were talking. She wished her problem and the way she was dealing with it had drawn Tom closer to her, but if anything it had pushed them even further apart. Sometimes she wondered whether she'd ever feel close to him again.

"Thanks for coming round, SJ."

"Thanks for asking me." It seemed that Tanya had forgiven her. She should feel relieved. So why did she feel so sad and churned up as she kissed Tanya goodbye, clipped on Ash's lead, and took him out to the car?

Chapter Twenty-Two

Perhaps it was because the anniversary party, which had been looming like a thunderstorm on the horizon, was now just three weeks away. Her mother had been on the phone twice this week, ostensibly to confirm they were still bringing the wine, and had they done anything about glass-hire? But really it was to check they were still definitely coming.

SJ had assured her they wouldn't miss it for anything. But the thought of seeing Alison again, of having to introduce her stunning and manipulative sister to Tom, made her shake more than giving up the booze had done. Knowing she couldn't even have a nerve-calming drink to take the edge off the experience made the whole thing worse.

She glanced at her watch. Despite what she'd told Tanya – because she hadn't wanted to overstay her welcome – Tom wasn't going to be home for another couple of hours. Suddenly, the thought of going back to an empty house filled her with dread. They still had wine everywhere – Tom had said there was no way he was chucking it all out – and SJ was scared of its pull.

Perhaps she should take Ash for a walk while it was a bit cooler. He was one of the reasons she'd driven to Tanya's. He liked to stroll around a nice park, but he wasn't so keen on hard pavements these days, so she tended to drive him somewhere. Maybe they could go somewhere different for a change.

Instead of turning for home, she headed out of London. The one thing she really missed about

Bournemouth was the seaside: the flat blue infinity of the sea; the cries of the gulls; the sharp tang of ozone and seaweed. Suddenly she knew where she wanted to go and, glad at least to have a purpose, she drove through the Rotherhithe tunnel, picked up the A13 and headed for the coast. She'd had a friend who lived in Westcliffe on Sea once, near Southend, and while she didn't remember the beach being all that big, at least she would be able to smell the sea and the place was familiar to her, which felt comforting – and Ash would love the feel of the sand on his paws.

Forty-five minutes later she was on the coast road. When she'd been here with her friend Carol they'd always walked, and parking was obviously at a bit of a premium. But even looking for a parking space was a hundred times better than sitting at home being tempted to open a bottle of Chardonnay.

Oh, why had she thought about Chardonnay? For a few moments the idea of an ice cold glass of wine hovered in her mind, calling to her like a lighthouse beacon to a sailor on stormy seas. She could taste its dryness on her tongue and feel the coolness slipping down her throat, and then the delicious soporific effects of the alcohol easing its way around her body.

Her fingers tightened on the steering wheel. Shit, shit, shit. Get rid of that thought. Get rid of that thought now!

Gloria Gaynor's *I Will Survive* blasted out of the radio. It was amazing how many songs had lyrics that pertained to alcohol – not that they were meant to be about alcohol, of course; they were meant to be about love. But it was uncanny how well they fitted what she was feeling now. *"I will survive,"* SJ sang along in time with Gloria. *"I will survive – hey – hey."*

206

The song faded. The craving didn't. The DJ started wittering on about how much he was looking forward to getting home for a cold beer in his garden.

SJ spotted a parking space. Thank God. She pulled into it and turned off the ignition and the radio, along with it. Somewhere in her head the voice of *Alco* was taunting her – how had she ever thought she could do this? Even with Kit's support and encouragement, even with Dorothy's kindness, she must have been mad to think she was strong enough to beat alcohol. It was all around her – she would never be able to escape its seductive siren call.

Alco's voice hammered away in her head like some evil troll with a pickaxe. Tap, tap, tap against the rock face of her mind. How could she be a real alcoholic anyway? Real alcoholics didn't have jobs and decent husbands. They had ravaged faces and great big bellies and yellow skin and raincoats. Oh God, she was slipping into stereotype land.

For some reason she thought of Dorothy, with her clear blue eyes and serene smile. *"If ever you want any help with anything, hen ..."*

SJ slid her wet hands off the steering wheel, shakily got out of her car and liberated an interested Ash from the back. He pricked up his grey ears and scented the fresh salty air. It was a lot cooler here than it had been on Tanya's sheltered decking. SJ stared out at the choppy water. The power station chimney was silhouetted against a sunlit horizon and there was a brisk breeze coming off the sea. It whipped her hair around her face and smashed a little common sense into her mind.

She was not going to listen to *Alco*. It was tempting to put her hands over her ears – to block him out. Tempting, but probably pointless, as his voice was coming from inside her own mind. Her addict's mind, she thought bleakly, as she took Ash down on to the shoreline and set him free.

One day at a time, that was all she had to do. Her feet sunk into the damp shingle. One step at a time if that was easier. She struggled to get back the positive thoughts she'd had all week – the thoughts going to AA had put there.

That didn't work either and, walking beside the water with her dog strolling peaceably ahead of her and the mournful calls of gulls wheeling above her head, SJ had never wanted a drink so much in her life.

Her hands were still sweating – perhaps that was some kind of delayed withdrawal symptom but she didn't remember sweating hands being on the list. She'd have to check. She wiped them on her jeans. Then, on impulse, she stopped and phoned Tom's mobile which, his service provider informed her, was switched off.

Frustrated, and desperate now to talk to someone – anyone – to distract herself from thoughts of drinking, she scrolled through her list of numbers. Her finger hesitated over her parents' landline. Was it too early to say she'd contracted an infectious disease and could see no one for at least a month? Yes, probably.

Dorothy's mobile was listed below her parents'. She glanced at it, momentarily puzzled, before remembering Dorothy had insisted she have it.

"Call any time," she'd said, her beautifully manicured hand covering SJ's. "Day or night. I'm usually up till the small hours working."

At the time she'd wondered why Dorothy had thought she'd need to call. It was difficult enough

208

seeing her at Poetry and a Pint and trying to pretend nothing had changed. Had Dorothy known how hard she'd find this? With a swift glance to check Ash hadn't wandered too far, she stopped in the shelter of an old wooden sea break and called her.

Dorothy answered on the third ring and SJ took a deep breath. "Hi, it's SJ. I was just – er – wondering how you were doing?"

"I'm good, thank you, SJ, absolutely fine. How are *you* doing?"

SJ was tempted to say she was absolutely fine, too, but before she could speak, Dorothy added, "How's the not drinking going? Are you finding it tough?"

"Yeah – a bit," SJ confessed, wondering if she'd always been such a master of understatement. "Well, actually a lot. Actually, ever such a lot. I'm on the beach at Westcliffe on Sea. I've been fantasising about a bottle of Chardonnay ever since I got here."

"I take it you haven't got one with you?"

"No," SJ said, sighing deeply, and to her surprise Dorothy laughed. That wasn't supposed to happen. She was supposed to be sympathetic and tell her the craving would pass. Instead Dorothy changed the subject. "Did I ever tell you about the time I was on holiday in Dumfries?"

"No," SJ said with another sigh. "I don't think you did."

Dorothy launched into an account of being stuck in a hotel with nothing to drink and how in the end she'd been so desperate she'd knocked back a whole bottle of perfume.

"Scent contains alcohol," she explained.

"What did it taste like?" SJ gasped in fascinated horror.

"Disgusting. It was the most disgusting thing I'd ever poured down my throat – I wasn't too bad at that stage, you see."

The fact Dorothy didn't consider drinking perfume 'too bad' put things in perspective a bit. SJ would never consider any such thing.

"Did it work?" she asked, breathlessly. "Did it take the edge off the craving?"

"No, it didn't," Dorothy chuckled. "When I looked at the bottle properly I realised it was the kind of perfume that doesn't have any alcohol in it. So I'd just had myself a very expensive drink, pet. And it was all for absolutely nothing."

"My God," SJ said. "That's terrible." She wasn't sure which was worse – the fact that Dorothy hadn't satisfied her craving, or the fact she'd been desperate enough to drink a bottle of perfume in an attempt to do it.

And in the moments of silence that followed, SJ realised to her horror that she'd already prioritised the two things by the order in which they'd occurred to her. It was far more terrible that Dorothy hadn't satisfied her craving – God, did that mean she was already thinking like an alcoholic?

The silence went on so long that SJ wondered if Dorothy had hung up. She coughed experimentally.

"So then, SJ – how are you feeling now? Any better?"

"Yes, I am. Thank you, Dorothy."

"My pleasure. So tell me, hen, what have *you* been up to today?"

By the time she had finished talking, twenty minutes later, SJ realised that her hands were no longer

210

sweaty. The terrible tension in her muscles had eased off. The craving had gone.

"Thank you so much," SJ said, rocked with a humbleness that made her want to weep, because she'd just realised that Dorothy had known exactly how she felt, and exactly how long to keep her talking. And she must have been interrupting her work – Dorothy had often said that evenings were her best time for writing. "Thank you so, so much, Dorothy."

"Any time, pet. You can phone me any time you want to."

Chapter Twenty-Three

Another thing SJ had noticed since she'd given up drinking was that she'd started to remember things she hadn't thought about since they had happened – or at least not for a very long time – which wouldn't have been so bad if any of them were nice. But they weren't. Sometimes the memories were incomplete – she'd get fragments of the past flicking into her mind; random scenes that weren't connected would play out in her head like some surreal film. This usually happened at night when she was trying to get to sleep, which was virtually impossible when the only nightcap she allowed herself was camomile tea.

When she mentioned it to Kit he told her that alcohol was a very good memory suppressant, which was often why people drank, and that eventually the memories would work themselves out of her head.

"It might help if you talked about them," he added idly.

"To you?" she asked, half wanting to talk to him about them, and half afraid.

"It doesn't have to be me. You could see another counsellor, maybe a psychotherapist if you prefer?"

SJ shook her head. She trusted Kit, but she didn't want anyone else poking about inside her mind.

There was a small silence.

"Did you mean now?" SJ asked, noticing with a stab of alarm that they had forty minutes of the session left.

"If you like?" He gave her a half smile and said nothing else until eventually she said, "Okay ..."

Kit nodded, his dark eyes interested but not impatient, and SJ went on slowly. "A lot of things I remember are about my parents ..." He nodded again. "... This is probably very childish and stupid but I don't think they've really ever loved me." She bit her lip. "No – that's wrong. They do love me, but they love Alison more."

"And what makes you think that?"

"They always take her side," she said, swallowing hard. "They always did it when we were kids, and they're still doing it now." She paused. "Even when she slept with Derek they sided with her. Well, they were shocked for a while, but then as time went on they thought we should move on, put it all behind us. They didn't understand why I couldn't bear to be in the same room as her. They still don't."

Kit shifted in his chair but he didn't speak, and after a while she went on quietly. "They've never once said that Alison should miss a family gathering so I can go for a change. They don't blame her for breaking up my marriage. They just blame me for being an unforgiving cow." She could feel tears sliding down her face, but she couldn't stop them and she couldn't look at Kit. "It's their party in a week's time and I've got to take Tom to meet Alison."

"Are you scared it might happen again, SJ? Is that what you're thinking?"

She reached for the box of economy tissues and narrowly avoided knocking over the leaflet stand.

"I don't think I can do it without a drink," she said.

"Yes, you can. You're stronger than you think, SJ."

213

"I'm not," she said sadly. "I'm really not."

It was only when she had tidied up her face in the loo downstairs with the aid of some cold water and a paper towel and was outside again in the sunshine of the Soho street that she realised she had never answered Kit's question.

Was she afraid Alison would make a move on Tom?

Tom wasn't like Derek. Tom was a what-you-see-is-what-you-get kind of person, whereas Derek had been far more complex.

As far as she knew Tom had never lied to her – unlike Derek, who'd kept on lying, even when he must have known it was futile. Even when he must have known all his lifelines were used up.

"I've just been to see Alison," she'd announced on that evening five years ago, as she'd walked back into their kitchen.

"Oh, yeah – how's she doing?" There was nothing in his face. Not a flicker of apprehension, not an echo of remorse. She'd felt anger building.

"You know how she's bloody well doing – you slept with her on Saturday night." SJ didn't recognise her own voice; it was so choked with bitterness, every word twisted with pain.

Yet still for a moment he hadn't reacted. He'd just stared back at her, his eyes blank. For an awful moment SJ had thought he was going to carry on denying it. Tell her she was imagining things, being paranoid.

Instead, he scratched his nose, coughed, and cupped his hand over his mouth, almost thoughtfully. Not thoughtfulness, but guilt, SJ registered, remembering something she'd learned in psychology. People always touched their faces when they felt awkward or were about to lie – it was almost as if they could take some of the power out of their words if their hand was across their mouth. Make the lie not quite as potent.

"So?" she prompted quietly. "Tell me your side of the story. Is it true? Did you sleep with my sister as soon as I was safely in Dublin? Or has she made the whole thing up?"

"Um…" He took a couple of paces backwards, half turning so he was facing their kitchen window.

SJ followed his gaze. On their patio the rotary clothes line was strung with a line of his socks and pants, the Armanis amongst them, stirring slightly in the evening breeze. She could see the line of tension in his jaw.

She trembled. "For God's sake, Derek, just tell me what happened."

"I was off my face. I don't really remember."

"Well, Alison does." She moved across his line of vision so he was forced to look at her. "Alison remembers all the gory little details. She even remembers what boxers you were wearing. And what sheets…" she broke off, haunted by fresh images.

Derek shook his head and stared at the floor. A muscle was twitching in his cheekbone. His brown hair was ruffled like the feathers of a bird after a dust bath. He had never looked so beautiful. She had never hated him so much.

He cleared his throat again, spreading his hands in front of him; his wedding ring glowed dully in the golden light.

"I'm sorry, okay. I'm really sorry. Like I said, I don't even remember it – I was really pissed."

"But you still managed to do it. Was it good? Or did you just think, well I've tried one sister I'd better try the pretty one. Is that what you thought?"

"No. No, of course I didn't."

For the first time he looked shocked. When she raised her hands to slap him, hardly aware of what she was doing, wanting only to hurt, he didn't even try to defend himself. He just stood there mutely, letting her vent her rage and pain and grief.

She'd bloodied his nose and he hadn't tried to stop her. Afterwards, she'd sat at the kitchen table while he cleaned off the blood with a wet dishcloth at the sink. Then he'd turned back to her, his shoulders straighter now as if he somehow thought that it was done with. An eye for an eye, a bloodied nose for the worst pain he could have inflicted. SJ had felt wrung out, all the fight and anger gone. But she'd known he could never make up for what he'd done.

All through their marriage she had ignored it when he flirted with her friends because she had trusted him utterly. She had felt secure in the knowledge that he'd chosen her. That she came first in his life and always would.

But now that trust was shattered. She knew it could never be rebuilt.

While Alison had gone back to her adoring husband and been forgiven – sometimes SJ thought Clive would put up with anything for a quiet life – SJ had thrown Derek out and filed for divorce. The unbearable pain had slid slowly into black depression, but she couldn't take him back. She couldn't risk letting him do it to her again. She couldn't risk letting any man do that to her again.

216

Chapter Twenty-Four

There were twenty-four hours to kick off, and all SJ's fears about seeing Alison were swirling around in her heart. There was still time for something to crop up and detain her – but she'd had her hair done at Oliver's, just in case. He'd chopped off loads – SJ had watched in horror as it fell in chunks to the salon floor, but it did look better, she had to admit. To her surprise it didn't seem that much shorter, but it no longer turned witchy five minutes after she'd dried it.

She had a feeling she'd lost a bit of weight too. That was probably because she'd eaten very little lately – she was too nervous to eat. Or perhaps her wine-free evenings were beginning to make a difference.

"What are you going to wear?" Tanya had asked when she'd phoned the previous evening, and the question had sent SJ into a panic.

A frantic search through her wardrobe had increased the panic tenfold. It was ages since she'd been anywhere that required dressing up. Her old party clothes were all too small. Her Monsoon jacket needed cleaning and it was too late to get it done. Anyway, it wasn't really party wear.

When she'd mentioned it to Tom he suggested she buy something. Then he'd put his money where his mouth was and had given her his credit card. Her guilt at spending more of his money overridden by desperation, SJ had nipped into town and returned with two outfits, neither of which she was sure were suitable. She never had been able to make up her mind where clothes were concerned.

Now she laid them out on the bed and wondered whether she should phone Tanya and ask for advice. Finally, she did.

"I've got this long black skirt from Next, which sort of skims over my bulgy bits and hides my legs, and a floaty white gypsy-style blouse to go with it."

"Right ..." Tanya didn't sound very impressed. "Don't tell me – the other outfit includes black leggings?"

"Well, yes it does ...." SJ bristled. "What's wrong with black leggings?"

"Nothing's actually wrong with them, but you never wear anything else, so they're hardly special, are they?"

"So what do you suggest? I can't be bothered to take everything back."

"You must – I'll come with you. We can get you kitted out in something glam. I'll meet you outside Next in half an hour."

SJ wasn't sure she fancied the idea of something glam. It was okay for Tanya, who always looked stunning, but she had far too many lumpy bits that needed covering up. She pointed this out to Tanya as soon as she arrived, waving her Next bag defiantly.

"You're talking rubbish," Tanya said, without even a glance at the skirt and blouse she'd spent hours choosing. "Now let's get rid of these and find something more suitable."

To SJ's horror, Tanya's idea of 'something more suitable' turned out to be a tiny black shift dress with spaghetti straps.

"I can't wear that."

218

"Why not?"

"It's too short. Everyone will see my legs." Everyone would probably be able to see her knickers too, if she leaned forward, she thought glumly. She wouldn't even have been keen on that ten years previously, when there'd been a lot less of her.

"There's nothing wrong with your legs. Now humour me. At least try it on."

SJ did as she was told, then poked her head around the changing room curtain where Tanya was on guard so she couldn't do a runner.

"I'm not coming out, I feel naked. You'll have to come in."

"It looks gorgeous," Tanya said. "What do you think?"

"I'm not sure." SJ didn't want to admit she hadn't actually looked in the mirror because she knew she would look hideous. It had taken her ages to sort out the spaghetti straps, which had lived up to their name and tangled into knots.

"Well, I think it suits you. You look ever so slim."

"Do I?" SJ sneaked a glance and saw that while slim was a slight exaggeration, she didn't have any untoward bulges – the skirt skimmed rather than clung. Her arms looked okay too – they weren't flabby at all, which was a nice surprise; she hadn't worn any arm-revealing tops lately. Pity about her legs.

"All you need now is some nice heels, and the right bag, and some suitable bling. Come on, let's go and pay for the dress."

The shoes Tanya made her buy were lovely, feminine and delicate so even her size eight clodhoppers looked good. Her legs looked slimmer in heels, too. She felt like Cinderella. The right bag turned out to be a black clutch bag with diamante detail, but Tanya turned her nose up at the display of jewellery.

"Too expensive for what it is. You can borrow something of mine. Come on, let's head back and you can choose."

"Are you sure it's not too late?"

"No, Michael won't mind – he never goes to bed early. Come on. I want to get you sorted out properly."

Michael was watching a black and white film when they got back. It was the first time SJ had seen him to talk to since Tanya had told her about his penchant for cross-dressing. Although she'd waved at him across the squash court once or twice, they hadn't been out as a foursome lately – Tom had been too busy with work.

She'd been afraid she might feel differently about him, but when he leapt up and gave her a hug, she realised with relief that she didn't. He was still the same old Michael, with his boyish grin and floppy fringe. She pushed the images of Lizzie firmly out of her head as she returned his peck on the cheek.

"How you doing, SJ?" His eyes sparkled. "Been shopping? What have you bought?"

She got the dress out to show him, and he made all the right noises. Man-type grunts of approval, rather than Lizzie-type girly comments – phew!

"Tanya's going to lend me some bling."

"Uh huh. I'll leave you girls to get on with it then." With another quick grin he went back to his film, and they escaped upstairs.

"Right, all you need to do now is to put your hair up and you'll knock 'em dead," Tanya announced when SJ had got the whole outfit on again – complete with a chunky pink and gold necklace. "You look stunning."

220

SJ wouldn't have gone that far, but she had to admit she did look better than she'd done in the skirt and blouse, which had been more sensible A-level tutor than party girl.

"Don't forget nail varnish." Tanya scooped up two bottles from her dressing table. "One of these would look good. How are you feeling now?"

"Like I might actually be going, after all," SJ admitted, swallowing a choked-up feeling of gratitude. "Thanks, Tanya. I don't know what I'd do without you."

When she got home she hung everything in her wardrobe and told Tom he'd have to wait until tomorrow before he saw what she was wearing. She didn't want the short dress giving him ideas. They hadn't made love lately and she didn't know how she was going to manage it without the help of a few glasses of wine.

It struck her she'd have the same problem after the party – but the following night was aeons away. She couldn't think of anything beyond facing Alison.

While Tom was getting ready for bed she phoned her mother from the privacy of the lounge, guessing correctly she'd be up late doing party food.

"Sarah-Jane, I hope you're not ringing me with any last minute excuses about not being able to come, because I've got enough on my plate already."

SJ was about to make some indignant denial, but then she reminded herself Mum had every right to be worried. After all, that was exactly what she'd done on every previous occasion in history. "Of course not," she soothed. "I was just checking that everything was set for tomorrow – and there was nothing else you wanted us to do."

She was also harbouring the faint hope that Alison, by some miracle, had decided not to go. But her mother's next words dashed this to smithereens.

"Yes, we're all set. Your sister's done most of the food – she's a godsend. I couldn't have managed without her."

"Great."

SJ could hear the hollowness in her voice and maybe her mother could too, because she added gently, "She's ever so pleased you're coming, pet. It's going to be lovely having my two girls together again."

SJ wondered what she meant by *together*. Her mother probably had some rosy picture of her and Alison telling each other jokes over a G&T. Oh God, don't think of gin.

"And it's so long since you've seen the children, isn't it? Sophie's a proper young lady now – just like her mother. You won't recognise her. Kevin hasn't changed much, unfortunately. Alison caught him smoking in his bedroom the other day. I ask you." Her mother tutted her disapproval. SJ had a feeling she might like Kevin the most. He was obviously the black sheep of the family. They'd have a lot in common.

"Anyway, love, I'm sure you don't want to hear all this now. But I'm so pleased you and Tom are going to be there." Her mother's voice dropped an octave. "I do love you, you know, Sarah-Jane. I've hated all this upset. It means the world to me that you're coming."

It crossed SJ's mind that her mother might have had a couple of glasses of something herself. She wasn't given to unprompted declarations of affection.

222

"We're looking forward to it, Mum," she lied huskily. "Now, you go and put your feet up, and don't worry about a thing. Tom and I will see you tomorrow."

She hung up just as Tom came into the room, wearing nothing but his boxers. Considering he had a desk job and ate pasta whenever he felt like it, he was in pretty good shape.

"Everything okay, love?" He crossed the room and sat beside her on the window seat.

"I need a wash," she protested, as he slipped his arms around her waist and tried to kiss her.

"I'll help you get your clothes off."

"No need," she yelped as she escaped. When he came up to bed she pretended to be asleep, ignoring his hands as they ran over her body and discovered she was still wearing her pants. That should be a big enough clue, surely? She threw in a little snore for good measure and eventually Tom got the message and rolled over with a sigh.

SJ knew she wasn't being fair, but she couldn't have made love with him tonight if her life depended on it. Yet now he'd left her alone she was far too tense to sleep.

When she finally drifted off, her dreams were fragmented and filled with Alison. In one of them SJ and Kevin, who'd morphed into a twenty-five year old Bruce Willis lookalike, were running away from Alison down her mother's garden, each of them carrying a box of two hundred Marlboro.

"If I ever catch you smoking again, I'll kill you," Alison raged, as she closed the gap between them.

"In here," SJ gasped, yanking open the door of the summer house, shoving Kevin inside and instructing

223

him to hide behind the tomatoes. "She'll never find us in here."

She woke up, her heart thudding madly, as if she really had been running. It was three a.m. She got out of bed, fetched a glass of water from the bathroom and sat on the edge of the bath, sipping it and listening to the creaks and night noises of the old house and Tom's gentle snores from next door.

'You're stronger than you think, SJ.' Strange how it was Kit's voice, not Tom's that flickered into her head, offering reassurance and a smidgeon of comfort, like a tiny candle in the black old night.

SJ crept back across the landing to bed, wishing that Tom would wake up and reach out and cuddle her. He wouldn't even have had to speak; just the feel of his arms would have been enough. Perhaps if she woke him? But that wasn't very fair – and if she woke him and he was cross, she didn't think her wired emotions would cope. She curled up on her side and then spooned into the heat of him and shut her eyes.

The rest of the night was fragmented between restless sleep and nightmares. In the last nightmare she was sipping wine from the spout of a watering can.

SJ woke up with a sickening feeling of dread and her head pounding from the hangover. Oh God, she'd caved in and had a drink. Dorothy was going to be furious. Kit would shake his head and give her one of his serious raised-eyebrow looks, which were far worse than if he'd just told her she was a weak-willed silly cow. Tanya would be bitterly disappointed. Shame flooded through her – she'd been so determined, so sure she wasn't going to drink again. Drinking out of a watering can too. *Watering can!*

224

It took her a few moments to realise she hadn't been doing any such thing. As the echoes of the hangover flicked out of her mind, like little scurrying night demons that giggled as they ran, SJ heard *Alco's* taunting voice. She blocked it out – she knew now that the voice wasn't a separate entity, but her own doubts and low self esteem converging into one in her head. Trying to sabotage the good she was doing.

Fully awake now, she sat up. It was only five a.m. But there would be no getting back to sleep. She dressed quietly and went downstairs, feeling wearier than when she'd gone to bed. In the kitchen she lit a cigarette, breathed in the blissful smoke of it, let Ash into the garden and followed him out into the new day.

The dog stretched his long grey body, blinked and sniffed the air. A couple of sparrows were chirping away in the maple tree beside the summer house and the early morning light lit up the paving slabs outside.

SJ yawned and hoped the dreams had been sparked off by worry about seeing Alison again – and weren't some kind of premonition.

Chapter Twenty-Five

The day both dragged and raced. While Tom was doing paperwork upstairs, SJ cleaned the house in a rare spurt of domesticity. She didn't much feel like cleaning, but someone had to do it, and she was too restless to do nothing.

In between cleaning she smoked far too many fags, and shovelled painkillers down her throat. She might not have a hangover, but the headache she'd woken with was real enough. She knew she should probably have something to eat, but she didn't feel like eating. Still, at least she should look even thinner in her dress. That was a result.

Just after lunchtime, Dorothy phoned. "How are you feeling?"

"Awful," SJ confessed.

"Well, don't forget what I said. Make sure you have plenty to eat – before you go, I mean. Not when you're there and someone's trying to shove a glass of wine in your hand."

"Okay."

"Did you have a good night's sleep?" Dorothy persisted.

"No, not really. I had nightmares."

"Take your mobile to the party and if you get the slightest urge for a drink, you phone me. Okay?"

"Sure," SJ murmured, wondering how she was going to manage that in a houseful of people.

Hi, Dorothy, I'm gasping for a stiff drink. Can you talk me out of it, please?

226

A couple of people at meetings had advised her not to go to the party. They said it would be too difficult with barely six weeks of sobriety behind her, and SJ would have dearly liked to take their advice. But Dorothy had said that if the party was important, she should go just for a short time, but she should make sure she didn't feel hungry or lonely or tired. Well, she didn't feel hungry, but she felt very tired and very alone.

Tom had been more distant than ever lately. He hadn't even questioned the number of texts she'd been getting, most of them from Dorothy to see if she was okay. She could be having an affair for all he knew. SJ wished it was that simple. An affair would have been a logical reason for her lack of interest in the bedroom, but she had the uneasy feeling that she hadn't lost interest. The longer she went without alcohol, the clearer her head became. She'd never been that interested in sex with Tom. She had thought, at first, that they just needed practice; she'd been wrong, and she had never had the courage to tell him.

Tanya phoned too. "How are you doing? You all set for tonight? You will phone me if you have a problem, won't you?"

At this rate, she'd be spending more time on her mobile than talking to party guests.

"Who are you talking to?" Tom appeared in the kitchen doorway and SJ jumped.

"Only Tanya. Bye, Tanya, I've got to go."

She hung up as Tom yawned and stretched his hands above his head. His face was crinkled with tiredness and he blinked a couple of times. "I suppose we ought to think about getting ready. It's quite an early start, isn't it? Do you want first go in the bathroom?"

"No, you carry on. I'll be ages, and I've got to do my nails first."

It took three goes to get her nail varnish on. Her hands were shaking too much. And why was it that whenever you'd just painted your nails you got an urgent itch right inside your ear that couldn't wait the required time for them to dry – which was always much longer than it promised on the bottle.

When she heard Tom come out of the bathroom, she went up and had her own shower and got changed. She could hear Tom whistling in the bedroom – one of them was obviously looking forward to it then. She put on the dress, sorted out the straps, pinned up her hair and studied her reflection.

Tom wolf-whistled as she came out of the bathroom.

"Blimey, I'll be the envy of every man there. You look amazing. You should wear dresses more often. You've got gorgeous legs."

"No, I haven't. They're too fat. And I'm getting cellulite at the tops."

"What rubbish. You're beautiful." His eyes narrowed in appreciation and SJ shivered. He hadn't looked at her like that for a very long time.

She put her hands out in front of her – ostensibly to check out the colour of her varnish: hot pink chocolate, whatever that was supposed to be; they were more peach than anything else – but really to see if they were still shaking.

They were.

228

"Tom, I don't think I can go through with this," she said, glancing up at him. "I can't face Alison, I really can't."

"SJ, darling…" He must be intent on going; he never called her darling. "We don't have to stay long – but we DO have to go. Your mum and dad will be really upset if we don't."

"They probably won't notice," SJ said in desperation. "They'll be surrounded by people."

"We can't let them down. We're taking the wine."

She wished he hadn't reminded her about that. "That's another thing I'm worried about. I'm going to be surrounded by all these people drinking. I don't think I can cope."

"Why not? I mean, it's just will power, isn't it?"

SJ blinked. Was that really what he thought? That she didn't have any willpower and that's why she frequently drank herself into oblivion, no matter how much she hurt herself and anyone else who happened to be in the vicinity? It was obvious from his expression that he did.

"Are you saying I haven't got any will power?"

"I don't think you've got any when it comes to alcohol – no. You can't have – or you wouldn't get so drunk."

"It's not about willpower, Tom. It's an illness. It's recognised as an illness – alcoholism – ring any bells? You must have heard of it."

He was smiling. He was actually SMILING. As if this was just some simple little matter that they'd sorted out and resolved, just by her going to a few AA meetings.

"Well, you're certainly ill when you drink too much. I agree with you there." Gently, he took her

229

hands in his. "You'll be fine. I know you will. In a couple of hours' time you'll be wondering what you were worried about."

SJ doubted that very much, but she knew when she was defeated. Short of faking an urgent illness on the way over, she couldn't see a way out. She supposed she could pray the car broke down en route, or that a gang would rob the off licence just as they were picking up the wine and hold the two of them hostage at gunpoint. That would be good as long as they didn't actually shoot them – she could probably sell a story like that to the Nationals and make some money.

Not that God usually answered her prayers – the miserable old bugger.

Aware that Tom was still holding her hands and seemed to be waiting for her to say something, she made an effort to pull herself together.

"You look great, too," she said, and he did. He was wearing black trousers – how come men could get away with it? And the jacket he'd worn at their wedding. It still fitted him perfectly. None of the clothes she'd had when they got married fitted her now.

"So are you ready then? I said we'd pick the wine up just after five."

Why did he have to keep mentioning wine?

Feeling a surge of irritation, she grabbed her bag and followed him to the front door.

As they stepped outside she caught movement out of the corner of her eye and turned to see a butterfly – a red admiral – was caught in a cobweb strung between the window and the front wall of the house. Its wings fluttered frantically as it tried to escape but only succeeded in entangling itself further in its prison.

In the corner of the web a large striped spider appeared, attracted by the movement. SJ shuddered. She hated spiders. Torn between wanting to rescue the butterfly and not wanting to go within touching distance of the spider, she paused.

Catching her look, Tom stepped forward, carefully freed the butterfly and set it on the grass. They watched as it shook out its wings, as if not quite believing it was free, before fluttering away like a piece of bright satin.

How odd that Tom understood some of her fears so well, yet he was oblivious to how afraid she was now.

"What?" he asked, pausing and raising his eyebrows.

"I was just thinking what a sweetie you are. I bet that butterfly thought its number was well and truly up."

"Well, I could hardly watch it struggle." He smiled at her and she looked at him, standing there in his dark suit, his eyes suddenly vulnerable.

Yet you can stand there and watch me struggle with the hardest battle of my life. She ached with loss. *Oh, Tom, where did we go wrong? How come we look so normal on the outside when we're in bits below the surface? When we don't communicate any more – when you haven't a clue how I feel? Do you know how much I want to fly off somewhere? Escape to some peaceful land where there is no wine and no temptation? Do you know how scared I am, Tom?*

"What?" he asked again, and this time he tilted his head slightly so a triangle of sunlight slanted across his face and highlighted the grey glints in his hair. SJ could smell roses and hear the muted coos of a pigeon somewhere close by.

231

"I was just wondering what you were thinking," she said huskily. And she knew that their disintegrating marriage was her fault. How could he be expected to read her mind?

"I was thinking that if we don't get a move on, we're going to be late," he replied, putting an arm around her shoulders and propelling her firmly in the direction of his car.

Chapter Twenty-Six

Rather to SJ's dismay, but not to her surprise, her prayers about the car breaking down went unanswered. With hindsight, she probably shouldn't have called God a miserable old bugger. Neither was there a hold-up at the off licence. A spotty-faced youth who didn't look old enough to be selling alcohol offered to help Tom carry the cases out. SJ shrunk lower in the passenger seat as they loaded the wine and exchanged jokes about drinking it.

Oblivious to her tension, Tom drove on towards Romford, with the wine bottles clinking tantalisingly in the back. How was she going to get through the next few hours? Perhaps she should have asked Kit if she could be let off not drinking just for this one night. She could start the sobriety again first thing in the morning. It wasn't too much to ask, was it? She shouldn't be expected to face Alison without a drink in her hand. Especially as everyone would be trying to press drinks on her – even Tom probably, seeing as he obviously still hadn't got the message.

She'd contemplated telling her mother she'd given up drinking, but she knew that such a confession would lead straight to an inquisition and she didn't feel ready to tell her parents she had a full blown drink problem. She knew alcoholism was an illness – she was living it – but deep down, even she occasionally wondered if she was just pathetically weak-willed. How were her straightforward, totally traditional parents ever going to be able to understand?

As Tom pulled into a space directly outside her parents' house, she touched his arm.

"I don't feel well," she said, which was true. She felt sick with nerves.

"We're here now." Tom didn't sound in the least bit sympathetic. "Come on, let's take this in and let them know we've arrived. They'll be wanting to get the drinks set out."

Feeling both trapped and depressed, SJ went ahead of him. Why was he so hell bent on meeting bloody Alison anyway? Did he really have no understanding of how she felt? No, come to think of it, he probably didn't. She'd already established that he didn't understand her at all.

SJ trembled as she stood on the doorstep with the gift-wrapped package for her parents. She and Tom hadn't been able to think of a suitable joint present for a ruby wedding anniversary, so in the end they'd bought her mum a ruby necklace and her father a bottle of forty year old port and wrapped them in a box together. The port had been Tom's idea – SJ wasn't even sure her dad liked it, although Tom seemed to think he did. SJ didn't like it much either, but she was so desperate for a drink now she'd have given it a try. Good job it was gift-wrapped and out of sight.

"Has no one answered the bell?" Tom asked her, as he placed the box of glasses on the path alongside the wine.

SJ shook her head, not wanting to admit she hadn't rung it in case Alison let them in.

"Maybe they're all out in the garden then. Perhaps we'd better give it another ring," Tom suggested, and did just that.

234

After a four second delay, which felt like forever, SJ's mother opened the door – to her intense relief.

"Hello, loves – oh, is that for us? Isn't it beautifully wrapped? Did you do it yourself? Jim, come and give Tom a hand, will you, pet? Go through to the lounge, SJ, love, and tell me what you think of the decorating."

Red balloons and red streamers clashed horribly with the terracotta walls and carpet. It was enough to make you feel sick, even if you didn't already. SJ took several deep breaths, which made her feel dizzy, and laid the box on the floor beneath a table that heaved with plates of food.

Mum had really gone to town. There were pork pies, cut into quarters; cheese and pineapple on sticks; vol-au-vents with some unidentified grey filling; a leg of ham; a whole salmon; three bowls of salad – sensible salad, iceberg lettuce, tomato, cucumber and radish and none of what her mother referred to as fancy leaf rubbish. Several plates of sandwiches were still covered with cling film, and four plates of quiche with little placards announcing they were vegetarian. Her sister's handiwork, SJ suspected; Alison had been a vegetarian since she was at school.

Dad had protested when Alison suggested they all try this new way of eating, but Mum had capitulated, as she always did to her younger daughter, her princess.

SJ glanced around the room, which led out on to a conservatory, which in turn led on to the huge back garden. Aunt Edie, Dad's sister from Barnsley, and Uncle Simon were installed in cane chairs, already getting into the swing of things by the look of it. They both held giant glasses of red wine. Beyond them she could see more relatives and some of her father's darts

235

team, milling about admiring the geraniums. A red and white striped tent blocked out the light at the end of the garden. Dad was right; it was more like a marquee than a gazebo. She was never going to get through this without a drink.

Still, at least there was no sign of Alison – perhaps God had decided to answer her food-poisoning-her-sister prayers instead then. Good old God.

Catching her glance, Aunt Edie heaved her plump, flower-patterned body out of the chair and gave her a beaming smile. "Oh, look, there's Sarah-Jane, love. Dahling, come and give your Auntie Edie a hug. Don't you look smashing? Doesn't she look smashing, Simon?"

Please don't say, "Hasn't she grown?"

"Hasn't she grown, Simon?"

At the same moment, her mother appeared in the lounge doorway and, sensing escape from one of Aunt Edie's strongman hugs, SJ turned towards her.

"Isn't Alison in here, pet? She popped out to get some tonic. We were worried about running out with you around. I hope she won't be too much longer."

With luck she'd be caught up in a multi-car pile up and be eternally detained. SJ was horrified at her thoughts. Surely she didn't wish her sister dead? Just permanently absent would have done.

"Isn't that dress a little short?" her mother added before withdrawing. SJ's confidence dropped another notch. Oh, what she would have given for a nice large glass of Chardonnay. She had her mobile in her clutch bag. Perhaps she should call Dorothy now. No doubt she had a few more perfume stories tucked up her sleeve to warn SJ of the evils of drinking.

236

She contemplated dragging Tom out to the garden. They could hide in the marquee. Hey, perhaps it would be possible to hide from Alison for the entire evening – even if they were in the same place. That was an idea she hadn't considered.

She hugged Aunt Edie dutifully, kissed Uncle Simon, and denied that she'd grown very much in the last ten years – except perhaps outwards.

"Nice dress," Simon leered, his beaming red face so close she could smell the wine on his breath. She'd never noticed alcohol on anyone's breath before. How odd.

Then, excusing herself on helping-her-mother grounds, SJ bounded into the kitchen, the suggestion of hiding on her lips, just in time to see her father popping a slice of lemon into a glass already brimming with sparkling liquid.

"There you go, love – a nice gin and tonic to start you off, complete with ice and a slice, just how you like it. And to say thanks for bringing the wine – it's a lovely gesture." He beamed at her, but SJ was too busy staring at the glass he was holding out. He didn't need to tell her what it was – she could smell the juniper berries from here. Oh God, oh God, oh GOD. What should she do now? If she said she didn't want it, he'd get very suspicious.

And it would be ungrateful and selfish, wouldn't it? Like saying you didn't want a slice of someone's birthday cake when you were on a diet. She hesitated, hoping Tom would rescue her. Fat chance. He was flirting with her mother by the cooker.

"Go on, love – we got that in special. No one else is on the gin."

So it would be wasted as well. She looked back at her father's beaming face. She took the glass. It wouldn't hurt to hold it, after all. She could pour it over the roses when they went outside. Yes, good plan. The roses could probably do with a decent drink. No doubt they were sick to death of the horse manure her father shovelled over them every Sunday morning.

The front door slammed and, as if from a long way off, she heard her mother's over-bright voice. "Ah, I expect that's her now, Tom. You must come and say hello, she's been dying to meet you."

Was she not even going to be allowed to introduce him herself? If it had to be done, she should be the one to do it. She could hear Alison's voice in the hall.

Feeling as though things were sliding out of her control far too rapidly, SJ stared into her gin and tonic. She raised the glass to her lips, sniffed it and was swamped with an overwhelming compulsion to down it in one. No one was looking at her – no one cared if she was sober or not. Mum, Dad, Tom – they were all looking towards the door. Waiting for Princess Alison to make her entrance.

SJ had one final battle with her conscience, and lost. She took a sip at the same moment as her sister walked into the room.

Chapter Twenty-Seven

SJ had dreaded this moment for years. She'd imagined lots of scenarios. In her more positive moments she'd imagined that Alison had put on masses of weight and let herself go and looked a mess. She would shuffle across the room, peering out through bedraggled hair extensions, and sniff a little and say, 'I'm so sorry, sis, about what happened. Can you forgive me?'

SJ wasn't quite sure what she'd have said in these circumstances. Her imagination had never extended that far.

In her less positive moments, Alison had looked as gorgeous as ever and she'd smirked and raised her eyebrows and said something like, 'Well, well ...' Her sister had always been fond of the phrase *well, well* ... 'We meet again at last. I'm so glad you've got over this silly feud.'

The reality was completely different. Alison hadn't put on weight, at least not as far as she could tell. She'd had her blond hair cut into a slick bob, which made her face look elfin, and she was wearing black jeans and a pale blue bodice over which her boobs spilled. SJ felt suddenly overdressed. Why had she let Tanya talk her into buying this dress?

For a very long moment they stared at each other. Alison wasn't smirking either. She looked a little shyly between SJ and Tom and then she blinked a couple of times and came across the space between them.

"It's good to see you, sis. I was really pleased when Mum said you were coming."

No one else said a word. A kind of hushed expectation had settled over the kitchen.

SJ wondered what they thought was going to happen. A grand reconciliation, possibly – a big hug. Neither she nor Alison had ever been into hugging.

Aware that everyone was waiting for her to say something, she said, "It's good to see you, too. This is Tom, by the way. Tom, meet my sister, Alison."

It was almost an anticlimax. Why ever had she been so worried about it? Okay, so the top was a bit provocative, but apart from that, Alison didn't look like a maneater, as she turned her attention to Tom and held out her hand. "Very pleased to meet you, Tom. I've heard lots about you."

"Ditto," Tom said gravely, and Alison had the grace to blush.

Tom didn't seem to have noticed the drink in her hand – he'd been talking to her mother when Dad gave it to her. SJ took another surreptitious gulp.

The rustling of carrier bags heralded the arrival of Clive, Alison's husband – he was obviously chief tonic water carrier. Perhaps he'd been waiting outside in case there was a fight – he'd always avoided confrontations.

"And this is my husband, Clive," Alison introduced the two men.

Unlike his wife, Clive had put on weight. The buttons around his midriff were under some strain. His brown hair was thinning on top, and he looked older than Tom, even though he wasn't.

The kitchen was getting crowded and SJ felt lightheaded. She realised her glass was almost empty. She hadn't even tasted it – what a waste. She was, however, aware of the slow feeling of intoxication spreading through her veins. That would be lack of food, no doubt

– not to mention abstinence: nearly six weeks of abstinence. She'd really blown it this time, too, not just dreamt she had.

"Would you like a refill?" Alison was asking. "I'll join you if you don't mind? I like the occasional G&T."

SJ held out her glass. What the hell. She was talking to her sister again for the first time in nearly five years. If that wasn't cause for celebration, she didn't know what was.

With the bottle of gin in one hand and a half empty bottle of tonic in the other, Alison manoeuvred her out into the garden and SJ saw a teenage girl sitting on the grass, texting rapidly into a mobile. Her blond hair was cut into a short bob – she looked exactly like Alison had done at the same age. SJ supposed it wasn't surprising. That was genetics for you. Out of nowhere, she felt a pang for the child she might never have.

"Sophie," Alison called, and the girl glanced up. "Come and say hello to Auntie SJ."

"What for? She's never been interested in me."

I deserve that, SJ thought, feeling her heels sinking into her parents' lawn and her heart sinking with them. "Leave it," she murmured. "She's right – I haven't been much of an auntie."

"Sophie. Where are your manners? Come here now."

The girl rose reluctantly and came across, her beautiful face mutinous. She had deep blue eyes and high cheekbones and a mouth that SJ guessed was more attractive when her lips weren't so tightly pursed.

"Hello." She stared SJ out, daring her to smile, so SJ decided not to bother and finished her refill instead. There was a small silence while she struggled for something to say. "How's school?" sounded too trite and auntie-ish. Likewise did, "Long time, no see." She felt her face burn under her niece's cold gaze. In the end she settled for, "Sorry I haven't seen you for so long. We'll have to catch up sometime."

But not now – definitely not now. Possibly later, when she'd consumed a great deal more alcohol and was feeling less paranoid and insecure.

Her phone buzzed in her bag with the arrival of a text and, grateful for the distraction, SJ hooked it out, saw it was Dorothy, and switched it off. She'd sort out what she was going to say to Dorothy later, too.

"Where's your brother?" Alison asked Sophie.

"The last time I saw him he was having a fag behind the greenhouse."

SJ almost dropped her glass as she remembered last night's dream. Perhaps it had been a premonition, after all.

"He'd better not be smoking." Alison's voice was sharp and she marched across the lawn. She had the gin so SJ followed her. Oh dear, she felt pretty drunk already. She'd have to watch herself.

Still, at least if Alison was with her she couldn't be chatting up Tom, so it wasn't all bad news.

Kevin wasn't behind the greenhouse. If he had any sense he'd have seen his mother coming and scarpered. Not that Alison looked as though she'd be easily put off. She poked around behind the nettles that grew rife at the bottom of the garden – their mother's boot-camp regime obviously didn't extend this far – and SJ wondered with a growing sense of unreality if Alison seriously expected to find her errant son in their midst.

At least she and her sister hadn't grown up in this house, hence there were no memories here of shared fights and childhood happenings. SJ wasn't sure

242

whether that was a good or bad thing. She'd never liked this house much. Ex-local authority and solidly built, it was drab in both shape and design. The only thing it had going for it was the hundred foot garden, which had been an allotment when their parents had moved in.

"The little sod better not have been smoking," Alison muttered, and SJ noticed her neck and collar bones were already a little flushed from gin. She'd only had half a glass. Or perhaps that was embarrassment at seeing her after all this time. She wondered idly whether Alison would apologise. Perhaps she felt she didn't need to. SJ didn't imagine she'd been beating herself up all this time over sleeping with Derek.

"So what's been happening with you then, SJ?" Alison sat on a wrought iron bench, which had obviously been polished for the occasion, and patted the space beside her. "Let's have a catch up before we do the socialising bit. It's been ages."

SJ sat beside her, but before she could open her mouth Alison was off again.

"Where shall we start? Shall I go first? Did Mum tell you about my new salon? I've got this great little place in Wanstead. Not big or anything, but brilliant for passing trade. Dad helped me do it up – it's got this marble-effect floor and I had these gold taps fitted, not real gold obviously." Alison's laugh tinkled across the balmy air. "But you do need to project the right image, don't you? I think it's very important. Oh, and you'll never guess who came in the other day." She paused for dramatic effect, but not quite long enough for SJ to ask who. "Only Adam Macclesfield."

Adam who?

"He's the lead singer of *Empty Vessel* – they're a rock band, you must have heard of them. They are

243

soooo IN. He's absolutely gorgeous. Shorter than he looks on stage. Aren't they always? Mind you, everyone's short compared to us lanky things, aren't they?"

Her laugh tinkled again. The gin and tonic she still hadn't finished had obviously gone straight to her head. SJ wondered if it was too soon to ask for a refill.

"He only came in to enquire about Botox – do you believe that? I wondered if those lips of his were real – he looks like a young Mick Jagger. Mind you, we'll have to be very discreet if he wants it done. It's not the sort of thing I want the girls to go gossiping about. If word got out that his sexy pout is nothing but Botox, then my reputation would be on the line."

Not to mention his reputation, SJ reflected. "Mmm," she murmured, thinking it wasn't so bad sitting here in the early evening sun listening to her sister talk trivia. The gin had dulled her nervousness. She might even offer some personal information of her own in a minute. That's if she could get a word in edgeways. Not that she could compete with gold taps and rock stars.

Above the marquee the sky was clear blue and beyond the surrounding rooftops it was almost lilac. SJ lit a cigarette and stretched her arms above her head – she was starting to feel very relaxed. She could fall asleep out here. Curl up on the bench and wake up when the party was all over. The party she'd been dreading all these weeks, which had turned out not to be so bad after all. Why had she been so worried?

"I suppose we ought to get back," Alison was saying. "Do you want another gin to take with you? Once Auntie Edie spots the bottle we'll have had it. Between you and me, Mum thinks she's a right old

244

soak. Mind you, you're not doing badly, are you? Do you always drink so much?"

"I haven't had a drink for well over a month," SJ said truthfully, holding out her glass. She might as well get shot for a sheep as a lamb. She wasn't sure that was quite the right expression – but what the hell. She got to her feet a little unsteadily, and traipsed after her sister.

She could cope now. The drink was helping, not hindering. She took another deep drag on her fag. She could cope with whatever the party chucked at her. In fact, she couldn't wait.

Bring it on.

Chapter Twenty-Eight

The marquee wasn't as big as it looked from outside, perhaps because a lot of people were shoe-horned into it, all of them talking animatedly.

It was baking beneath the canvas, and the air smelt of mown grass and real ale – most of the marquee's occupants were downing pints of the stuff. SJ caught the odd phrase as she and Alison weaved beneath the red and white striped heat.

"Best flights money can buy – I tell you, it's worth the investment."

"I couldn't believe it when he threw that triple twenty – but you've gotta hand it to him. Old Charlie always comes up with the goods."

"Bloody darts," Alison said, close to her ear. "Dad must have invited the whole team. They've probably got a board set up in here somewhere. Mum wouldn't let them put one in the house."

SJ looked around for it and tripped over a guide rope.

"Whoops – steady," Alison giggled, grabbing her arm and saving her from ending up flat on her face.

"It's these heels," SJ said, thinking it was a miracle she hadn't spilled any of her drink. She really must get a grip. She felt as though she'd been here hours, but a quick glance at her slightly blurred watch face told her it was barely six thirty.

She and Alison elbowed their way between the beer-bellied darts players and their equally large wives until they were standing in one corner of the marquee.

"What do you think of the lights? I helped Dad set them up last night." Alison gestured towards the red and white spotlights that were stretched on wires just beneath the canvas ceiling. They didn't look as if they'd be up to the job of anything other than giving a muted glow when the sun went down.

"Must have taken some doing," SJ said, wishing suddenly for the comfort of Tom. Where was he anyway? Oh, yes, in the house. She really ought to get back to him. He'd be wondering where she was.

"I think I should find Tom. He doesn't know anyone."

"He knows Mum and Dad. Don't worry about him. He'll be fine. Do you want another drink? Oh, just a sec. There's Kevin. He's got a bloody pint of lager in his hand, the little sod. Honestly, SJ, that child will be the death of me. Never have kids. They're not worth it. Stay there. I've got to sort him out."

"Okay," SJ said, no longer sure what she was saying okay to: a drink; not having kids; or staying put. Possibly all three. She sank down onto a handy garden chair, lit another fag and watched Alison thread her way gracefully towards a tall figure whose face was obscured by a hood but who very definitely had a pint in one hand – and a fag in the other. SJ felt a wave of sympathy – poor Kevin had obviously thought he'd be safe amongst the beer-swilling darts players, and was blissfully unaware his mother was on his case.

Unfortunately someone had moved across her line of vision so she could no longer see what was going on. Doubtless Alison would give her all the gory details later. And at least it was someone else who was in trouble for a change instead of her.

247

SJ wasn't aware how much time had passed. It was all a bit of a blur. One or two people came and talked to her, although she couldn't remember much of the conversations. When they realised she didn't know anything about darts they drifted away again. Although one nice man brought her a pint to be going on with – as she looked like she'd run out.

"Terrible about the guy who shot all those people in America," he said, handing it over.

"Mmm." She smiled benignly and after a while he went away. She watched a bee buzzing around the tap of the beer barrel. She hoped no one would get stung and kill the bee. She liked bees, with their black and yellow honey-full bodies. If anything, the volume of voices had increased since she came in. She couldn't hear any individual conversations, just a babble of sound, which reminded her of being at a swimming pool with her head beneath the water. She was surprised the neighbours hadn't complained. Perhaps her parents had invited them too.

Every so often the nagging thought that she should be somewhere else surfaced, but SJ couldn't remember where the somewhere else may be, so she stayed put until the need to go to the loo became urgent and she realised she'd have to head back to the house.

The freshness of the evening air was a welcome relief after the muggy heat of the beer tent and the lawn felt squishy beneath her feet. For a moment SJ's head spun and she paused to get her bearings. The lights of the house seemed miles away. She made slow progress towards them. It was like wading through quicksand. The brush of something against her calves was a shock – she didn't remember the grass being that long.

Glancing downwards, she was amazed to see she'd wandered off the lawn and was standing in a flowerbed. Mum would kill her. Hastily, she brushed earth off her shoes, reinstated two flattened plants by leaning them against their associates and continued her journey, the urge to pee growing with every step. Hopefully no one would be in the loo; she was close to bursting.

As she drew nearer the lit kitchen window she could see her mother deep in conversation with a woman she didn't recognise. There was no sign of Tom. Yes, of course, that's where she should be – with Tom, because he didn't know anyone. There was no sign of Alison either. Oh well, she'd have to sort that out in a minute.

No one was in the bathroom. Thank you, God. The relief of emptying her bursting bladder was marvellous. Her mother hadn't spotted her going past the kitchen doorway and up the stairs either. Thank you, God, again. "Good old God, I'm sorry I called you a miserable old bugger. You know I didn't mean it."

SJ washed her hands and then, realising her shoes still had bits of earth clinging to the heels, rinsed them off in the sink, and dried them on a fluffy white towel. Hmm, that hadn't been such a bright idea. The towel now looked filthy. She contemplated stuffing it in her bag and sneaking it into the washing basket downstairs, but her bag was way too small for the stuff already crammed into it, let alone a towel.

Plan B was to rearrange the towel on the rail so the dirty bits weren't showing. Mission accomplished. You'd never know it wasn't pristine. SJ giggled as she put her shoes back on, unlocked the bathroom door –

which took several attempts for some reason – and stepped out into the hall.

She could hear voices coming from her parents' bedroom – the soft musical notes of a woman's voice and the deeper muffled sound of a man's. SJ leant against the wall to catch her breath, a horrible feeling of foreboding stealing through her. What if it was Alison and Tom?

That was pretty unlikely. Tom had already told her he didn't fancy Alison. She frowned. No, he hadn't. She hadn't actually seen him since they'd been introduced, so he couldn't have done. She was getting her wires tangled. It had been Derek who said he didn't fancy Alison. She'd believed him – and look where that had got her.

It would be best to investigate. She made her way along the landing towards her parents' bedroom. Damn walls. She was sure they weren't usually that close together – she kept bouncing off them.

Outside her parents' room, she paused again. She could hear soft giggling now. It sounded like Alison. SJ felt her heart sink – all that being nice to her earlier and getting her drinks had just been a ploy. Well, no bloody way was she getting away with it this time.

With adrenalin pounding through her very soul, SJ flung open the door, tripped over a coat that was on the floor and sprawled headlong into a mirrored chest of drawers that was much closer to the door than she remembered it being and also, for some reason, not against the wall. There was an almighty crash as the chest of drawers, a bedside light on top of it, several small bottles and a box of her mother's jewellery, tipped backwards under SJ's weight and hit the floor.

SJ ended up on the carpet beside it, tangled up in the wire flex from the lamp, which had gone out – although she wasn't sure it had ever been on – and with a shower of her mother's beads around her neck and a bottle of her mother's favourite scent by her nose. Prada – she'd have recognised its distinctive smell anywhere. In the dim light that filtered through the undrawn curtains she could make out the outline of a couple in the coat-covered bed. Neither of them was big enough to be Tom. She didn't think either of them was Alison either. In the split second of silence that filled the room after the crash, SJ tried to refocus her eyes.

"Is that you, Auntie SJ?" came a small shocked voice from the direction of the bed.

SJ closed her eyes and groaned. No wonder it had sounded like Alison – it was Sophie. The poor girl must have slipped up here for a cuddle with her boyfriend and – judging by the pounding of numerous feet on the stairs – she'd just drawn the attention of half a dozen people to what should have been a private event.

Oh My God. She certainly wasn't going to win any favourite auntie competitions now.

Chapter Twenty-Nine

Tom's voice was the first one she heard, closely followed by her mother's. "Whatever's happened? Is that you, Sophie?"

Light flooded the room and SJ closed her eyes, working on the principle that if she couldn't see them, they couldn't see her. This worked for all of thirty seconds. Then she felt hands on her shoulders.

"SJ, for heaven's sake. Are you drunk?" Tom's voice was edged with panic.

"*Courshe* I'm not drunk." Batting his hands away, she sat up, which was a mistake as the room started to spin.

"Someone moved the drawers," SJ protested, stumbling to her feet, but no one took any notice. She could hear her mother berating Sophie and whoever the poor girl was in bed with.

"It's disgraceful behaviour, my girl. Your mother is going to be very disappointed. You should be studying for your GCSEs."

What on earth did GCSEs have to do with anything, SJ thought, as she bent to gather up beads and scent bottles?

"I'm really sorry. This is all my fault." She'd been about to say she thought Alison was trying to seduce Tom, but she'd caused enough mayhem already.

As Tom and her father heaved the chest of drawers into an upright position once more, SJ noticed the mirror was cracked. A diagonal line zigzagged across the middle and she caught a glimpse of her rumpled reflection. Distorted and ugly. Her hair had come loose from its chignon and her mascara was smudged beneath her eyes. The all-day lipstick that Tanya had recommended was the only part of that still looked pristine, which proved what a good liar lipstick could be.

"Do you think we'd better go?" she asked Tom.

"I think we'd better get you sobered up," he said with a quiet sigh.

SJ and Tom were sitting in the conservatory, sipping coffee. To her immense relief, no one else at the party seemed to have noticed anything amiss. There was a lot of drunken chatter going on and one or two people smiled in her direction. SJ smiled back happily. She couldn't have upset too many people then. With a bit of luck no one except her immediate family would ever find out about the little incident upstairs.

The only thing that was slightly puzzling was that it was now ten thirty. So she'd lost a couple of hours somewhere. How very odd. She had a sudden vivid image of talking to Auntie Edie, who at this moment was snoring in the cane chair across the other side of the room, an almost empty gin bottle at her side.

Fragments of their conversation bounced into her head.

"Hello, love, one for the road?" Auntie Edie looked up at her through bloodshot eyes.

"I probably shouldn't," SJ murmured, sneaking a quick glance over her shoulder to see where Tom was.

Struck with a sudden brainwave, she held out her coffee cup for the gin.

"Oh, go on then – just to keep you company."

Tom would think she was still safely drinking coffee. What an excellent plan. Why hadn't she thought of it earlier? What was the point of being an alcoholic if you didn't have some sneaky back up plans in place?

Puzzled, SJ looked back at the still snoring Aunt Edie. When exactly had that conversation taken place? She didn't recall talking to Edie at all this evening, apart from when she'd first arrived. She didn't recall being in the conservatory either until now. She took another sip of coffee. Definitely coffee, and not gin. Perhaps she'd imagined it. Disorientated, she glanced through the connecting doors into the lounge. A pair of red balloons, one half deflated, lay forlornly by the door and another fragment of memory flicked into her mind.

She'd been standing in front of the decimated buffet table, which looked as though a horde of hungry pigs had descended on it and had a good snout around. All that was left were a few egg and cress sandwiches with curling edges. Funny how egg and cress sandwiches were always the last to go. SJ scooped them up and ate them. Pity about the salmon – salmon was her favourite. Oh well. There were a couple of pieces of Alison's vegetarian quiche left too. She ate these and felt almost normal again, although she was aware that it took a long time to get back to her chair.

And no sooner had she settled down back in it than one of her mother's Cat Protection League friends came into the room with a plate held aloft.

"Mushroom vol au vent, SJ?" She smiled as she strolled across the terracotta carpet. "There's not much else left, I don't think."

Tom shifted beside her and she was jolted back to the present. Perhaps she should go and check the buffet

254

table and see if she'd imagined that bit too. But she wasn't sure she could walk in a straight line.

Instead, she slipped her fingers into his. "Are you enjoying yourself?"

His hand felt tense and he didn't meet her eyes. "What do YOU think?" What was that supposed to mean? Why did he have to answer a question with a question? Life would be a lot less confusing if people were more honest with each other. Honesty was a good thing – a very noble and lovely thing. No one should have guilty little secrets eating them up from the inside out. If more people were honest about their innermost thoughts and feelings then the world would be a much happier place.

The next thing she was aware of was being in the kitchen at twenty to twelve, surrounded by a circle of her family. Tom, Mum and Dad, Alison, Sophie – even the errant Kevin was there.

He was hoodless now, and minus both fag and pint of lager. SJ focused on him with difficulty and tried to pick up the thread of conversation. They'd obviously all been talking about something, but she had no idea what. She felt disorientated – as if she'd just woken up, but she couldn't have just woken. She was standing up. It was very disconcerting.

Kevin looked like he was drinking orange juice. Probably a cover; you could hide all sorts in orange juice. SJ gave him a wobbly smile and decided to err on the side of humour. "I bet there's gin in that orange, isn't there, love?"

Kevin, who had the same blue eyes as his mother and sister, didn't smile back. No one was smiling. They were all looking at her with quiet sorrow in their eyes.

255

Or was it sympathy? SJ began to feel uncomfortable. What was going on? She'd obviously missed something.

Tom, who was closer than anyone else, ran a hand through his hair and sighed.

"I'm really sorry. I don't know what to say. I don't know what to do with her. I just don't know what to do about all this."

"Don't you worry yourself about it now, Tom. It'll all seem brighter in the morning. You can sort it out properly then – work things out between you. I'm sure there's a logical explanation." That was her mother, and it took SJ a few seconds to realise they must be talking about her. She glanced at Tom in puzzlement. All she'd done was ask Kevin if he had gin in his orange – it was hardly the crime of the century.

She opened her mouth to say something else and then, to her dismay, the cupboard she was leaning against moved sideways violently and she found herself on the kitchen floor with her head wedged against the fridge. A magnet of Blackpool Tower lay alongside her nose and she was aware of her mother's voice.

"Oh dear, oh dear. You could stay, Tom, if it's easier. I don't want her to be sick in your nice car."

Charming. She didn't even feel sick. "I'm not drunk…" she began, as the words ebbed and flowed somewhere above her. "I haven't touched a drop for three hours."

Or at least that's what she wanted to say. She wasn't sure she'd managed to get the words out. Her head was pressed against something hard. Frowning, she concentrated on focusing her eyes once more. Success. She could see a collection of fluff in between

256

the fridge and the sink unit, and what looked like a pea that must have rolled under there.

An escapee pea. There was a pun there somewhere. An ESCAPEA, no less. SJ giggled at her own wit, and entertained herself with visions of it hopping off her father's plate, just before it was about to meet its maker and rolling under the fridge to hide. And now the poor little pea was all alone – all alone with the dust and the fluff on the kitchen floor.

A refugee pea. No, a refupea – no, that didn't have the same ring to it. Suddenly the pea's fate struck SJ as terribly, terribly sad. No doubt it had thought it was off to a new and better life, but had ended up in the darkness all alone.

Chapter Thirty

SJ came slowly into wakefulness and wished she hadn't. She felt like death – in fact death would have been preferable. Her whole body hurt. Her stomach felt like an empty churning cement mixer. It rumbled and gurgled and there was a very unpleasant stink in the room.

She was lying on the sofa in their lounge. There was a red plastic bucket by her side – that was the source of the stink. Ash was curled up on the rug by the fireplace. And Tom was sitting in an armchair watching her. Not speaking, not moving, just looking at her with an expression she'd never before seen on his face. Disgust.

She smiled uncertainly. He didn't smile back. He just carried on looking at her. SJ began to feel unnerved.

"What?" she said at last, moving her head a fraction and wishing she hadn't because several demons with pickaxes were hammering away inside her skull.

"I could ask you the same question." Tom spoke in a flat grey monotone. "What? Yeah, what, SJ? What the fuck did you think you were doing? Have you any idea of the hurt you've caused?"

SJ hadn't, but the fact he'd said 'fuck' – which he never said – in the same flat grey voice he'd used to say 'what?' gave her a pretty good clue she'd upset him.

"What did I do?" She spoke very quietly and slowly to cause the least possible movement.

"Do you really not remember?"

"No," she whispered, wanting very much to cry. She must have done something really bad for him to be looking at her – speaking to her – like that.

"Did it involve taking off my clothes?"

He shook his head, and SJ felt about under the duvet and discovered she still had them on. Well, that was something. She'd have hated to hear she'd performed a striptease for her parents and their guests.

Her mind flicked back over the previous evening: the bench with Alison; the marquee with the darts players; the bedroom with Sophie – that had been quite bad, but surely not unforgivable; the conversation with Aunt Edie; the kitchen at the end. The scenes rolled over in her mind, but there was nothing that struck her as being particularly awful. Not awful enough to make Tom look at her like this. Hang on a minute – hadn't she knocked over a dresser in the bedroom? That had caused one hell of a disturbance.

"I know I had too much to drink. I'm sorry. But it was a party – you're supposed to have too much to drink at parties. You said so yourself."

"There's a difference between having one too many and drinking the whole place dry." There was contempt in his voice. SJ flinched.

"I'll give Mum a ring and apologise later. Don't worry. She'll understand."

"She already understands. You told her you were an alcoholic, SJ. You told a whole roomful of people – including most of the darts club – you were an alcoholic."

"Oh."

"Yes, 'Oh'." Tom's voice still hadn't risen from flat grey. It was disconcerting and she was beginning to

259

feel sick again. The proximity of the bucket wasn't helping.

"You also told them WHY you were an alcoholic."

Unease rose alongside the sickness. "What do you mean? What did I say, exactly?"

"You said it was my fault you'd started drinking. You said you'd never loved me. That you'd only married me because you didn't want to get hurt again. You said the love of your life had been Derek, but after what Alison did, you'd realised you couldn't carry on being married to him, so you settled for me. You said you had to drink to blot out the pain of settling for second best."

SJ didn't say anything. Now she understood why he was speaking in grey. If he let any emotion into his voice he would break. She could see the deep raw pain in his face. His arms rested along the arms of the chair, his hands apparently relaxed, but his fingers were trembling.

SJ had never seen Tom in such pain before. She had never seen anyone in such pain. And it was down to her. It was all down to her.

"I'm so sorry," she whispered, knowing it wasn't enough. Nothing she could say would ever be enough.

By the fireplace, Ash had put one paw over his nose. It was a position he often lay in, like a bird with its head tucked under its wing, but at this moment it seemed to SJ as though he was trying to blot out the sounds of their voices. Blot out the pain that was filling the room like a great black shroud. A shroud gently placed by unseen hands over the death of their marriage.

"It's not true," she said, hating herself for it, but wanting to say something – anything – to take away the pain she'd caused.

"Isn't it? I'm not so sure, SJ. You haven't wanted me much lately, have you? Physically, I mean. I may be naïve, but I'm not completely stupid."

There was no denying this. SJ groaned. She was going to be sick. Stumbling to her feet, she just made it to the bucket and, heedless now of her husband's presence, she emptied a little more of the poison from her body. Retching into the bucket, heaping more foulness over what it already contained. When, gasping and beaten, and still with the taste of bile in her nostrils and throat, she'd finally finished, she rose weakly and, without looking at Tom, carried the bucket through to the toilet where she disposed of the contents and bleached it. Oh, that she could bleach out her body and mouth in the same way.

Feeling marginally better, SJ gulped down a handful of Nurofen, found a re-hydration sachet she kept for hangover emergencies in the cupboard and forced herself to drink a pint of water. The effort of so much activity drained her and she went slowly back into the lounge.

Tom was sitting where she'd left him. Wary of approaching him because she knew he would shrug her away – and she wouldn't have blamed him – she sat on the settee again, tucking her knees beneath her like a child.

"I'm really sorry, Tom. I was way out of order. I always talk rubbish when I'm drunk. I know some people tell the truth when they're drunk, but I don't, I never have."

"So none of what you said last night was true? It was all drivel, was it? Just because you'd poured half a brewery down your neck?"

She nodded vehemently. She had no memory of saying the things Tom had just told her, which terrified her. How could she have caused such devastation without even knowing she had done it? The only saving grace was that she doubted her drunken ramblings could be proved one way or another. All that mattered now was to take the pain off his face. She would spend the rest of her life making up for his pain. She would have to.

'What? Even though you know in your heart of hearts that what you said is true?' whispered a voice in her mind. Not *Alco* this time – he'd been conspicuous by his absence during yesterday's spree – but the voice of her conscience. The voice of her conscience continued relentlessly.

'Even though you know you DID marry him because you didn't want to be hurt again? Do you really think it's better to continue with this lie than tell him the truth?'

SJ became aware Tom was speaking again. "So it's not true about our friend, Michael, being a cross-dresser either, then? That he likes to dress up as a woman and have people call him Lizzie?"

SJ stared at him in horror.

Before she could deny it, Tom went on softly, "Where did that come from, SJ? Is it some warped little fantasy you've got? Perhaps, deep down, it turns you on thinking of men dressing up in women's clothes. Does it make us more vulnerable or something? More easy to manipulate, maybe?"

262

SJ closed her eyes, knowing she had to stop him. Stop this before it got any further. She had to convince Tom he was right – that her ramblings about Lizzie were the product of an unbalanced mind. Even if he thought he'd married some kind of pervert. That was preferable – anything was preferable to him knowing it was true.

"Of course it's not true about Michael. That's ridiculous. My God, I really was drunk, wasn't I…?" She tried a casual little giggle, which came out as a sob.

Tom raised his eyebrows. "I don't know what to believe any more. But I am going to find out." He glanced at his watch and stood up, a slight frown on his face.

"Where are you going?"

"I'm playing squash with Michael at eleven thirty. Had you forgotten? I'm not surprised. You never did think of anyone but yourself."

"Please don't say anything, Tom. He'll be embarrassed – it's such a mad idea. Please just forget I ever mentioned it." She was gabbling, but she couldn't seem to stop.

Tom jangled his car keys thoughtfully. "Michael won't be embarrassed. I know him better than that. It'll probably give him a good laugh." He paused in the doorway. "Unless, of course, it's true! In which case I'll assume the same of the rest. I'll assume that far from spouting rubbish when you're drunk, you actually tell the truth."

SJ caught up with him at the front door, her head spinning with sickness and shame. "Please, Tom, don't say anything to Michael. It's stupid, you know it is."

She held onto his arm, partly to stop herself falling and partly to stop him from going. But he brushed away her hand, his eyes cold.

"Yeah – it sounds stupid, doesn't it? But me thinks *the lady doth protest too much.* See you later, SJ. Your head should have cleared a bit by then and we can have a proper chat."

He unlatched the front door and she made another grab for his arm. "Tom, please? Wait. I just need you to listen to me for a minute. Please?"

Barely glancing at her, he shook her off, more forcibly this time. "I've had enough of listening to you. I thought I'd made that clear." The front door slammed in her face.

Shocked, she fumbled to get it open again. Her fingers weren't working properly. Neither were her legs. It was like being in one of those dreams where she was trying to run from the baddies and her feet were stuck in mud. By the time she got the door open Tom was already in his car, the engine running. She tripped down the last step, only partially regaining her balance and almost falling, putting out her hands to save herself. "Fuck it."

Tom gave her a look of such disdain that, even from behind glass, it froze her into stillness.

"Wait," she shouted, straightening up, brushing gravel from her hands, but he was already reversing out onto the road and driving away.

She ran back inside, adrenaline sharpening her movements. Where was her phone? She had to phone Tanya. She had to warn her that Tom was coming to see Michael.

She finally found her phone in the bottom of her bag. There were three missed calls from Dorothy. Shit.

264

She wasn't looking forward to talking to Dorothy. With sweating fingers she pressed Tanya's number.

"The mobile you have phoned is switched off."
Shit, shit, shit!

They didn't answer the landline very often but she tried it anyway, listening to it ring and ring, visualising Michael looking at Tanya. *"Are you going to get that?"* *"No. Leave it. It'll just be someone trying to sell us something."* And then she realised they wouldn't be there anyway. Or at least Michael wouldn't. He would meet Tom at the sports centre. Tanya often went with him for a swim.

Maybe a text. No, she couldn't possibly explain this in a text. She would have to drive over to the sports centre. She would be over the limit but hey, how much worse could it get? No one was likely to stop her. She could drive in a straight line. She *hoped* she could drive in a straight line.

Her car keys weren't on the hook. Where the hell were her car keys? She couldn't even remember the last time she'd driven her car.

They weren't in her bag, or in the pockets of any coat she could remember wearing lately – and time was running out. Tom had been gone ten minutes. He would nearly be at the centre. He would stroll in and Michael would smile at him, all unsuspecting, blithely unaware that his most private and intimate secret was about to be chucked rudely in his face. Sweet gentle Michael. SJ couldn't bear it. Breath catching in her throat, she began to sob.

Blurting out the intimacies of her best friend's marriage was unforgivable. Tanya had trusted her implicitly and she'd let her down. Not just let her down, she had betrayed her. The best friend she had ever had.

265

She might just as well have stabbed her in the heart. In fact Tanya would probably have found that less painful.

Still sobbing, she sank to her knees on the floor by the front door. She hadn't thought she could feel any worse than when she'd opened her eyes an hour earlier, but she did. She felt worse than she'd ever felt in her life.

She had let everyone down. She would never be able to make up for the hurt she'd caused. Tanya and Michael would never forgive her and she would never be able to forgive herself. The future yawned ahead of her like a massive, accusatory black hole and she knew she couldn't face it.

She couldn't stand the pain. Not for another hour, not for another second. Getting unsteadily to her feet, she went across the hall and stood in the doorway of the lounge. Tom had put a new bottle of gin on the optic last week. She had no idea why – he didn't even drink gin, and she'd given up. But she'd blown that one, hadn't she? Just like she'd blown everything else in her life.

Leaning forward, she unclipped the bottle from the optic and stood it upright on the bar. It was amazing how something that looked so much like water could be so lethal. There was enough here to knock her halfway to oblivion. She hesitated, feeling strangely detached. Oblivion suddenly seemed like a very good option. The only option. How many glasses would it take to get her to oblivion? On autopilot, her movements stiff and jerky like a puppet's, she moved behind the bar and began to take out glasses from the shelf beneath and stand them on the bar.

Four crystal tumblers, two pewter tankards, five little shot glasses Tom used for whiskey chasers if ever

266

he was in the mood, and one commemorative glass with *Sarah-Jane and Tom, married 2009*, inscribed on the side.

She lined them up carefully along the bar. She lined them up in order of size, smallest first. And then she began to fill them up with gin. It reminded her of the dolls' tea parties she and Alison used to have as kids. They had a red plastic tea set back then and they'd used water, not tea, and they would argue over who got the biggest teacup. But gin was far better than either water or tea and, best of all, Alison wasn't here to argue about who got what. Alison wasn't going to get her hands on any of these glasses. They were all for her. All for SJ. Finally, she had found something that Alison couldn't get her hands on.

She smiled as she reached the end of the line. She had rather short-changed the last glass but she didn't suppose that mattered. She also had a thumping headache – but that didn't matter either. Gin was the oldest painkiller in the world. That was what they said, didn't they?

Oblivion – right then. With the same curious sense of detachment she picked up the first glass. It was one of the shot glasses. Its contents were gone in a heartbeat. SJ reached for the next glass. Gin wasn't very nice neat. It was much better with tonic, but she didn't think they had any. And after a while she couldn't taste it anyway.

Oblivion.

She wondered how long it would take.

Chapter Thirty-One

Beep, beep, beep. Beep, beep, beep. All she could hear was the steady rhythm of the monitor, measuring her heartbeats. *Beep, beep, beep.* Proof positive that she was still alive, although she ought not to be. By rights she should be dead. For a few seconds anger surged and the monitor quickstepped to its rhythm. Why hadn't they left her to it? Why had they bothered to resuscitate all this heartbreak?

"Are you conscious …" Doctor Maria Costello was asking her now, "… of the danger you placed yourself in? Last Sunday afternoon you drank almost a full litre bottle of gin. I'd like you to tell me why."

SJ shook her head. She couldn't stop sobbing. She was holding the blue tablecloth-like sheet to her face like a comforter, but it wasn't helping.

The doctor held out a box of tissues and SJ tugged out a handful and wiped her eyes, but she couldn't stop the pain. It poured out of her, on and on and on.

"Take your time, Sarah-Jane. We've got plenty of time. You were at home, do you remember?" the doctor prompted gently and SJ nodded.

"What day is it?"

"It's Tuesday afternoon. Tuesday 7th September."

Oh God, so it was after the party then. Her parents' party – that must have been on Saturday. Of course it had been on Saturday. She remembered standing in the kitchen with her family all looking at her in disapproval (Kevin had been there) and there was something about

268

a pea. Had she been lying by the fridge? Had she imagined that bit? Please let her have imagined that bit.

Another more disturbing memory crawled in and she tried to sit up, but it hurt so much she gave up and lay down again. "Are my parents here?"

"They've been here for the last two days. They've just gone to get something to eat. Your husband's gone with them. They'll be back very soon, I'm sure."

Two days. Where had the last two days gone? "Oh my God," she said, finally. "Oh my God."

SJ didn't know how much longer the doctor sat there. Or what else either of them said. Time seemed to blur in and out. At some point she was aware of her parents coming back in, of her mother sitting by the bed and stroking her head like she'd done when she was ill as a child: a rhythmic, soothing touch that sent her drifting back off into blackness.

She was aware of Tom being there some of the time, too – pale and rigid and silent. She closed her eyes when she saw Tom. She didn't want to face any of them. It was all too painful and raw and every time she cried – which seemed to happen all the time – it hurt a little bit more. She was still only getting snippets of memories. Fragments of the party and fragments about the conversation she'd had with Tom when she'd begged him not to go round to Michael's to ask him about the cross-dressing. She would have given a lot to be able to have lost that conversation but she guessed blackouts didn't work like that. You couldn't pick and choose which parts of your life you wiped out.

Sometime around the Tuesday evening – or it could have been the Wednesday evening, she'd lost

269

track – SJ opened her eyes and saw Kit and Dorothy standing beside her bed.

"How are you doing, hen?" Dorothy gave her a huge smile, the warmth of which made her want to cry again, but which also made everything suddenly seem more bearable.

"Food's improved by the look of it," Dorothy remarked, sniffing the air, and SJ realised that it was teatime and that hospital staff were bustling around with trays and cutlery. At some point she'd been moved out of ICU and on to a main ward. She didn't remember that happening.

Kit smiled at her too, pulled up two chairs, their legs scraping the floor, and gestured for Dorothy to sit down. He was wearing jeans and a white T-shirt and a smart brown leather jacket she'd never seen before. He looked tanned, although not all that relaxed. She had the feeling he was uncomfortable in a hospital.

"You missed your appointment," he said, raising his eyebrows, "so I thought I'd drop by."

"That's well beyond the call of duty," she managed, embarrassed, but also hugely pleased to see him.

"Duty doesn't come into it," he said, and rummaged in his pocket. "I was going to get you some grapes, but I thought these might be more appropriate." He gave her a little paper bag of what turned out to be boiled sweets. "Good for throats," he went on conversationally.

"Thanks." She blinked. "I think my throat might just about manage one of these."

"Not much fun having your stomach pumped – even when you are out for the count." Dorothy's voice was matter of fact. "I was awake for two of mine. I

270

swear they were rougher the second time when they forced the tube down my throat. Mind you, the nurses had all been going off to a party when I turned up on the ward, half dead. I was holding up the proceedings. They weren't very happy."

SJ blinked. Trust Dorothy to upstage her. "I am never having my stomach pumped again," she said. "I am never drinking again either. God, even the thought of it …"

Dorothy leaned forward and touched her arm. Her face was serene. "One day at a time, hen, that's all you need to worry about. Is it okay to have one of those?" SJ held out the bag and Dorothy helped herself. "Thanks, pet."

SJ looked at Kit. "When I first came to S.A.A.D I saw a man coming out of the pub across the road. It wasn't even lunchtime, but he was totally pissed. He could barely walk. I didn't think I was the same as him. I didn't think I was a proper alcoholic."

"And what do you think now?" Kit asked, his dark eyes holding hers.

"I think I just haven't got quite as far down the path as that man. Well, I hadn't," she amended.

"Well, as you know, alcoholism's a progressive disease," Kit said quietly. "There are stages. Some of them can last for years."

"You don't have to do this on your own," Dorothy put in. "I've made some of the best friends of my life in AA. In the past I only had drinking buddies. Now I have friendships forged in hell."

"Don't you mean in heaven?" SJ asked her with a weak smile.

"No, my darling, I don't." Dorothy paused to crunch her sweet. "Friendships forged in the fires of

271

hell last a lot longer than the friendships you might find in some namby-pamby heaven."

"Some people liken alcoholism to being on a train," Kit said, helping himself to a boiled sweet, the leather of his jacket creaking as he moved. "Once you're on it the ultimate destination is death. But you don't have to stay on the train. You can get off it any time you like."

"It's a pretty straight choice at the end of the day," Dorothy said. "Admit you're an alcoholic and give up drinking – or carry on drinking and die." She smiled sweetly. "It's a tough one, I know. It took me ages to make up my mind. But I think you might be a bit more sensible than me."

SJ shuddered. "I'm not very sensible," she said. "But I do know …" Her voice cracked a little as she looked into their concerned faces. "I do know now that I want to get off the train."

Chapter Thirty-Two

"I blame myself. I should have seen it coming. I should have stopped you. I should have been around more." Tom sat at their kitchen table, his head in his hands, his voice full of self-recrimination.

It was awful. And it was made more awful by the fact they'd had this conversation many times over the past few weeks. She'd been out of hospital for over a month, but however hard SJ tried to move on from what had happened Tom wouldn't let her.

His initial anger and distress had morphed into an endless inward look at himself. As if he was personally responsible for her overdose. It was hard to cope with and although she'd told him over and over there was nothing he could have done – she was responsible for her own actions – he couldn't seem to accept it.

SJ wasn't sure how many more times she could bear to go through the same old cycle, but she tried again anyway.

"You know that's not true, Tom. I was the one who poured the stuff down my throat, both on that Sunday and on all the other days before it. My alcoholism has nothing to do with you."

He looked at her and she could see herself reflected in his eyes. A small brown person, somewhat diminished – that's how she'd seen herself lately. Thanks to Kit.

The last time she'd seen him he'd put a basket of stones on the table in front of her and asked her to pick out the one she thought represented herself.

Slightly bemused, but willing to do anything he asked in the hope it might help, she'd rummaged around and had found herself right at the bottom of the basket. A small brown stone, dull and lifeless – like one of thousands you saw washed up on the beach, its edges rounded into smoothness by the constant pounding of the sea. The shine the water had given it was long gone.

"Why did you pick that stone, SJ?" Kit's gaze had held hers and she'd shrugged. "What is it about that particular stone that reminds you of yourself?"

"There's nothing special about it. It's the same as millions of others, waiting for its moment to shine and sure it will never come."

SJ had surprised herself with these words, so unthinkingly spoken. She'd expected Kit to home straight in on them and talk about self-esteem. They'd already established she had none and it was one of the areas they were supposed to be working on. But instead he'd directed her back to the basket and asked her to pick out everyone else who was important in her life.

Five minutes later, they'd stared at her collection of stones. A shiny white pebble for Alison, a lump of black onyx for Tom, a piece of sandstone for Mum, a chunk of granite for Dad, and a strikingly pretty stone threaded with blue for Tanya. The blue stone had a hole in its centre.

SJ pointed to it and whispered, "That's where her heart should be. Only I plucked it out, didn't I?"

She had phoned Tanya when she'd come out of hospital and Tanya had told her in barely a whisper that she never wanted to see her or hear from her again. And SJ had known that she meant it. There was no going back.

274

"What's important," Kit said, drawing her back to the room, "is the position of the stones. Look at how you've positioned them in relation to each other."

SJ looked and saw what he was getting at. Her own stone – the little brown stone – was set back from the rest. The nearest to it was Tanya's stone. The group of family stones formed a semicircle beyond that, and the furthest away from the brown stone was Tom's.

And now, as she looked at the dark shadows beneath her husband's eyes and the onyx blackness of his hair, she thought yes, Kit Oakley knew a thing or two about psychology. Her counsellor might not be a shrink in a suit but he had got it in one about her perceptions of distance – and he'd never even met her husband.

Only a table separated herself and Tom now, but emotionally they were aeons apart. Always had been and always would be, she was beginning to think. She got up and went across to him, but even when she was touching him, her hand on his shoulder, she didn't feel any closer.

"Maybe you could come along to one of my counselling sessions?"

"I'm not getting my dirty laundry out in front of a stranger. It's bad enough we're in this god-awful situation without spilling it all out in front of someone else."

"But that's what counsellors are for. It's not like we're going to be judged. It really helps to talk things through with someone who knows what they're doing."

Blimey, she'd come a long way since the early days. She believed it now – believed in the power of the spoken word. She should have known about the power of words already, especially when she considered what

275

her job was – or rather her ex-job. That had been another little bombshell God had decided to drop on her.

"Sorry, we're having to cut some of our part time courses this year," her curriculum leader had told her when she'd phoned about her contracts. "Another consequence of government cuts, I'm afraid."

"But my students' pass rate was 98%," SJ had gasped.

"It's no reflection on you. I'm very sorry."

So she was out of a job, too, except for Poetry and a Pint, which didn't make very much profit unless she had more students. Her rapidly decreasing income had hardly registered at the time. It had been insignificant amidst the rest of the chaos in her life.

"Then how about coming to an AA meeting, Tom?" she went on gently. "Or maybe even Al Anon? That's for families."

He shook his head. "I'm not sitting in a room with a bunch of drunks."

"You hardly ever see any drunks," SJ said truthfully. "They're all on coffee – decaf, most of them. Or camomile tea. Or Lapsang Souchong. The ones that are really worried about cross-addiction drink nothing but hot water with a slice of lemon in it."

She was trying to lighten the mood, but she could see from Tom's tense frown she hadn't succeeded.

Realising she still had her hand on his shoulder, which felt as hard and unforgiving as stone, she moved away, perched her bum on the edge of the washing machine and looked at him.

"Do you want us to get a divorce, Tom? Do you think there's any point in carrying on?"

276

It felt weird to be asking him that. Weird to be standing in the warmth of their dream house in their dream kitchen, which was still toast-scented from breakfast, and asking him if he wanted a divorce.

For a moment she let her gaze travel around the untidy room. Their breakfast things were still on the side. There was a smear mark of something on the dishwasher and on the hooks above the kitchen shelf one of the cups was hanging the wrong way round. Tom would have noticed that once, and corrected it. He hated lack of order. A large bluebottle was in its death throes on the terracotta window sill. SJ chewed the nail on her thumb – the only nail she had with some chewing capacity left in it – and wondered what he'd say. Was their marriage in its death throes too? It certainly felt like it.

"I don't know what to think. I keep wondering if this is just a phase. Your alcoholism, I mean." He stumbled over the word and SJ could bear it no longer.

"It's not a phase, Tom. I'll always be an alcoholic, if that's what you mean? For the rest of my life I'll have to go to meetings."

This thought, which had once made her shudder, now calmed her. She felt safe at meetings. For that brief hour and a quarter she knew she wouldn't drink. Neither would she be tempted – there were too many reminders of the devastation it caused. The rooms where she'd once felt out of place – as though she'd stumbled into a nightmare life that wasn't her own – now felt like home.

"I'll always have this problem," she said, more softly. "But it is my problem. You don't have to deal with it."

277

"I don't think I can deal with it." He met her eyes, still shaking his head as if in recognition of his own thoughts. "I've always done what I thought best by us, SJ. I've always worked hard to get the things I thought you wanted."

"And I've always messed it all up again," she said quietly, knowing he was struggling to ask for the truth that was at the heart of all this. Did she love him? Or had she really only married him because she couldn't face being hurt again? Because she'd given up on love?

He screwed up his face. Here it came.

"What you said at the party – about not being in love with me when we got married. Was it true?"

She could see what it had cost him to ask her. Ask her in the coldness of daylight, when there was no glass of wine to hide behind, either for him or for her – when they were on the level playing field of reality. Such courage deserved honesty. There was no point in giving him false hope. Because whatever else had changed within her, she couldn't change the facts.

"I didn't love you in the way I should have done," she said, wishing it could be otherwise. For Tom's sake, as well as hers. He was a good man. He deserved to be loved. Everyone did. Hard as it was, she had to give him the chance to walk away, to find that happiness with someone else.

For a long moment he didn't speak, but his shoulders had slumped. Now it was he who looked diminished. SJ watched him silently.

"I don't want a divorce – not yet, anyway." His voice was gruff with pain and she struggled to keep in her own tears. She'd made self-pity into an art form. It was time to be strong.

"But I think it would be best if we had a trial separation."

"Do you want me to move out?"

He nodded slowly. "I'll pay for you to live somewhere. Give you a chance to get yourself sorted out with another teaching job. It's the least I can do."

It was a generous offer in the circumstances, and she was torn because he couldn't afford it. She'd seen his bank statement when it came with the morning post.

"I'll stay with a friend," SJ suggested. That would be tricky – she didn't think she had any left.

The same thought had obviously occurred to Tom. "You could stay with your parents?" he said.

"Yes, I'm sure Mum would let me have her spare room." She was just as sure she didn't want to go there. Mum had been on her case constantly since the hospital and while SJ wasn't surprised and while she felt terribly guilty that she'd put her parents and Tom and even Alison through such a trauma, she couldn't have faced going back to live at home.

She had put off going round for A Proper Chat too, which was what her mother had been nagging her to do for the last couple of weeks. She said she was busy preparing lesson plans for the coming term. Mum was going to find out that was a lie sooner or later, but the truth was she couldn't face anyone at the moment.

It was difficult enough to look at herself in the mirror, let alone make eye contact with anyone else.

"What about Ash?" Tom's face was freer now – less haggard, as if the decision had lightened him. "I can't look after him – I'm not here enough."

"I'll take him with me." Wherever I go, she added silently. Because no way was Ash going into some dog sanctuary. She might have devastated everyone else in

279

her life, but she wasn't abandoning her beloved dog, too.

"You don't look very well," Tom went on, as if noticing her pallor for the first time.

"My period's due," SJ lied, because this was easier than admitting the thought of being on her own scared her witless. Her marriage might have been for all the wrong reasons, but it had given her security.

"I could nip up the shop and get you some painkillers if you like? Do you need anything else? Are you okay for – you know – other stuff?" He reddened and SJ felt a tug of tenderness.

He still couldn't bring himself to say Tampax – buying them for her was a task he'd avoided for their entire marriage – yet now they were on the rocks, he was offering.

"I'm alright for everything else," SJ said, swallowing a huge lump in her throat. "Thanks anyway."

He nodded, looking mightily relieved and she felt the ache inside her growing into a massive well of despair. However badly they'd started, they had been happy – well, they'd had their moments, but it seemed awfully strange to be ending it like this – two strangers, who'd never really known each other at all.

Chapter Thirty-Three

Dorothy came to the rescue by offering SJ her spare room.

"Thanks, but it's not just me, I come complete with elderly greyhound," SJ said, wanting Dorothy to have all the facts before she committed herself.

"I like dogs."

Hugely relieved, SJ didn't give her another chance to retract her offer and – to Tom's obvious relief – she and Ash moved into Dorothy's terraced house, which was in Bermondsey, not that far from where Tanya and Michael lived.

"I doubt it's what you're used to, but it's big enough for a lass and a wee dog," Dorothy had said, as she'd shown her the spare room, which was modern, with fitted wardrobes and a huge double bed with a lemon-coloured duvet that matched the walls, and a bookcase crammed full of Dorothy's books.

"I'll have plenty of bedtime reading," SJ quipped.

"It'll take you years to get through that lot," Dorothy said with quiet pride. "There's a lifetime of experience between those pages." She'd hesitated in the bedroom doorway. "I don't want you getting drunk and throwing up on the carpet, mind – it's new."

"I'm not drinking any more," SJ had muttered sheepishly, and this had been met with a snort.

"Well, if you've a yen to start it up again, you'd best bear in mind I know every hiding place there is in this house."

One evening, over dinner, Dorothy asked SJ if she fancied going to an AA convention.

"What exactly is an AA convention?"

"It's the same as a meeting – except they get outside speakers and they go on for longer – anywhere between a weekend and a whole week. This one's a mini-convention, so it's just Saturday."

"How much do they cost?" SJ asked, wishing money didn't have to be a consideration for everything, but it was. She hadn't let Tom support her financially; it was time she stood on her own two feet so she'd got a job in a bistro, which she hoped wouldn't have to be permanent.

Although actually it was quite good fun being a waitress again – Mortimer's was a lot more upmarket than Pizza Express. It was the lower half of an Art Deco building in Hackney and had stone floors and white lace tablecloths and a gay Spanish bar manager who enjoyed camping it up.

"Oh, not another recovering blooming alcoholic," he muttered when he'd tried to give SJ an expensive glass of wine that had been poured out by mistake and she'd said she didn't drink. "Still, I suppose at least that means you won't be necking all the profits." He tossed back his Hispanic curls and minced up and down the floor with the wine on a silver tray. And in the end SJ had fallen about laughing.

She didn't put him right one way or the other – as Dorothy had frequently told her, the reasons she didn't drink were no one's business but her own. But she got on well at Mortimer's.

The customers liked her – she got more tips than anyone else because she was always clowning around and making people laugh. Even on her darkest days she

282

concentrated on making people smile. Making people smile felt good. It didn't atone for all the people she had hurt so badly, but it helped somehow.

Dorothy cleared the plates from the table and SJ came back to the present with a start.

"This particular convention doesn't cost anything, hen – and you get a free lunch."

"Well, that clinches it, then," SJ quipped. "When is it?"

"The last weekend in November – the 25th, I think."

SJ felt a flicker of pain – the 25th of November was Tanya's birthday. Whatever else had happened between them across the years they'd never missed each other's birthdays.

"What is it?" Dorothy asked, catching her look. "Do you have other plans?"

SJ explained. "I've known Tanya since senior school and we always do cards and wine for normal birthdays and champagne for big birthdays. It's tradition. And now I'm never going to see her again."

"You wouldn't have taken her wine this year, even if you were still close." Dorothy's voice was gentle.

"No, I suppose not." SJ blinked back tears. "I can't go near wine. I don't trust myself. I can't even bear to look at it in supermarkets. I have to close my eyes when I go past the alcohol aisles." She grimaced – this had already caused two near miss accidents, one with a mum and toddler, and one with an old gent with a white stick, who was legitimately allowed to stumble into things because he couldn't see where he was going. "Will it always be like that?"

"No, it won't." Dorothy took their plates over to the sink, turned on the tap and then came back to the

283

table. "I don't know how long it will take you. We're all different. But I can tell you honestly that if someone waved an open bottle of Scotch under my nose now I wouldn't be tempted. And it's been like that for more years than I can count."

SJ sighed. She couldn't imagine not wanting to drink, which had come as quite a shock. She had thought that the horror of taking an alcohol overdose would have been big enough – painful enough – to make the prospect of ever drinking again abhorrent. But it hadn't been like that.

The further away that nightmare time got, the more she began to think that maybe one drink wouldn't hurt after all. Quite often she could smell alcohol, even when there was none around to smell – some sort of weird olfactory hallucination. And to think she'd imagined she didn't have a drink problem.

Dorothy patted her shoulder and the gesture was so tender that SJ felt the tears come properly now.

"I don't think I can do this." She could feel her voice husking over the words. "I don't think I can stand it. The thought of never having a drink again – ever in my life – is terrifying."

"Och! It's not forever though, is it? It's just for today. These next few hours, these next few minutes if you like. Just keep it in the day."

Over the next couple of months life at Dorothy's settled into a pattern: walking Ash, going to work, and meetings. SJ was pretty much left to her own devices. Dorothy spent ages tapping away at the keyboard of her Apple Mac, which lived on a bureau in her lounge.

"I keep it there because I like having the telly on while I write," she confided.

"Doesn't it put you off?" SJ asked, surprised. "I'd have thought it would be really distracting."

"Not at all. If I find something distracting, I allow myself to be distracted and watch it for a while. Sometimes it's helpful for my story, and I just weave it into the plot. I find writing is like knitting. The raw material of fiction is life and I reach out for it and knit it into my stories. You can't reproduce life without living it a little."

Dorothy smiled serenely while SJ digested this.

"Life for a recovering alcoholic is about balance," she went on. "We tend to be extremist by nature. That's often how we got into such trouble in the first place. You take a look around the rooms, Sarah-Jane. Most of the people in meetings are self-employed. That's because they don't get on very well working for other people. They don't like being told what to do, for a start. They're far too rebellious."

"Mmm," SJ agreed. She could relate to that at least.

"Many recovering alcoholics do so well at their own businesses that they become millionaires," Dorothy added.

SJ nodded. That was good news. She would have liked to work for herself – she didn't need to be a millionaire, but some more money would be nice. She smiled at her thoughts. Waitress to entrepreneur millionaire was probably a bit of a quantum leap; still, there was no harm in aiming high.

"But to go back to what I was saying, we do need balance in our lives. I don't work because I need to. I'm sixty-five, you know – I could have retired ten years ago, financially. I still write stories because I enjoy

285

writing them. If I let it take over and didn't get a little distracted at times, my life would be all out of balance."

Dorothy was very wise, SJ reflected, not for the first time. She hadn't realised she was a pensioner. She didn't look like one.

"So have you thought any more about this convention? Do you think it's something you might enjoy? Or don't you fancy hanging about with a load of ex-drunks for the day?"

"I couldn't think of anything I'd rather be doing," SJ replied, realising with surprise that it was true.

"And will you be sending your friend a card for her birthday?"

"Yes, I will." SJ wished she didn't feel so upset about Tanya. They'd had rows before, across the years, but nothing that had ever come close to this. It still filled her with grief that she and Tanya would never again go for a girly chat and swap confidences.

When she'd moved into Dorothy's, she'd sent Tanya a change of address card. There had been no response – and she hadn't been surprised. A small part of her still hoped they'd be friends again, one day – but the realistic part knew they probably wouldn't. Some things could never be forgiven.

Nevertheless, she spent ages choosing a birthday card for Tanya. Her hand hovered between the *My Special Friend* cards and the more jokey variety they usually bought each other. Neither seemed appropriate and in the end she'd chosen a card with a skylark in full flight across the backdrop of a setting sun. Inside, she'd written simply: *Happy Birthday. Hope you're okay. Thinking of you. SJ x*

Then she'd posted it before she could change her mind. Afterwards, she'd wondered if perhaps she

286

should have left out the kiss. But it was too late now. Tanya probably wouldn't answer it anyway. Why should she?

Rather to her disappointment, because she'd hoped he might, Kit didn't show up at the convention. She told him all about it at her next session, and he smiled at her enthusiasm.

"What?" she said, pausing for breath.

"I was just thinking that if you could see yourself now, compared to the person you were when you first walked in here, you wouldn't believe it."

"What do you mean? I can't be that different."

"Oh, you are, SJ. You're much more relaxed, happy, confident – it's great to see."

"How very rewarding for you," she muttered, feeling slightly irritated that he obviously still saw her as a client, and was oblivious to her as a woman.

He laughed. "I didn't mean it like that."

"I've lost masses of weight," she pointed out, deciding to give him a helping hand on the old perception front.

"I'd noticed," he said equably, and SJ found herself wondering when exactly he'd noticed. She'd never once caught him looking at any part of her except her face, which was exasperating because she spent a lot of time on her appearance when she came to see him – as she did when she went to meetings. It was something she'd noticed the other women did too. There were some beautiful girls in AA.

She'd suspected she might see Kit differently without the aid of alcohol-tinted glasses. She'd also thought that splitting up with Tom might be sad enough to bring her back to reality where men were concerned, but if anything she liked Kit more than she had before. It still touched her that he'd come to visit her in hospital, but it went deeper than that.

She liked the warmth in his eyes and the tiny lines around them that crinkled up when he smiled. She liked the way his short brown hair spiked now he'd had it cut. She wondered if he used gel or if it was natural. She liked his hands, with their strong stubby fingers and short nails – she'd spent many a night in bed at Dorothy's imagining what it would be like to feel his hands moving over her skin.

Now and then she'd allowed herself a brief fantasy about what it would be like to kiss him.

"SJ…" His voice broke into her thoughts and she jumped guiltily. "Talk to me – tell me what you're thinking?"

No way was she telling him that. If she confessed to one tenth of what was in her head, he'd suggest she see another counsellor – and then she'd never set eyes on him again. And he was the only bright spot in these days of abstinence.

"Why?" she asked, playing for time as she tried to conjure up a suitable answer – one that wouldn't have him marching her out of the door.

"Because that's what we're here for – and because – well – you looked happy for a moment there – so it's not all bad, is it?"

His voice was unusually hesitant. He never sounded hesitant. Maybe he felt the same. After all, it happened, didn't it? Counsellors fell in love with their clients all the time – well, they did on telly. There'd been a plotline about it once on *Sex and the City*. She couldn't remember the outcome – bugger, she wished she'd paid more attention.

288

SJ smiled. For a brief moment she visualised herself telling him he was the reason she was happy. That actually she was in love with him – well, a little bit in lust with him at the very least. But she knew if she told him that she wouldn't be able to retract the words. He'd be morally obliged to insist she didn't see him again. And she couldn't bear not to see him again. Life would be a great deal emptier without him in it. No, it was far better to keep everything on a nice safe fantasy level.

"How's it going with Tom?" he asked. Maybe he had picked up on her thoughts, after all.

"I don't think there's going to be any happy reconciliation. Tom's not in a hurry to divorce me, but he doesn't want me to move back in either. And I really don't blame him."

"But you haven't been tempted to drink on that?"

SJ shook her head. "I get tempted occasionally, but I'm not going to do it. I only have to remember what happened last time."

He raised his eyebrows, and she said quietly, "When Dad gave me that gin and tonic at the party – complete with ice and a slice – I had no idea what it would lead to..."

"Congratulations," Kit interrupted, and she looked at him in surprise.

"What?"

"You got the right drink," he said with a smile. "It's the first drink that does the damage. It takes ages for most alcoholics to get their head around that. They think it's the fourth or the fifth – or the final bottle they can't even remember guzzling."

She blushed. "Yeah, thanks very much for reminding me of that!"

"You're welcome," he said, unrepentant. "You've got a very good sponsor too, haven't you?"

"Dorothy's amazing. I don't think I could have done it without her. And I've made a few friends at meetings." That had surprised her. How normal people were – and yet also how diverse. She'd met nurses, teachers, waitresses and office workers; not a tramp on a park bench in sight. The only thing they all had in common was they couldn't drink like other people. They couldn't stop at one.

"So you've got plenty of support then?" Kit said. "Plenty of people around you who'll help you stay sober?"

Suddenly realising what he was getting at, SJ nodded. "I should stop coming here, shouldn't I? Free up the appointment for someone who needs it more than me?"

"I'm not saying that. I've told you before – you can come as long as you need." Kit's face was serious.

"But it's true, isn't it? I can't keep coming here forever. I have to stand on my own two feet sooner or later."

The thought of not seeing him any more left her feeling impossibly bleak. And ironically it was this that decided her.

Deep down, she knew she only kept coming because she was a little bit in love with him. And while the old SJ would have found this a perfectly good reason to continue, the new more mature SJ knew it wasn't.

When they stood up at the end of the session, she looked at Kit and said softly, "Don't book me in next week. I think I can probably cope from now on."

"Are you sure?" He stood a few feet away from her, his dark eyes solemn.

The prospect of never seeing him again filled her with grief. A massive ache had started in her heart and was rising up into her throat. She couldn't swallow.

Clinging to her self-control, she forced herself to meet his eyes. "I can phone if I change my mind, can't I?"

"Of course you can. We'll still be here."

She had to get out before she lost it completely. The ache was increasing. In a minute it would spill over and she would cry. And that would be silly – she should be thrilled she no longer needed to come to an addiction counsellor, not devastated.

"Stay safe, SJ," Kit said softly, and she nodded again. Bloody emotions – they'd been far easier to deal with when she'd been able to bury them. There was so much she wanted to say, but she knew she would never get the words out.

In the end, all she could manage was a mumbled, "Thanks," before she fled. But when she was outside once more on the familiar street, it struck her that Kit didn't need her to go into long thank you speeches anyway. He probably knew exactly how she felt. He always had.

Chapter Thirty-Four

SJ told her parents she was an alcoholic on Christmas Day, just before dinner. She was amazed that the subject hadn't come up before, but it hadn't although, in some ways, perhaps this wasn't so surprising because her parents' views on alcoholics were the same as SJ's had once been. They were sad old men in raincoats who sat on park benches swigging bottles of meths.

SJ's troubles – while they might have involved alcohol – clearly had more to do with her marriage breaking up than anything else. Her time in hospital hadn't been talked about since. It was as though her parents wanted to forget it had ever happened. SJ wanted to forget it had ever happened too, but she couldn't leave them in happy ignorance about her alcoholism because from the moment she'd arrived they'd been trying to press a glass of shandy on her.

"I can't have just the one, Dad, I really can't."

"Don't be so bloodeh ridiculous," her father responded, with a slightly drunken grin. "We won't let you near the hard stuff, don't worry."

"But I'm an alcoholic, Dad. That means I can never drink anything safely again."

Her mother banged down the Yorkshire pudding tray – they had Yorkshires with every roast, even turkey – tucked a strand of damp hair back off her hot face and also smiled.

"Pack it in, Sarah-Jane. We had enough of all that nonsense at the party."

"It's not nonsense, it's true," SJ said, with a growing sense of unreality. "I'm not drinking because I'm an alcoholic – a recovering one. That's what we're called when we stop."

"Oh, isn't she a case, Jim? Listen to her." Her mother prodded a Yorkshire experimentally and half turned from the stove. Something in SJ's expression must have alerted her because suddenly she stopped smiling. "I know you had all that trouble before, and I know you get carried away sometimes, but everyone does. Don't they, Jim? You mustn't think you're any different from anyone else."

It was echoes of Tom all over again. Feeling a rising sense of panic, SJ went on desperately. "I'm sorry, Mum, I shouldn't have sprung it on you like that, but I am different. I've been seeing an addiction counsellor. He even came to visit me in hospital. I've been seeing him for the last six months."

Now she had their attention. They were both staring at her with varying degrees of shock and she wished she hadn't said anything, but only fleetingly. If she'd been braver she'd have told them before.

Dad had been about to take a sip of his pre-dinner pint, but now he put it down so forcefully that froth spilled over the edge of the glass.

"Is that why Tom threw you out? Because he couldn't handle living with a drunk?"

She flinched. "We've been through all that, Dad. And no, I didn't move out because of my drinking. I moved out because we're not right together. We haven't been for a while." 'Ever' would have been more truthful, but that was between her and Tom.

The inquest went on and on. How long had she known? Why hadn't she said anything before? Who

293

else knew? Was she sure? The latter question was asked with such regularity between the hundreds of others that SJ would have wondered if she really was sure – but for the fact that her last drink had almost ended her life.

Then again, she only had to look back on how much her thoughts and attitudes had changed since she'd stopped drinking to know the answer to that one.

The further she got from daily drinking, the clearer her head had become, and the surer she was that she'd had all of the personality traits of an alcoholic for many more years than she'd drunk daily.

With hindsight, she could see how much of a double life she'd been living. It had been necessary to have two SJs. There was the public one, who'd been a supportive wife, a dutiful daughter, a witty and entertaining tutor, and a sympathetic friend.

Then there was the private one: the SJ who'd needed to down a bottle of wine and half a dozen gins every night so she could face going to bed; the SJ who'd woken sweating and panicking in the early hours, when the alcohol-induced oblivion had released its grip; the SJ who was crumbling inside and was desperately afraid of what she was becoming.

She didn't need to be that person any more. She could be the person she'd always dreamed she could be. The person she'd thought she was until she'd stepped into that dingy little counselling room.

Ironically, the best thing about telling her parents on Christmas Day was that they told Alison as soon as she arrived with Sophie, Kevin and the long-suffering Clive.

Alison – to SJ's shock – was the least surprised of anyone.

"I thought you had a problem," she said, fixing SJ with her cool blue gaze as they sat down to eat. "Table looks nice, Mum. Did you get these crackers from Morrison's? Why have we got two each?"

"They were buy one, get one free," their mother said proudly. "But they had a sell by date."

Alison shook her head in disbelief. "What on earth have they got in them – food or something?"

"Luxury items."

"Luxury price too," their father chipped in. "Should have been half the price they were."

SJ giggled, but no one else seemed to pick up on the irony of this.

Alison turned her attention back to SJ, who was sitting beside her at the dining room table, which was covered with a red and green holly patterned tablecloth. "Do you remember that musician I was telling you about at the party? Adam Macclesfield – the one who came in to the salon about Botox?"

SJ nodded, wondering where her sister was going with this.

"Well, he's a recovering alcoholic – I mentioned it to you when we were chatting. Don't you remember?"

"No," SJ said. Mind you, that wasn't surprising. There was so much she hadn't remembered about the party.

"Adam's been sober a couple of years now, and he's got a very stressful job – what with all those groupies chasing after him. So if he can do it, I'm sure you can. You haven't got any stress in your life, have you? Being a waitress is a doddle compared to being a rock star."

SJ ignored her sister as she spooned roast potatoes onto her plate. Once she'd have fiercely resented this slightly patronising summary of her life – but now she felt secure enough not to react to Alison's teasing. How things had changed. "This smells delicious, Mum," she said, breathing in the mix of turkey and cranberry sauce. "Does this sauce have any wine in it?"

"No, but the gravy does – oh my goodness. Don't let her have the gravy, Jim. Everybody – keep the gravy away from Sarah-Jane."

SJ wondered what they thought she was going to do – grab the jug and pour it down her throat by the spout. No one seemed to have any such compunction about leaving their brimming glasses of Cava in front of her.

"There's no shame in being an alcoholic," Alison went on breezily. "It can happen to anyone. It's an illness, not a moral failing. I know you said at the party you were drinking because of Tom, but that's not true. You were probably born an alcoholic. I was talking to Adam about it. It's exactly the same as being born diabetic – or asthmatic, like Kevin." She picked up her son's inhaler from the table as she spoke. "Which is why I get so cross when I catch him smoking.

"Does anyone want any more sprouts?"

"Not for me, thanks, Dad – Sophie will have some, she's hardly got any veggies on her plate."

"I hate sprouts."

Alison shot her a glare. "Everyone hates sprouts. I expect it's in your genes, Sarah-Jane. I mean, we all know Aunt Edie's an old soak. And Grandpa George was an alcoholic too, wasn't he, Mum?"

How on earth did she know that? SJ wondered. Grandpa George had died before they were born, and

296

his name was hardly ever mentioned. She glanced at her parents, who were listening to this conversation in open-mouthed amazement. She was pretty amazed herself. Never in her wildest dreams had she imagined Alison might understand something that Tom had completely failed to grasp, let alone be prepared to announce it to their parents, thereby painting her in a completely different light in their eyes.

"Are you a real alky?" Kevin asked, his face alight with a mixture of horror and admiration. He and Sophie hadn't been told about her stint in hospital. Well, not the reason for it anyway. It had been brushed under the carpet like every other scandal that had ever happened in their family.

"I mean, have you done stuff like fall over in the gutter and puke all down your front when you're drunk?" he persisted with barely concealed glee.

"Kevin, stop that kind of talk right now – people are trying to eat," Clive said, glaring irritably at his son.

SJ winked at Kevin and offered him a cracker. "Tell you later," she mouthed behind her hand.

Sophie narrowed her eyes in disgust, but SJ could tell she was quite interested in knowing the answer to Kevin's question, too. Perhaps she could end up being a proper auntie to her sister's children, after all – the kind of auntie who could be a dire warning of the dangers of getting involved with drink and drugs. Being a dire warning sounded a lot more fun than being a good example.

After dinner, while their parents gorged themselves still further with nuts and mince pies in front of the telly, Alison ordered Clive and Kevin to do the washing up and steered SJ purposefully into the conservatory.

"Is it really over with Tom?" she asked, her voice unusually soft. "I thought he was quite a sweetie at the party."

"He was – he is," SJ amended. "But yes, it's really over. There's no way back for me and Tom. I think we'll stay friends. I really like him. But we don't want to stay married."

Alison twirled a lock of blond hair around her index finger. "I'm sorry to hear that."

"Don't be. We should never have got married in the first place. I know that now."

"It's a pity, he was much better for you than that prat, Derek," Alison went on thoughtfully.

SJ felt her hackles rise, but where once she'd have jumped down her sister's throat, now she didn't. She just waited, wondering what was coming next.

"I've never apologised about all that stuff with Derek, have I? I know I probably should have done, but I couldn't bring myself to do it."

SJ wanted to ask why, but it was obvious Alison had something to get off her chest. She'd stopped twiddling her hair, but there was a flush across her collar bones. As usual her sister looked stunning in a pale lemon blouse with tiny pearl buttons and a matching row of pearls at her throat. But SJ didn't feel inferior any more. The endless sessions with Kit had given her so much more than a way to stop drinking.

"The reason I didn't apologise was… well…" Alison hesitated, uncharacteristically vulnerable. "Sarah-Jane, don't take this the wrong way, but actually I think I did you a huge favour. If he was prepared to drop his trousers for me – and believe me, he didn't need a lot of persuading – well, he'd probably have done it for any woman. So if it hadn't been for me, you

298

might not have found out what a total bastard the guy was."

SJ snorted in a mixture of amusement and outrage. She was NOT letting that one go by – no matter how much she tried to turn the other cheek these days and see the other person's point of view.

"You don't half talk a load of old bollocks sometimes, Ali."

Her sister's eyes widened in annoyance. Perhaps she should have been more subtle. Now they were finally both under the same roof she didn't want to start a fight and ruin their parents' Christmas. She reminded herself she hadn't started it. Alison had – she was obviously still trying to find a way of justifying her self-seeking behaviour by pretending her motives were altruistic.

"It is not rubbish. It's true. Derek was a…"

SJ put her hands in front of her, palms facing forward. "Enough. You didn't get off with my ex-husband because you wanted to show me that he wasn't worthy of me. You just had too much to drink – and you fancied him. And let's face it, you didn't think I'd find out."

Her voice had been louder than she'd intended and Ali's face had gone the colour of their parents' terracotta floor tiles.

"What's with all the shouting?" said an interested voice from the door. Kevin was grinning broadly and SJ wondered with a stab of guilt how much he'd heard.

"By the sound of it, Mum's rewriting history again." Sophie stood behind him, her lips set in a disapproving twist. "You said that Auntie SJ didn't talk to you any more because you didn't get on with her

299

first husband – and you told her what a dodgy geezer he was. You didn't say you'd actually…"

"Shut up, the pair of you. This is a private conversation between me and your aunt. And besides, you're supposed to be washing up."

"You shouldn't shout, though, if you want things to be private."

"Nanna said we were to check for dirty plates," Kevin added, picking up a coffee mug and a bowl still half full of peanuts from the table."

"I said SHUT UP! And put those bloody peanuts back."

SJ swallowed a smile as Sophie and Kevin backed out of the room and turned her attention back to her sister.

"You were lucky Clive didn't throw you out." SJ decided to press home her advantage with uncharacteristic ruthlessness.

"Yes, I know." To her surprise, Alison's eyes were suddenly awash with tears. "I am sorry, Sarah-Jane. I know what I did was awful."

Some of SJ's anger melted in the face of her sister's obvious distress. "Yes, it was," she said, softer now. "I know you've never liked me that much, Ali, but I still didn't think you'd do something like that."

"Why do you think I've never liked you?" Alison rummaged around in her bag for her compact. She sounded quite surprised.

"Cutting the tail off My Little Pony because you wanted to make a wig for your Barbie; swapping my best top for those sparkly jeans you used to wear night and day; pretending to be ill so Mum and Dad couldn't come to my school play." SJ counted on her fingers as she went, and noticed her nails were growing back

300

nicely. She couldn't have bitten them lately. "Not to mention hiding my English assignment on the Brontes – I know that was you. Need I go on?"

"I was jealous. I did most of those things to get Mum's attention because I thought she loved you better than me."

"What? Now that really *is* ridiculous."

"No, I'm serious. She never stopped going on about you. All I ever heard when I was growing up was, 'Why can't you be more like Sarah-Jane? More sensible, more grown up, more responsible'. I was sick to death of you being held up like some paragon of virtue."

She sounded quite miffed and it was SJ's turn to be surprised, although actually several of those phrases rang true. She'd overheard Mum saying them herself. Maybe her childhood hadn't been as black and white as it seemed either. Maybe all children thought their parents loved their siblings better than them.

"I'll get us a nice glass of wine." Alison couldn't resist a smirk. "Oh no, you can't, can you? Never mind, I'll have yours. I'll get you an orange juice, shall I?"

"I'll get the drinks," SJ said, not entirely sure her sister wouldn't be tempted to slip a gin into hers in the misguided belief that what the eye couldn't see the heart wouldn't grieve. Although, on second thoughts, perhaps she was misjudging her again – she'd seemed pretty clued up earlier.

"Cheers," Alison purred, stretching her hands above her head and arching her back like a contented cat. "While you're out there, make sure they're not slacking with the washing up. I don't want Mum doing anything – she's done enough slaving in the kitchen today."

301

"Sure."

"Oh, and Sarah-Jane…?"

"Yes," she said, hesitating in the doorway and glancing back at her sister, who looked nothing like the monster she'd once perceived her to be. It was strange how twisted her thinking had once been.

"I'm glad we're talking again. I've really missed having someone to have a good old barney with."

Chapter Thirty-Five

Tanya didn't respond to the Christmas card SJ had sent. Neither had she responded to the birthday good wishes. But on Dorothy's advice SJ didn't try to contact her again.

"The right time to make amends will come along," Dorothy told her softly. "But there's no rush, hen. You just get yourself sorted out for now. Get a bit of sobriety behind you."

So SJ spent the first few months of the New Year looking into the possibility of doing more teaching privately. She couldn't face going back into Adult Education; her heart wasn't in it any more. She didn't think she'd get enough students to fill more than one Poetry and a Pint class, but she was contemplating teaching other forms of word craft in a fun environment. Creative Writing appealed, or Making Shakespeare Fun. That would be excellent in her room at the Red Lion. It had just the right atmosphere for studying old plays.

"I'm also thinking about changing the name from Poetry and a Pint to something more appropriate," she told Dorothy, one evening after dinner. "Something that's not quite as alcohol related."

"Such as?" Dorothy looked interested.

"That's the trouble, I can't think of anything that's not alcohol related – Poetry and a Pina Colada keeps buzzing round my mind for some reason. And the only other thing I can think of is Poetry and a Peanut." She sighed.

"I think you should probably leave it as it is," Dorothy said. "Pint doesn't have to mean alcohol anyway, does it?"

SJ giggled. "No, you're right. If it isn't broke, don't fix it – and I do like teaching at the Red Lion, even though it's a bit of a trek now. But I'd quite like to do some other classes that aren't academic as well."

There were a lot of possibilities. Adult Literacy had always appealed, although she planned to do that on a voluntary basis – just for the sheer satisfaction of introducing people to the joy of reading.

She and Tom had decided to make their separation permanent and she'd agreed to a small settlement, which covered the money she'd put into the house when they bought it. She'd agreed that he could pay it in instalments so he didn't have to sell the house. It was the least he deserved, she thought idly, when she went over to talk to him about it one bright evening when the air was balmy with summer.

He looked older and wearier than ever, and she guessed he was still working all hours. Although the kitchen was warm because he'd been cooking, the rest of the house felt cold and unlived in. Outside, the grass needed cutting and the flowerbeds were overgrown with weeds.

They discussed finances and how Ash was and SJ felt more relaxed with him than she ever had in the past.

As she got up to go, she said softly, "Tom, I know I owe you a huge apology. It must have been hell living with me. I'm so sorry."

"It wasn't hell." He smiled at her. "Besides, you weren't the only one at fault. Who'd want to be married to a husband who was never here?"

304

"And who'd want a drunk for a wife?"

"Don't beat yourself up, SJ. I never noticed your drinking and hey – I always did like my pub paraphernalia, didn't I? Some might say I was lucky, I collected the ultimate in breweriana – a real live alcoholic."

SJ laughed. It was the last thing she'd have done a year ago. And it was the last thing he'd have said a year ago, too. She wondered what had brought about the change in him.

"Are you seeing anyone?" she asked curiously.

"Who'd have me?" He reddened, and suddenly she knew she was right on target. There was someone else.

Meeting her eyes, he nodded. "You always were a mind reader, SJ – pity I wasn't the same with you – but yeah, okay, there is someone. It's early days, but I've been on a few dates with my boss. She does even longer hours than me, but at least we see each other at work."

"Be happy," she told him. And she meant it.

As she left Kentish Town and headed back towards Dorothy's, SJ reflected there were only two people left to make amends to now – Tanya and Michael. She decided to leave this for a while longer.

Summer moved slowly into autumn and one beautiful Saturday in late October, SJ woke up, knowing it would be today that she would go and make her peace. She had no idea why she felt it so strongly, but just that Dorothy, so wise and patient, had been right. Deep down in her bones, she just knew.

Chapter Thirty-Six

Ringing Tanya's doorbell was far scarier than when she'd first pressed the buzzer at S.A.A.D, all those months ago. SJ wasn't sure what she'd do if Tanya slammed the door in her face. All she knew was that she had to do this because she couldn't live with herself if she didn't try, just one more time, to make amends properly.

There was a new car in the drive, a BMW Sports – Tanya had always wanted one of those. No one came, and SJ's stomach crunched and churned. Fear always made her feel sick. Perhaps they were out. She was about to turn away when she saw movement behind the frosted glass. The door swung open.

"Can I help you?" asked a Bet Lynch lookalike with a towel turbaned round her head. She must have just got out of the bath.

"I'm sorry to disturb you. I'm looking for Tanya and Michael Wiltshire. Do they still live here?"

"No, love. We bought the place off them – ooh, six months ago."

"Did they leave a forwarding address?"

"Yeah – I'll get it for you."

"Who is it?" A man's voice called from the depths of the house.

"I'm a friend. Sarah-Jane Crosse."

"Won't keep you a tick."

When she came back her face was different – guarded where before it had been open. "Sorry, we don't have an address after all. Must have lost it." She made to close the door and SJ took a step forward.

"Please, could I just leave you a number …?"

She shook her head, clearly embarrassed. "Sorry, love."

SJ knew there was no point in pressing it. Tanya and Michael hadn't wanted her to catch up with them. And she wasn't really surprised. Feeling hot, despite the crisp autumnal air, SJ got back in her car and drove slowly home.

Dorothy was working, her fingers flying over the keyboard, when SJ committed the cardinal sin of disturbing her. She took in a coffee to soften the blow and put it by her elbow.

For a while she was ignored and then Dorothy tutted and stopped typing. "Well now you've broken my train of thought, you may as well tell me what's on your mind. Did it not go well?"

"They'd moved. What if they had to leave the area because of me?"

"Och - isn't it funny how we assume the world revolves around us! It rarely does, you know."

"Ouch."

"Perhaps you could try her office."

"That's tricky. Tanya works from home. But I could go and see Michael. If I had the nerve," she added, half to herself.

"Come on now, SJ, you're not giving up already. That's not like you!"

"No, I didn't mean it like that. Michael's an entertainments manager. He works in a club. I have enough trouble with the alcohol aisle in Tesco," she said wistfully. "How am I going to cope with a club?"

Dorothy patted her arm. "You're not going in there for a drink though, are you? Just concentrate on the job in hand. You'll be fine."

SJ hoped she was right as she parked outside The Cage that evening. She'd decided there was no point in hanging around. Now she'd made up her mind to see Tanya she wanted to get it done.

There were already a few people queuing to go in, and a bouncer was chatting to a woman near the entrance. SJ had never liked clubs much – she found them intimidating. She took a deep breath and walked to the head of the queue.

"I'm here to see Michael Wiltshire – would you please tell him it's Sarah-Jane Crosse." Would he come out and see her? She thought he might. If only to make sure she wasn't about to blab to his colleagues about his private life.

She was right. Less than five minutes later, Michael appeared. He looked embarrassed. His hands were buried in the pockets of his linen suit and his movements were agitated. Sweat sheened his face.

"What do you want?"

She nearly lost her nerve. Why had she decided to do this with an audience of bouncers and clubbers? Get a grip, SJ. She had rehearsed what she was going to say, which started with the line, "I'm not here to cause trouble," but it was too long and convoluted. In the end she just met his gaze steadily and said, "Please ask Tanya to call me. Please, Michael. This is my new mobile number."

Fleetingly she thought he might not take it, but he snatched the card from her hand and spun away, his pale suit swallowed up by the dark innards of the club.

308

She wondered if he'd throw it in the first bin he passed. She'd have to risk that. She could do no more.

Dorothy agreed. "Sometimes friendships can't be mended," she said. "But I hope I'm proved wrong."

After a fortnight of silence SJ had to accept that Dorothy wasn't going to be proved wrong.

And then she got the text.

If you want to see me, come to this address – Saturday. Ten a.m. Tanya.

The address turned out to be in Bermondsey, not all that far from where they'd lived before, but the house looked bigger than their last one. The fact that Michael's car was in the drive made her feel even more apprehensive. But then she owed Michael a huge apology too, and it hadn't been appropriate to make it outside The Cage. So it was right he should be here.

Once more she'd prepared the words in her head. But in the end, when Tanya opened the door, all she could manage was a squeaky, "Thank you for seeing me."

For a long, long moment, Tanya didn't speak. SJ could see half a dozen emotions in her eyes. Pain, regret, guilt, embarrassment, surprise, but the overriding one – the one her face eventually settled into – was sorrow.

"Please can I come in?"

"Michael's here," Tanya eventually managed, a small sigh escaping from her lips – which were beautifully made up, even on a Saturday morning.

"I know. I want to see him too."

Tanya held the door open and SJ stepped into the unfamiliar house. The hallway was wider, the carpet was fluffier, and the stairs were in a different place, but everything had the same smell. That mix of citrus furniture polish underlaid with the Classique scent Tanya always wore. Maybe her senses were heightened, SJ thought, trembling. They said that happened to men who were walking to the gallows. That the last breath of air was the sweetest they ever knew.

She followed Tanya through to the kitchen, where Michael was sitting at the table reading a paper.

"We've got a visitor."

"So I see." His face tightened as he stood up, and SJ's heart felt as if it were on some invisible ratchet that had just been knocked down several notches. She could almost hear the clunk, clunk in her chest.

"I know I'm probably the last person you want to see, but I'm here to say I'm sorry. So very sorry about what I said – what I've done to you both. I don't expect you to forgive me. I know I don't deserve that." Oh God, she was in danger of going into the I'm-not-fit-to-lick-your-boots routine that Dorothy had warned her about.

She attempted to straighten her shoulders and look Michael in the eyes – which wasn't difficult, as they were more or less the same height. Even though she felt much smaller than him. Much smaller than both of them. She cleared her throat and waited.

Still neither of them spoke. SJ wasn't sure what she'd expected, but it wasn't this granite mountain of silence.

"That's basically all I came to say. I – er – well – it's probably best if I get out of your hair now."

She was mid-turn, berating herself for being such a spineless coward, when Michael finally spoke. "Hang about, SJ. I'll put the kettle on. I'd offer you something

310

stronger – you look like you need it – but we haven't got any drink in the house."

"I don't drink any more…" she began, before realising it was his attempt at humour.

Behind her, Tanya pulled out a chair. "Sit down, SJ. We don't want you to go. Do we, Michael?"

His eyes said no and, feeling light-headed with relief, SJ did as she was bid and sat down. While Michael got mugs from the cupboard and spooned in coffee, Tanya folded the newspaper to clear space from the table. Such ordinary things – as though she were any other visitor, here for a normal Saturday morning chat and hadn't just walked back into their lives after a gap of more than a year.

"Have you really stopped drinking?" Tanya asked, settling opposite, her green eyes curious.

"It's coming up to fourteen months," SJ told her proudly, and waited while Tanya worked this out.

"I haven't had a drink since – well, since around the time of Mum and Dad's party." She'd never told Tanya about her final drink, or about ending up in hospital. She'd never had the chance. "I go to my meetings three times a week," she added.

"You still need them – after all this time?" Tanya sounded incredulous.

"They keep me sober. And besides, I've made quite a few friends." God, she was beginning to sound like Dorothy.

"Do you still see that counsellor of yours – Kit, wasn't it?"

SJ shook her head. "No – he packed me off into the big bad world. Well, actually I packed myself off. I had to grow up sooner or later."

"And what about Tom? Last time Michael saw him, he mentioned you weren't together any more."

"That's right. We're getting divorced."

"I'm sorry." Tanya reached across the table and took her hand, and for the first time since she'd walked into the house, SJ thought she might crumble.

"Don't be sorry. We weren't right for each other. We should never have got married in the first place."

"Even so, it's sad when a marriage has to end," Tanya went on. "Was it the drinking? Tom never could stand anything that was different to the norm, could he?" She glanced at her husband as she spoke. "He speaks to Michael now if they bump into each other at the sports centre, but he can't look him in the eye. I think he's scared Michael might make some sort of move on him."

"Not that I'm worried about Tom looking me in the eye," Michael added with a wry grin. "The main thing is I can look myself in the eye these days – in the mirror, I mean."

"Me too. I used to hate what I saw in the mirror." SJ clapped her hand over her mouth. Tactless. "What I mean is, I lost all my self-esteem – I didn't know who I was…" She was pretty sure she was digging the hole deeper so she shut up.

Michael made a little hmmph sound of amusement. "Don't beat yourself up. In some ways you did me a favour, SJ. I'm not ashamed of who I am any more. It's one hell of a relief to feel like that after so many years of despising myself."

"I know," SJ said with feeling. "But I'm still sorry for what I did. I shouldn't have told anyone about your private life –"

312

"It's okay," he said, slanting a glance at Tanya. "It's okay with us. Isn't it, love?"

Tanya nodded slowly. "I'm really glad you got in touch. I'd have contacted you sooner or later – only I wasn't sure exactly where you lived."

"Didn't you get my change of address card?"

"Yes, but I tore it up – I was still too cross with you back then. And I was damned if I was going to ask Tom where you were." She hesitated. "Oh hell, SJ, I'm sorry. But we've had a lot going on."

"Yes, so I see. Moving house... work...And the last thing you needed was an extra load of hassle from me."

"I wouldn't have put it quite like that," Tanya said diplomatically, but SJ knew she was right on target.

"I wouldn't have talked to me either," she said quietly.

Tanya blinked and stared down at her fingernails, which were pale pink with tiny silver stars. There was a small silence. SJ felt she should fill it but she didn't know quite what to say.

"You're looking very well."

"Thanks." Tanya exchanged glances with Michael. SJ wondered if she was outstaying her welcome. She'd finished her coffee. She didn't want to go, but she didn't want to be annoying either – maybe they'd only let her in out of kindness.

She shuffled through her bag for her car keys. If Tanya looked relieved she'd take it as her cue to leave.

"Actually, SJ, the truth is, I was a bit scared about getting in touch again." Tanya bit her lip. "I thought you might hate me. After all, I knew you had a drink problem – I knew you couldn't help being an..."

"An alcoholic," SJ supplied gently.

313

"Yes..." Tanya blushed. "You'd told me about it enough. And I knew you'd split up with Tom, but I didn't stick around, did I? I deserted you in your hour of need."

"No, you didn't," SJ gasped, amazed Tanya felt like this. "I hurt you beyond belief."

"Enough," Michael interrupted sharply. "Let's forget about the shitty past, shall we – or we'll end up going round in circles all day. You're here now, SJ. That's all that matters."

Chapter Thirty-Seven

When SJ left Tanya's she was on cloud ninety-nine, which was ninety times higher than cloud nine. They were friends again, but it wasn't as if they'd never been apart – it was better. She felt as though the three of them were soldiers who'd survived being on the front line and had come through it stronger. There was an unbreakable bond between them.

She felt so euphoric she had an urge to buy them both a present and so instead of heading back to Dorothy's, she drove into the city centre, parked in a multi storey and went shopping. What should she buy them? Nothing over the top – something silly would probably be best. There would be plenty of time for serious presents. She went into a card shop and was looking at the huge array of novelty teddies they had when someone brushed against her arm.

Glancing up, she realised in a heartbeat of shock that it was Kit. He must be on a teddy hunt too. He looked as surprised to see her as she was to see him. It was pretty silly really – they lived in the same area; at least she presumed he lived somewhere nearby. In some ways it was amazing they hadn't bumped into each other before.

Kit spoke first. "Hello, SJ, how's it going?"

It was eleven months since she'd seen him, but his gravelly voice still did odd things to her insides. She thought she'd got over all that. It was all very well being in lust with your counsellor when he was actively counselling you – it was almost inevitable, she'd consoled herself when she'd tried to get him out of her head afterwards – but discovering he still had the power to reduce her to a quivering wreck when she bumped into him in civvy street was unnerving.

She took an involuntary step backwards to get away from the force-field and just missed falling over a display stand of ruby wedding anniversary cards. There was obviously some sort of synchronicity at work, she thought, as Kit put out a hand to steady her.

It was the first time he had ever touched her and it felt like an electric shock – SJ had always thought electric shock moments in the romances she occasionally read were a bit of a cliché and must be rather unpleasant, but there was nothing unpleasant about this one. She glanced up at him through her eyelashes – was she flirting? – and said the first thing that came into her head. "Hey, Kit, do you fancy a coffee?"

Realising belatedly that this was a very bad idea because she'd be devastated if he said no, she racked her brain frantically for a way to retract it. But as usual her brains had turned to mush in his presence and before she could think of a single phrase in the English language that sounded exactly like, 'Do you fancy a coffee?' but which actually meant something else entirely, she heard him say, easily, "Yeah, sure. Why not?"

Five minutes later, clutching her bag of teddies and feeling mightily relieved she'd dressed up and washed her hair to go to Tanya's, she followed him into Starbucks.

"You're looking well," he said, as they sat with two steaming lattes in front of them. "So how's life?"

316

God, he was gorgeous. She had to get a grip. Maybe this feeling was an after- effect of the euphoria she'd felt since leaving Tanya's. She knew it wasn't. It was down to him. Kit-induced euphoria – he'd always been able to evoke it by the bucket load – and he hadn't lost the knack.

"I'm great," she mumbled. "I'm fine – I'm…" She was never this tongue tied. "Absolutely great. How are you? Who's your teddy for?" She knew she couldn't have sounded more inane if she'd tried.

"My sister's just had a little girl – Chloe – so I've become an uncle for the first time. I'm going over to see them later."

SJ realised with a sense of wonderment that it was the first bit of personal information he'd ever told her about himself. This rather put things in perspective. How could you possibly be in love with someone you didn't even know? It had to be infatuation.

Feeling better now she'd got that sorted out, she told him about Tanya. "I couldn't choose," she confessed, aware he was eyeing her bulging carrier curiously. They both laughed and, more relaxed now, she found herself explaining about the visit and how much it meant to her that Tanya had agreed to see her.

It was odd sitting opposite him somewhere other than S.A.A.D. The balance had shifted. For once, it wasn't SJ who was doing all the talking. He seemed quite happy to talk about himself too when she prompted him. They drank their lattes and ordered more and SJ was amazed when she looked at her watch and discovered two hours had flown past. She glanced at him, but he didn't seem anxious to leave. He hadn't so much as checked his watch since they arrived.

317

"Can I ask you something?" she ventured, as the coffee shop emptied out around them. "Something personal, I mean?"

"Something else personal, you mean," he corrected, but he was smiling so SJ carried on, encouraged.

"It's a bit more personal than what we've been talking about so far. You don't have to answer if you don't want to."

"I won't," he said. "But go ahead. Try me."

"When we first met I thought you might be a recovering alcoholic, like me – I mean, obviously not like me back then, because I was still a practising one. I mean like me now. But you're not, are you?"

He gave a half shake of his head, but before he could say anything, she went on haltingly.

"Yet you seemed to know how I felt all the time. What I'd do – how things would pan out. All the feelings and stuff. How did you know all that? Did you just go on a good training course?"

"No. I didn't need to." He held her gaze, his dark eyes steady. "Cocaine was my choice of drug, SJ. But there were other things – let's say I had a misspent youth. A distant misspent youth," he added. "I stopped all that insanity – oooh, more than twelve years ago."

"Ah," she said, feeling a mixture of emotions. Pleasure that he'd trusted her enough to tell her now, and relief – which she decided was probably an odd reaction, but she'd have been terribly disappointed if he told her he'd just been on a training course and hadn't really *known* how she felt.

"Thanks for being so open," she said, feeling enormously touched.

"My pleasure." He raised his eyebrows. "I think it's possible to counsel addicts effectively without having been one yourself, but it's easier if you've had some of the same experiences. There's more identification."

He leaned forward, put his chin in his hands and stared her out. "My turn to ask you something personal."

"Sure, go ahead, although I shouldn't think there's much you don't know about me already, is there?"

"Did you ever get things worked out with Tom? How's married life, these days?"

SJ told him what she'd told Tanya and he nodded thoughtfully. "Are you seeing anyone else? Have you fallen for anyone in your meetings yet?"

"No," she said, smiling. "I haven't met anyone I wanted to fall for."

Apart from you, she wanted to add. But she doubted he felt the same way. He was probably only being nice. He'd always been nice. And this catch-up chat was just a kind of unofficial extension to her aftercare plan.

"In that case, how do you fancy doing this again? Having coffee, I mean – say no if you don't want to. I won't be offended."

"I do want to," she blurted out before he decided to change his mind. "Very much. If you're not too busy, I mean." Bugger, where had all her hard earned self-respect gone? She'd almost bitten his hand off. "You're not just asking me because you think it would be a good thing to do?"

"I'm asking you because I enjoy your company – I always have. But neither of us was in a position to meet socially before. It wouldn't have been ... appropriate."

319

As he spoke, he reached across and touched her hand, and she felt another million or so volts bolt up her arm.

"And you think it's appropriate now?" Her voice was a husky whisper.

"It wouldn't have been if you were still with Tom. Or if I hadn't left S.A.A.D. But I'm not working there any more. They closed the place down a couple of months back – lack of funding."

"But that's awful. What about those…" She'd been going to say poor addicts, but instead she said, "…people who need to go there?" She didn't feel like a poor addict any more.

"It's not the only centre in London." Kit smiled at her. "Don't worry."

"Are you working at another one now then?"

"No, I'm working at the homeless shelter in Hackney – I thought it was time for a change." He coughed and went on uncertainly. "I couldn't counsel you again, even if you wanted me to – being as I'm no longer in the profession. So it would be okay for us to meet again – socially, I mean. That's if you wanted to?"

His fingers were still touching hers. It was incredible. Some good feelings at last – blotting out all the awful ones. She didn't think she'd ever had such an amazing morning in her life.

"Then yes," she added, looking up into his dark eyes and seeing herself reflected there. Not a small brown person any more, but a full size one – shiny and whole and strangely beautiful.

320

Chapter Thirty-Eight

Nightshades was the kind of club SJ wouldn't have ventured into in the past unless she'd been extremely drunk. It was dimly lit, smelt of spilt beer and sweat, and had an air of relaxed seediness. Across the small stage at one end of the room, the word NIGHTSHADES was spelled out in pink and purple bulbs. SJ wondered why they'd left off the DEADLY. A couple of ancient paper chains and some threadbare silver tinsel draped over the stage were the club's only concession to Christmas.

She glanced around. They were early and the place wasn't as full as it would be later. A guy wearing a cowboy hat and a waistcoat lined with silver bullets sat at the nearest table, supping a pint. His face was a mass of piercings. He had three studs in his nose, a couple of rings in each eyebrow and another row in his upper lip. SJ wondered how he got on at airport security.

At the bar a couple of transvestites, one brunette, one blond, perched elegantly on stools. Both wore miniskirts and fishnet stockings and had scarlet nails. They were almost a cliché, SJ thought happily. They made Michael, who was sitting opposite her, look like a class act.

He looked comfortable dressed as Lizzie. The silver pencil skirt and black sequinned top suited him. His highlighted wig curled softly around his face. Blusher accentuated his high cheekbones and his eye make up was far better applied than SJ's ever was. She was almost envious. Catching her gaze, he winked at her.

"You enjoying yourself, sweetheart?"

She nodded. "I never thought I'd say this, but yes, I'm having a great time. I'm looking forward to the main act. What's her name again?"

"Sybil Starlight." Tanya, who was beside her, grinned and leaned across to squeeze her fingers. "Are you really okay? You're not finding it too tricky being surrounded by people drinking?"

"It's okay at the moment." SJ glanced at Tanya's glass of orange juice and wondered if it was a concession to her.

"If I get tempted to down Michael's wine, I'll nip outside and grab myself a lungful of traffic fumes, don't worry."

"I'm really proud of you," Tanya said, her green eyes soft, and SJ swallowed. She was proud of herself, too. A whole fifteen months without a drink. A whole fifteen months during which she'd survived the end of a marriage and managed to move her relationship with her family, even Alison, on to a much more satisfying level. Well, Alison wasn't actually talking to her at the moment – they'd had a fight over a pair of Calvin Klein jeans that had been reduced to £10 in TK Maxx. But SJ had seen them first by a whisker – and she was more broke than Alison. And it was hardly her fault if Alison wanted to sulk for a fortnight.

At least she was getting on well with Kevin and Sophie, who seemed to like having a *dire-warning* for an aunt.

SJ felt strong. She no longer feared what the future would bring. She no longer wanted to blank out difficult feelings. She was comfortable in her own skin.

322

Like Michael, she thought, shooting him a glance. They had both grown into their new identities.

"I'm proud of you, too," she told Tanya. "It hasn't been an easy couple of years, has it? When did you change your mind about coming to places like this?"

"Very recently." Tanya raised her eyebrows. "I feel a lot more secure than I used to – I know we're going to be okay." She gestured around them. A few more men had drifted in – the dress code ranged from ripped jeans normality to pink lace and feather boa outrageousness. SJ saw one guy who was dressed completely in black leather, but wore the most beautiful pair of jewelled stilettos she had ever seen.

"This is less serious than going round someone's house – everyone goes a bit mad at Christmas, don't they?" Tanya's eyes sparkled. "Oh God, I can't possibly keep this to myself any more. We haven't told a soul yet, SJ, because it's very early days, but I'm pregnant again."

"Oh, Tanya, that's fantastic news." They leaped to their feet and hugged. "You must be over the moon."

"We are. I thought it would never happen again. After Maddie, after all those miscarriages, all those tests."

SJ could feel Tanya trembling a little in her arms. "It's the best news I've heard in months. I won't tell a soul."

"I know you won't."

SJ blinked rapidly. Over Tanya's shoulder she saw Michael cotton on to their conversation and raise his glass in their direction.

"I know we're a bit unconventional – as parents go." There was nervous laughter in Tanya's voice, and SJ knew she had her fears for the future – her doubts

323

and her insecurities. "But I also know we'll get through. We love each other. We can get through anything." She took a sip of her orange as they sat back in their seats. "I'm just sorry you didn't have the same support from Tom."

"It was different for us. I didn't love Tom in the first place. I hadn't got over Derek. I couldn't love anybody. Not even myself. And once he knew how I felt, what would have been the point in staying with me?"

"But he walked away at the first sign of a problem, SJ. If you hadn't been an alcoholic he might have stayed."

SJ shook her head, even though she knew she would never talk Tanya round on this one. Rather ironically, considering all that had happened – Tanya was a conventionalist when it came to marriage.

"I'm glad I'm an alcoholic," she said truthfully. "Well, a recovering one anyway. I know myself better because of it. I know who I am and what I want."

"Talking of what you want," Tanya muttered, raising her eyebrows, "how's that gorgeous man of yours?"

SJ smiled. "He's not mine," she said, feeling suddenly shy.

"But you are still bringing him round for dinner on Boxing Day?" Tanya pressed, her eyes sparkling.

"Of course."

"Good, because we're really looking forward to meeting him. Was it just chestnuts you said he didn't like?"

"Yes, but he said not to worry if you're putting them in the stuffing. He'll just skip the stuffing."

She and Kit had had a very interesting discussion about stuffing after that conversation, SJ reflected, which had nothing whatsoever to do with chestnuts. She felt her neck turning pink at the delicious warmth of the memory.

"Here's Sybil Starlight," Michael observed, as a drag queen in impossibly high heels and a long black dress covered with glittering silver stars tottered onto the small stage.

The crowd roared in appreciation. SJ smiled at Michael at the same moment as Sybil began to strut her stuff, swinging her hips provocatively before launching into an old Beatles song: *With A Little Help From My Friends.*

That was appropriate, SJ thought, as Sybil sang on in her gloriously husky voice. You didn't get far without your friends: your real friends, that was – the ones who forgave you and loved you and accepted you for what you were. She knew exactly what Dorothy had meant now about real friendships being forged in hell. Friendships that could withstand the extremes of pain and come through still shining were the strongest friendships of all. They had to be.

The song ended to rapturous applause and Sybil launched into her next number. It was a long while before it was quiet enough to speak again.

When Tanya and Michael were up dancing, SJ sneaked outside for a fag – she'd thought no one had seen her go but when she lifted her head from lighting it, she saw Tanya had followed her out.

"You shouldn't come near me when I'm smoking, it's bad for the baby," she cautioned.

"If I stay in there she'll be born deaf," Tanya said, "so it's six of one and half a dozen of the other. Besides, I wanted to ask you something."

"It wasn't something else about Kit, was it? You're going to meet him in less than forty-eight hours…"

"It was nothing to do with Kit," Tanya said, as SJ blew smoke in the direction of Big Ben, whose lit-up face was just visible above the roof tops.

"It was about you. What you said earlier about being glad you're a recovering alcoholic. Is that how you really feel?"

"Mmm, yeah, it is actually. I'm always honest about how I feel these days – that's Kit's fault."

Tanya nodded thoughtfully. "I was on the internet earlier looking at some statistics. Did you know that there are over a hundred million alcoholics in the world – give or take?"

"No," SJ said. "Shit. Are there?"

"Yes there are – and only a million of them will ever recover."

SJ shivered and Tanya narrowed her green eyes. "Do you know what that makes you, SJ?"

"Haven't a clue," SJ said, with a lot more flippancy than she felt. Was she about to get some dire warning about the dangers of relapse? Would Tanya ever really truly trust her again? She could see that her friend was blinking away tears and when she finally spoke, her voice was husky.

"It makes you one in a million, Sarah-Jane Crosse! That's what it makes you."

Acknowledgements

Janine Pulford, Jan Smiles, Jan Wright, Mel, Duncan Mac, Ian Burton, David Kendrick, Cathy Kendrick, Richard Jeffries, and especially to Peter Jones, Alison Neale, the proof fairy and my long suffering agent, Becky Bagnell. Many thanks guys; your help and advice was amazing.

Other Della Galton Titles

The Novel Writer's Toolshed for Short Story Writers
From SoundHaven, 2013
Genre: Non-Fiction

How to Eat Loads and Stay Slim
by Della Galton & Peter Jones
From SoundHaven, 2013
Genre: Non-Fiction

The Short Story Writer's Toolshed
From SoundHaven, 2012
Genre: Non-Fiction

The Dog with Nine Lives
From Accent Press, 2010
Genre: Fiction

Helter Skelter
From Accent Press, 2007
Genre: Fiction

Passing Shadows
From Accent Press, 2006
Genre: Fiction

9475042R00195

Printed in Great Britain
by Amazon.co.uk, Ltd.,
Marston Gate.